MINK ISLAND

Brent Purvis

Cover Design: Joanie Christian Design
jchristiandesign@gmail.com
Salmon Design: Ella Purvis

ALSO BY BRENT PURVIS

Jim and Kram Funny Mystery Series:

Tsunami Warning

Hooligan Arm (available summer of 2016)

DEDICATION

to Marci

on our 17th Anniversary

it's all bliss, right?

PROLOGUE

Craig, Alaska – June 1st

It was raining. Not a torrential downpour or anything that extreme, but rather a slow, steady drizzle. The temperature was in the mid-fifties, and the wind was blowing. The steady wind caused the rain to slant sideways as it fell. It was the kind of weather that was depressing, and it was the kind of weather common to the islands of Southeast Alaska. It was Jim Wekle's first day on the job.

In fact, Lieutenant Jim Wekle had taken his first step onto Prince of Wales Island a mere three and a half hours earlier. He had arrived on a float plane, checked into his temporary housing above *The Port of Call* bar, and barely had time to meet his staff when the call came in.

"We don't get many floaters wearing bikinis." A young trooper named Tavis Spurgeon made the comment. Straight black hair was barely evident beneath the young man's Stetson. His tall hat was covered in a wrinkled plastic wrap, protecting it from the rain.

"How often do you get floaters around here; clothed or otherwise?" asked Jim Wekle. Both troopers were standing on a rock covered in mussels and barnacles, peering down into a kelp bed exposed by a low tide. With the tide so far out, the troopers' vantage perched far above the water's surface. A girl wearing nothing but a green bikini with white polka-dots bobbed in shallow water against the base of the rock. She was face down, tangled in the kelp strands, and obviously quite dead.

Tavis said, "Couple times a year. Last floater was a few months ago. Long-time resident, Henry Dorts. He went out in his skiff to pull his crab pots and took a wave sideways. Found him floating several days later under the docks in Klawock."

The rainwater began seeping through the sleeves of Jim's shirt. The wind kicked up and blew spray directly into their faces. Sensing that the weather conditions were getting to his new superior, Tavis commented, "You should have been here last week. Weather was beautiful, sunny, almost seventy degrees."

"Good to know." The news didn't make Jim feel better.

A wave caused the dead girl to hit the rock rather hard. Tavis cringed and said, "Dumb girl. Thought she could go for a swim in these waters. That stuff isn't more than about 50 degrees. Between the temp and the current, she didn't stand a chance."

The Lieutenant squinted as he skeptically scanned the girl's body moving with the action of the waves. The two Alaska State Troopers stood close to ten feet from the water's surface gazing down into the saltwater, but the distance and movement of the body didn't keep Jim

Wekle from noticing something just below the green bikini strap.

"It wasn't the water temp or the current that killed this girl."

Tavis responded, "How can you be sure?"

Wekle pointed down at the body and said, "There's a bullet hole in her back."

1

Craig, Alaska is a small town located on the western shoreline of the massive Prince of Wales Island. Prince of Wales is the largest of many mountainous and tree covered islands that make up the Alexander Archipelago of Southeast Alaska. The town of Craig has only about twelve hundred full-time residents and, being quite remote, these residents can only leave the island by air or by sea. There are no bridges that connect Prince of Wales to the rest of the world. There are no Alaska Airlines jets that land in Craig, either. Most travelers, to and from the mostly uninhabited island, come and go on either a float plane or a state-run ferry boat.

Jim Wekle's recent promotion to lieutenant within the ranks of the State Troopers organization landed him the top position of a small station located just a mile outside of the Craig city limits. Jim had arrived earlier on a float plane. He hated flying on small planes, but he followed his orders and made the short flight from Ketchikan without incident. His prompt relocation from Anchorage landed him in the rain capital of the world. Jim Wekle hated rain.

It took Wekle and young trooper, Tavis Spurgeon, the better part of the morning to fish the dead bikini-clad floater out of the water. They had managed to secure the looped end of a rope around one of the girl's legs, but didn't have the heart to pull her body up the barnacle-laden rock. Her skin would have been torn to shreds. Tavis informed his new boss that the wind and jagged rocks poking up out of the water made it too dangerous to use a boat in order to extract the girl. It was decided that their best course of action was to wait for the tide to come up.

The weather was miserable. Wind varied from steady flutter to gale force. The rain drizzle was relentless. Visibility was abysmal. With the girl's lassoed knee tied off to a tree on shore, Jim Wekle sought refuge under a tall cedar tree that seemingly grew straight up out of the dark rock. He sat down on an old fallen log and lit up a cigar. The smoke wafted up and over the officer's bare, soaked Stetson.

"You know, it is policy to wear our rain protectors," Tavis spoke with a patronizing tone.

"I don't wear shower caps!" Jim's answer was short and gruff. He puffed away on his hand-rolled Dominican.

Tavis continued, "It's just that these hats are expensive and they told us at the academy that..."

"Look, let's get one thing straight right now." Jim Wekle threw darts with his eyes that seemed to pierce Tavis' skull. "I'm your boss. You don't tell me what to do. I couldn't give two shits about what they taught you at the academy. I don't wear shower caps. And these are Stetsons, NOT HATS!"

Tavis didn't speak much the rest of the morning. That suited Lieutenant Wekle just fine. Jim wasn't in the mood to make new friends. Two cigars later, the tide had risen enough to slide the body safely to shore. By noon, an EMS crew had finally taken the girl away in a body bag. Jim was tired, hungry, wet, and grumpy. He assigned Tavis to patrol the highway for speeders and then went to the station to unpack his personal items into his new office. The Trooper Station was located inside a light yellow double-wide stuck on a semi-flat chunk of rock. Salmonberry plants, ferns, short spruce, and tall cedar trees surround the station. There was only room for four vehicles to park on crushed rock in front of the small building. Jim Wekle parked his state-issued cruiser sideways across three of the parking spots. He didn't care. A dented white Nissan was parked correctly in the fourth spot.

"Hi there, boss. Remember me, Shelly? We spoke on the phone yesterday. Wow, a floater on your first day here. Poor girl, thinking she could wear a bikini in Southeast Alaska. What was she thinking anyway? Heard you had to wait out the tide. Some first day, huh? You get wet out there?" The verbal onslaught came from Shelly Gurtzen, long time dispatcher and office manager for the Craig Station of Alaska State Troopers. She had seen quite a few officers come and go over the years. The Lieutenants especially seemed to have a short shelf life for enforcing the law on Prince of Wales Island.

Shelly typed on her computer as she spoke in

continuous strands of banter, "Poor girl. Anyone I.D. her yet? Her description doesn't ring a bell to me, but then again, I don't hang out with the seventeen to twenty-five-year-olds. Probably came up for a charter or for summer work. Poor girl. Oh well, this is rugged territory and you can't just go jumping in the water thinking it's California or something..."

Jim removed his drenched Stetson and hung it on a coat rack to drain. He replied, "Shelly, is it?" She nodded. "Shelly, I think I will be in my office for a bit. I have a little unpacking to do."

"Oh, sure. I'm sure you have lots to do, first day and all. They dropped off a couple a boxes of your stuff from the float plane. They're sitting next to your desk..." Shelly continued typing on her computer while she spoke. She was still talking when Jim closed the door to his office.

Jim sat down in the chair behind his desk. It was surprisingly comfortable. He leaned his elbows on the desk and rubbed his temples. His damp hair dripped on some paperwork that he hadn't looked through yet. He wondered how his life could have come to this; alone on an island in Alaska. Why couldn't it be an island in the South Pacific or in the Bahamas? He loved sun and sand and girls in bikinis... Oops. Scratch that last one, he thought. Poor taste after this morning's events. He closed his eyes and continued the temple rubbing, deep in thought.

A knock on his door snapped Jim back to reality. It was Shelly. She held up a brown paper bag. He waved her in.

"Boss, I thought you might be hungry. I ordered you some lunch. Porty's famous halibut sandwich. You're going to love it." Shelly set the bag down on the desk and began to back out of the office.

"Shelly, just a minute." She stopped and looked up with a perky expression. "Shelly, do we have any swimming pools here in Craig?"

"No, unfortunately. We almost passed our last school bond that included funding for a pool to be built behind the high school gym, but it failed by thirty-two votes. I served on the committee and went door to door. I saved the fliers for next time the bond comes up for a vote. These kids need a pool, don't you think?" Jim was sensing that Shelly liked to talk.

Jim asked, "Are there any tanning salons in town? A simple yes or no will do."

"No, but..." Shelly caught herself from elaborating.

"How about hot tubs? Any hot tubs in town?"

"Oh, yes. Quite a few actually. My husband was thinking about putting one in last year, but we spent the money on a trip south instead. Money well spent, if you ask me. Yep, got to get off the rock every once in a while or you'll go crazy. You remember that. Get off the rock at least once a year and go visit someplace that has

8

stoplights..."

"Shelly?"

She smiled and said, "Yes?"

"Thanks for the lunch."

2

A skinny, older man with long, white hair pulled back into a ponytail carried a heavy cabinet down a single lane ramp that led to a small boat dock. The man wore a bright green t-shirt with some kind of logo on the front. He had on old jean cut-off shorts and brown Xtratuf boots. After placing the cabinet in the bow of an aluminum skiff, the man walked back up the ramp and disappeared into the woods. A few moments later, he reappeared on the ramp, this time carrying a portable generator. After two more trips up and down the ramp carrying various odd-shaped items, the man in the green shirt covered all of his cargo with a blue tarp, started an outboard engine, and pushed off from the dock. The boat puttered away slowly, bouncing up and down with the waves.

Several minutes later, a loud voice from the skiff yelled, "Hot damn!"

The town of Craig, Alaska was situated on a rather tiny point of land surrounded by two bays; Port Bagial to the south and Crab Bay to the north. The town was strategically protected from the open ocean to the west by dozens of islands, some no more than an acre in size and some of them over five miles wide. The islands created a maze of inlets and passages that snaked around treacherous rocks and thick, tree-covered terrain. The actual town center was planted on top of a point of rock that was barely longer than one-thousand feet. There were only four streets that ran east-west and they were crossed randomly by seven north-south side streets. One road circumnavigated the southern shoreline of town accessing some of the city's nicer homes and the northern side of the point held the bulk of Craig's industry. Tucked away between Craig and the rest of Prince of Wales Island were two marinas, one on the north side and one on the south.

Traveling between the two marinas was the main highway that connected Craig with the Native village of Klawock, just seven miles up the island. Past Klawock, the highway split into two. One road snaked east up and down hills and through dense vegetation for about twenty-two miles to the port town of Hollis. The other fork in the road veered off to the north and eventually split into multiple logging and forest service roads. This road system created a virtual labyrinth that plunged forever into the vast wilderness of Prince of Wales.

The *Craig Inn and Port of Call* was located on the north side of Craig's main access road, wedged directly between the two marinas. The locals referred to the establishment simply as "Porty's," and it was one of the most frequented establishments in town. The two-story brown building had a restaurant and bar on the street level and several rooms to rent on the second level. It was one of only three restaurants in town, one of only two bars in town, and it was the only hotel in town.

Jim Wekle unpacked his suitcase and changed from his blue Trooper uniform into jeans and a flannel shirt. He was damp and cold and hoped that the flannel would aid with both. Jim walked out of his room, down the exposed staircase and entered through Porty's heavy wooden door. The main room was dimly lit and smelled of cigarette smoke. There were several locals positioned at a long bar that stretched the length of the room. Several tables were randomly placed on the floor surrounding a pool table, jukebox, and cigarette dispenser. Two younger men with red hair and pale skin were throwing darts in the corner next to the bathrooms.

Jim walked over to an empty table and sat down. Gazing at the walls, Jim was intrigued by dozens of pictures of shipwrecked boats. Most of the pictures were older and in black and white. Some were obviously more recent. Below each picture, a label indicated the boat name, year and location of the wreck. The *Miss B* hit a rock off Kaigani Straight in 1964. *Helga's Dream* smashed into the shore in 1983 trying to navigate the Wrangell Narrows at low tide. The *Fish Buyer* dumped a full load of salmon over the side after running aground north of Sitka in 1955. Jim noticed that the wall next to the jukebox was dedicated to plane crashes. Similar pictures of wreckage with tags listing years and locations were displayed. Over some of the plane crash pictures were handwritten notes, such as; "Miss you, Thatcher," or "Now you're flying in the heavens, Lenny."

A pretty girl with dark hair and tan skin appeared at Jim's table, "What can I get you?" She was Native Alaskan and had a pleasant smile. Jim could smell her perfume. It was a nice change from the mixture of smoke, beer, and burnt grease smells that filled the air inside Porty's.

"I'll have a cup of coffee, black."

The coffee was bad. The second sip almost made him choke. A few minutes after the coffee was delivered, the pretty waitress walked up to Jim and asked, "Can you settle a bet for us?" She nodded her head back toward the bar. The locals on bar stools had all turned their heads and were watching the girl.

"What brings you to Craig? They think you are here for a fishing charter, but I don't think so." She spoke with a deep, yet still feminine, vocal timbre. She brushed black hair away from her pretty face and wore a snarky smirk across her lips.

"What makes you think that I'm not here for a fish charter?" Jim was a little amused, but he didn't really like every local in the joint staring at him.

The girl chewed on the end of her pen for a bit, and then said, "You aren't wearing a raincoat, you don't have an umbrella, and I haven't seen you take any pictures with a camera yet. Those are usually dead giveaways for tourists around here. Plus, you're alone. Not many guys fly up here alone to go salmon fishing."

Jim said, "You're quite the detective. Okay, so what brings me to this little damp piece of paradise if I'm not a tourist or a fisherman?"

She studied him for a moment and then spoke, "You're in good shape and your hair is cut short. That usually means Coast Guard around here, but you're too old to be one of the recruits."

"Gee, thanks."

"And it's no secret that Trooper Dan just left, so I would guess that you are the new Statie in town." The girl stuck the pen cap back in her mouth and twirled it a bit. The snarky smirk reappeared as she asked, "How'd I do?"

Jim glanced at the locals and gave them a shrug. "She's on the mark there, boys," he said in a loud voice.

The girl stuck out her hand and said with a smile, "I'm Maggie. Welcome to Craig." The locals grumbled and turned back toward their beers. One of the men slammed a five dollar bill down on the bar.

Jim shook Maggie's hand and introduced himself. Maggie went back to the bar and swooped up the five dollar bill she had just won. The locals went back to drinking and cussing. Jim went back to sipping his tepid coffee. After a while, Maggie returned to Jim's table with a fresh pot.

"Maggie, does it always rain here?"

"Oh, you should have been here last week. Weather was beautiful."

"So I've heard."

Maggie filled up his cup with hot coffee and then asked, "Do you know how that girl died yet? I heard she went swimming in her bikini. Someone else said that she got shot. Hauler Steve over there said that she fell off a cliff, but he makes things up sometimes."

Jim sipped his coffee. "It's an open investigation right now. I really can't say much." Maggie started to return to the bar, and then Jim asked, "Hey Maggie. You ever see the girl before?" Jim switched on his smartphone and flipped it to a picture of the dead girl's face. He held it out for Maggie to see. The sight of a dead girl's picture didn't seem to faze her. From the looks of the pictures on the walls that surrounded him, Jim figured that seeing dead bodies was part of life in Southeast Alaska.

"Never saw her before. That's pretty typical of the slimers, though. They rarely come in here." Maggie walked away to fetch a Coors for one of the locals. The two men throwing darts motioned to Maggie that they were ready for another round as well. Once the clientele were content with their drinks, Jim grabbed his coffee cup and took a seat on a bar stool next to a balding man wearing orange suspenders with the word *Stihl* repeatedly written up and down the straps

Jim asked, "Maggie, what did you mean by *slimer*?" The bald man snorted and a couple of the other regulars chuckled to themselves. Jim felt as though he was missing something.

Maggie said, "You know...on the *slime line*."

The door opened and a giant, blonde-haired man followed by a portly, gruff-looking woman entered the establishment. They both wore rubber boots and smelled of fish.

One of the locals at the bar yelled, "Pringle!"

One of the dart throwers hollered, "Hey Pringle, smack into any buoys today?"

The other red-haired dart thrower gave his brother a high-five and asked, "Throw any of your customers overboard this time?" The boys cracked up.

The yellow-haired man named Pringle smiled and spoke with a booming voice, "Say all you want, boys. It was a good day. Limits on kings, including a thirty-five pounder. Big tips today."

The portly woman spoke in a tone of voice that would make most loggers proud, "Rain is back. That brings in the fish. Fish bring in the tips. Life is damn good today. Give me a beer."

Dan Pringle and his wife, Alice, ran a charter fishing boat. From the third week in May to the third week in September, Dan and Alice Pringle worked nonstop every day. They made an entire year's salary in four months by putting salmon poles in the hands of their charter customers, baiting hooks, landing fish, cleaning and flash freezing the filets, and packing it all into three-foot-long fish boxes for return flights to Omaha, or Dallas, or Memphis or wherever else their clients were from. The more fish people caught, the more the Pringles got tipped. Any king salmon over thirty pounds almost guaranteed a five-hundred-dollar tip. Most of Dan Pringle's charters had money to burn. Most of Dan Pringle's clients puked over the side of his boat before the first fish was landed.

Jim suddenly noticed that the two red-headed dart throwers had come up on either side of him. Jim recognized the taller of the two brothers as the pilot that had flown him in from Ketchikan earlier that day.

The taller pilot nudged Jim in the shoulder and said, "Pringle here is famous for running into things with his boat."

The brother chimed in, "Yeah, you should have been here last summer. Nailed an aluminum channel maker square on doing about thirty knots. Slammed into it so hard that he launched some fat dude from Oklahoma clear off the side of his boat."

The taller one finished the story, "The dude was so friggin' fat they couldn't pull him back onto the boat. Had to drag him a half mile through the water onto shore just to get him back on his feet."

Alice Pringle interrupted, "Yeah well, I'd rather go out with my husband than to fly with *Frightening Frankie*, here." She pointed toward the tall pilot that Jim had flown with earlier. The nickname made Jim feel a little uneasy since he had just put his life into Frightening Frankie's hands that morning.

The banter continued between the locals, but Jim pulled himself away from the bar and cornered Maggie. She was wiping down a table close to the dart board. He asked, "What, exactly, did you mean by the *slime line*?"

She smiled at his question, showing white teeth on her pretty, dark face. "Cannery workers, Trooper Jim. Every year they start showing up about this time and leave at the end of the summer. You know, college kids here to earn enough money to pay for a whole semester or more." Maggie went on to explain that the salmon canneries throughout Southeast Alaska employed temporary workers each year to slice open, gut, and process the thousands, if not millions, of salmon that came from the fish buyers. The fish buyers purchased the salmon from the commercial fishing boats during various openings, or seasons, throughout the summer. When the fish were in, the slime line worked day and night in order to process the fish as quickly as possible to prevent any spoilage.

"You might want to check the Stockade. My bet is that someone there will recognize your dead girl's picture." Maggie gestured toward the trooper's phone.

Jim asked, "The Stockade?"

"That's just the name for the barracks over behind the cannery. It's where most of the slimers stay for the summer."

The door opened again and Tavis Spurgeon walked in. He was wearing street clothes, and he ordered a beer since he was off duty. He nodded at his new boss, but sat at the bar next to an older man with black and white hair and a beard to match. The older man had a bit of a belly, but looked as though he had been in good shape at one point in his life.

Tavis put his arm on the shoulder of the man he sat next to and said, "Uncle Tank, how are you doing tonight?" Uncle Tank took a long pull on his beer can and nodded his head as if to say he was doing just fine.

Uncle Tank spoke loud enough for the whole bar to hear, "Your new boss over there treat you right today?"

Tavis answered, "Just fine, Uncle, Tank. Had a floater on his first day. You hear about that?"

Tank growled, "Cuz if he don't treat you right, you just let me know. I'll take care of it."

The comment made Jim feel as about as welcome as a preacher at a stag party. Jim paid for his coffee and said, "Goodnight, everybody." Few responded.

19

3

Jim's cell phone began ringing at 2:34am. It was the ECC, or Emergency Call Center. Small, isolated trooper stations, like the one on Prince of Wales Island, cannot manage a full complement of officers for round the clock law enforcement. The Craig Station only employed troopers Jim Wekle and Tavis Spurgeon. The only other employee was Shelly, the daytime dispatcher and office manager. During the off-hours shifts, which usually included the middle of the night, all 911 calls were routed through a Seattle-based call center. The emergency call would then be forwarded to the cell phone number of the on-call trooper. In this case, it was Lieutenant Jim Wekle that received the early morning wake-up call.

A 911 dispatch at the call center relayed the emergency call. The recorded message sounded in Jim's ear:

"It's two-damn-A-M in the morning. Some idiot is playing music out on his boat. You had better send someone to make him stop, or I might start shooting at him!"

"Sir, do not start shooting at anybody. Is your life or anyone else's life in danger?"

"Yeah! His life is, unless you get him to stop with the damn loud rock and roll."

20

The ECC dispatch had decided that she should relay the call since threats were made. Jim lightly cussed as he pulled on his uniform. The address given to him was out Port St. Nicholas Road, a winding two-lane street that followed the shoreline south of town. It was close to three in the morning when Jim arrived at the address. It was still dark out, although daylight was right around the corner. Early June in Southeast Alaska only saw darkness from about 11:00pm to about 4:00am.

As soon as Jim stepped out of his cruiser, he heard the music. It sounded like rock guitar. In fact, it was solo rock guitar, no other instruments. There was a humming sound that accompanied the guitar music, which sounded faintly like an engine running. Jim walked down a narrow path that led to the front door of the house. As soon as the front entryway became visible, Jim's heart skipped a beat. He startled and jumped back, instinctively putting his right hand on the butt end of his holstered sidearm. Unexpectedly standing just beneath the protective awning of the house's front porch, a gigantic stuffed grizzly bear stood erect on a man-made podium; front paws clawing the air as if frozen in mid-attack.

Jim knocked on the door of the house and a grey-haired man opened the door. He was wearing plaid pajamas and had a shotgun slung over his shoulder.

Jim placed his right hand back on his pistol and said sternly, "Sir, put your weapon down now."

"Oh this, sorry about that." The old man laid the shotgun down in the corner of the doorway. "Good thing you arrived. I was about to fire off some warning shots at this damn fool."

"That would not be wise." Jim stepped inside the man's home. "What's with the bear?" Jim motioned over his shoulder with his thumb.

"Shot that puppy on the Kenai Peninsula two years ago. Quite a specimen, don't you think?

"Friendly way of greeting your guests."

The old man led Jim through the house and out onto a large deck. In the clouded darkness, it was hard to tell, but the deck overlooked the water. Jim heard waves hitting rocks directly below him. The house appeared to have been built on pilings right above the saltwater, jetting out from the shoreline.

"There he is." The old man pointed directly out from the house at the silhouette of a dark figure in a small boat. The music seemed to be coming from the boat. From this vantage point, the sound was shockingly loud. Distorted rock guitar riffs that rivaled Eddie Van-Halen pounded Jim's ears. In between solos, the guitarist would pause and yell, "Hot damn!" During those brief moments of interlude, Jim detected that the humming sound emitted from a portable generator that was positioned in the bow of the small skiff.

The sudden reality hit Jim. There was a man in a

fifteen-foot aluminum skiff powering a massive guitar amplifier with a portable generator, floating in the bay, rocking out at three o'clock in the morning. The guitarist finished a solo which included furious shredding and went into a lick that Jim recognized from an old Pink Floyd song.

"Hey, that's from *The Wall* album. Good tune," Jim said. The old man did not seem amused by the fact that the trooper recognized the guitar riff.

Suddenly, a blast of light streamed out from the deck. The old man held a powerful spotlight in his hand. It searched the waves until it illuminated the musician on the boat. The waves in the bay kept the boat rocking making it hard to center the light, but Jim could make out a few features. The guitarist seemed to have long white hair pulled back into a ponytail. He wore a bright colored t-shirt and stood in front of a Marshall half-stack; one of the largest and loudest guitar amplification systems on the market. With the light beaming onto his boat, the crazed musician set his guitar down and flipped out both middle fingers directed firmly at the old man's house.

The guitarist yelled, "Eat shit, old man...Haaaahaaaahaaaa!"

The old man looked over to the trooper and asked, "Can we shoot him?"

Jim retrieved a bull-horn from the cruiser. Returning to the deck, he activated the portable sound device and yelled, "This is the State Troopers. You need to turn off your amplifier. It's three in the morning."

The guitarist cranked up the volume and went into a tirade of arpeggios up the neck of the instrument.

Waiting for a break in the music, Jim yelled into bull-horn, "You must stop playing your music so loudly, or I will be forced to dispatch the Coast Guard."

The guitarist immediately laid down the guitar and jumped to the back of the skiff. He fired up the outboard engine and jammed it into gear. The boat sped away into the blackness of night. Just before leaving earshot, Jim and the old man heard a faint, "Hot damn!" drift back their way.

All supplies that sustain normal life on Prince of Wales Island are brought in by float plane or barge. Mail and special order items are delivered once every weekday morning by a float plane that travels to and from Ketchikan. All other supplies, including groceries that are sold in Craig's lone store, are shipped in on Sea Tank Marine Lines. Large flat barges are stacked high with shipping containers and pulled by tugboat all over Southeast Alaska and up and down the inside passage from Seattle. Assuming weather or mechanical failure doesn't delay shipment, the barge docks on the north side of the town of Craig every Wednesday morning. Containers are unloaded and supplies are slowly dispersed to various entities throughout the island. This process takes the better part of a day, and residents find it fairly common to not see fresh supplies actually hit the shelves of stores until late Thursday morning.

As Jim was hungry for breakfast foods on a Wednesday, he was a little miffed to see that the Craig Market had actually run out of milk. What store runs out of milk? Settling for expired yogurt and granola instead of his usual Wheaties, Jim was already in a grumpy mood. Lack of sleep, due to the middle of the night rock concert, coupled with more constant drizzle outside didn't help Jim's mood. He knew that chatty Shelly and fresh-from-the-academy Tavis would probably send him over the top. Instead of heading to the station first thing after breakfast, Jim thought he had better go for a little walk.

The Stockade was pretty easy to find. The cannery was a large building with rusted metal siding built on pilings over the north-end water. Across the street and up a short flight of stairs, Jim could see a three-story building with faded maroon paint. Printed on a dilapidated sign hung sideways, the word "Stockade" presented itself atop the maroon building. Jim took the steps of the staircase two at a time. He heard laughter and smelled the pungent odor of marijuana smoke. A deck made of wooden planks jutted out next to the door of the Stockade. Varieties of green foliage spilled over onto the deck from the small patch of woods surrounding the house. A circular, wood-fired hot tub sat in the center of the deck and four red-eyed young adults sat in debris-speckled steaming water. The youths seemed oblivious to the rain that fell on their bare upper bodies. As soon as the college-aged kids noticed the State Trooper standing next to the tub, a hand that held a joint quickly disappeared beneath the water's surface.

A boy with shaggy brown hair and two lip rings spoke first. "Uh, officer. So good to see you this morning." The other boy choked back a laugh, which came out his nose. He had tattoos on his neck. The two girls in the tub looked terrified.

Jim decided to pretend he didn't notice the pot smoke, "Good morning to you guys. You all up here to work the slime line this summer?"

The kid with neck tattoos started giggling. One of the girls told him to shut up.

Lip Rings said, "Oh yeah, you know it. Power to the fish, man."

Neck Tattoos couldn't control himself. It was obvious that he was too stoned to deal with talking to a cop.

One of the girls said, "We were just soaking in the tub. We didn't smoke anything." Lip Rings shot her a look of terror.

Jim said, "Relax. I just want some information."

Neck Tattoos had no other recourse than to completely submerge himself in the water. Bubbles rose from where his head entered the water. Lip Rings got out of the tub and stoked the fireplace that heated the tub. He was wearing a Speedo. Jim didn't really want to see the skin tight bathing suit, but he couldn't help but notice.

Jim pulled up the photo of the dead girl on his phone and turned the screen toward the two girls in the tub, "You recognize this person?"

One of the girls curled her lip, "Eew. She doesn't look so good."

Jim said, "She's dead." The girl's face turned pale.

The other girl said, "We just got here last night. Rode the ferry in and hitched a ride into town. We don't really know anyone, yet."

Neck Tattoos came up for air, giggled some more, and descended again into the tub. Jim turned the phone's image toward Lip Rings and said, "How 'bout you? You recognize her?"

The boy studied the picture and looked up at Jim with a shocked face that was too sincere to be faked. Lip Rings asked, "Debbie's dead?"

"Yep. Fished her out of the water yesterday." Jim put the phone back in his pocket. "Debbie have a last name?"

Lip Rings sat back down in the tub and said, "Uh, started with an 'S'...common name. You know, like Smith or something. I don't remember for sure." Bubbles kept emerging from where Neck Tattoos was submerged.

Jim asked, "She been here long?"

Lip Rings said, "No, a week, maybe two. Came up too early. The fish don't really start coming in for a while. I figured she got tired of waiting and hit the road. This place doesn't really start paying much until the sockeye and pinks are running."

"When did you notice that she was gone?"

"Couple days ago, I guess."

Jim was fairly certain that Lip Rings was telling the truth. He usually had a pretty accurate read for honesty. The trooper asked, "You work here before this year?"

"Yeah, third summer in a row. Tough work sometimes, but it pays. I'm an engineering major at UW, and I've only had to take loans for a couple thousand so far. Best summer work ever, man. I'll probably ride the ferry home with over twenty grand in the bank." Jim made a mental note. Twenty grand sounded like a lot of money. People have been killed for a lot less.

Jim asked, "You bankroll much yet this year?"

Lip Rings said, "Not much salmon to be canned yet. I heard that there are plenty of kings out there, but they usually filet and freeze those puppies. Canning will fire up soon, though."

Jim noticed that the bubbles had stopped. "You might want to bring your buddy up for some air soon." Jim wrote down their names and thanked the college kids for the information.

Halfway down the stairs, he heard Neck Tattoos emerge and say, "Dude, that was a close one. Is he gone? Let's light up another one."

4

Prince of Wales Island is the third largest island in the United States, behind Hawaii and Kodiak. It is over 135 miles long and almost 50 miles wide; larger than the state of Delaware. The island has over 1000 miles of shoreline due to the various inlets and points of land that surround the mountainous terrain. Only a handful of communities exist on the island and most were founded due to the fishing, logging or mining industries. Several small Native Alaskan villages still exist and a couple of isolated fish resorts reside on its shores.

There is an extensive road system of over 2,000 miles that sprawls throughout the island, but only about five percent of these roads are paved and well maintained. The rest are remnants of the logging days gone past and are only used sparingly by hunters or locals that really know their way around.

With the commercial fishing industry in decline and the logging industry almost non-existent, communities throughout Southeast Alaska turned to tourism and charter fishing in order to survive. Cities like Ketchikan, Sitka and Juneau see mammoth cruise ships full of eager tourists disembark on their docks daily during the summer months. These visitors bring in millions of dollars that are spent on "authentic Alaska crafts," most of which are made in China. These cruise ships bypass the small communities on Prince of Wales Island. The visitors to Craig during the summer months either fly in on a float plane from Ketchikan for a fishing charter, or they drive off of the ferry boat with their RV looking for a true Alaskan adventure. These tourists tend to be a little heartier and savvy than the cruise ship clientele, or they prove to be dumb as a box of bear turds.

Jim and Tavis got the call from Frightening Frankie. Frankie was flying the morning mail run in from Ketchikan when he spotted the RV that had slid off the logging road and wedged itself between a spruce tree and a tiny waterfall. The two occupants of the RV had taken refuge on the roof of the vehicle and were waving frantically at Jim and Tavis as they drove up in the state-issued Jeep Cherokee.

The retired couple had driven miles out a secluded gravel road with hopes of seeing wildlife. They thought the road conditions would be fine as they had seen an eight-year-old sign posted that said, "This road to be paved, courtesy of the Rural Island Vitalization Act (RIVA 2005 – Senator C. Travors)." Being that the sign had been riddled with bullet holes; the tourists should have taken a clue. Miles into the Alaskan wilderness on a road that was not fit for a recreational vehicle, a 2010 Luxury Coachman Plus had failed to navigate a corner cut short by a fallen tree. The driver had unsuccessfully compensated for the obstruction and plowed the rectangular-shaped behemoth down a short ravine and

31

directly into a barn-sized rock.

The crash had cracked the front window of the RV and a waterfall splashed through the windshield, quickly filling the lush living space with four feet of ice-cold mountain runoff. This forced Bill and Gladys Fetcherson from Mt. Pleasant, Utah to promptly exit the vehicle.

Gladys was clutching her yapping poodle when she slipped while descending the steps of the side door. Falling on her ass directly in the middle of a soaked chunk of moss, Gladys accidentally released the small dog from her clutches. The poodle was excitedly turning circles and yipping with high pitched vocal spasms in a small clearing next to the accident. The overly excited poodle was not more than fifteen feet away from Gladys when the eagle's talons latched on. Snookums, the small yapping dog, embarked on the finale of its life with a journey high above the trees. A bald eagle had spotted its lunch and planted spiked feet firmly into the back flesh of the tourists' pet and lifted it from the earth with grace and precision. The miniature canine could be heard yapping overhead for more than a half mile into the flight. With the sight of her Snookums being snatched from the ground by a massive raptor, Gladys released a shrieking screech from her position on the moist moss. Bill was in too much shock over his prized RV being filled by the waterfall to attend to his frantic wife.

The events had traumatized the Fetchersons to the point of delusion. Certain that there was a bear in the woods next to the waterfall, and with nowhere else to hide, Bill and Gladys ascended the aft ladder of their 2010 Luxury Coachman Plus and waited for hours on the roof of the RV before signaling a float plane that flew overhead. Roughly ninety minutes after waving furiously at the float plane, Bill and Gladys Fetcherson were ecstatic to see a white Jeep Cherokee with a State Trooper insignia rumble up the bumpy rural road.

Jim and Tavis were eventually able to guess the right logging road based on Frankie's aerial description. When the troopers rolled up to attempt the rescue, they were quite surprised to see the elderly couple clutching each other in terror on the roof of the wrecked RV. It took some calm coaxing, but eventually, Jim talked the couple off the roof and down the ladder.

What the Fetchersons had thought was a bear turned out to be a root ball of the overturned cedar tree that partially blocked the road. It wasn't until Jim made Tavis scale the root ball and jump up and down on it that the Fetchersons would finally calm down. Cold, hungry and drenched, the shivering tourists were checked into a room at the *Port of Call* until they could make arrangements for salvaging their wrecked vehicular home.

Jim made a deal with Tavis. If the young trooper would complete the paperwork on the RV rescue, Jim would agree to be on-call each night for the rest of the week. Tavis eagerly accepted the offer and went right to work on the rescue files. Tavis was excited to be officially off-duty as he had his eye on a couple of girls that might be interested in dating an officer of the law.

Jim sat at a corner table at Porty's and plopped a file folder down in front of him. Most of the faces up at the bar he now recognized. Apparently, Maggie wasn't working, but a young man that looked as though he could be related to her walked up to Jim's table.

"What can I get you, officer?" Jim had already changed into normal clothes, but it wasn't a surprise that all the locals knew who he was.

"Cup of coffee, black."

"You don't drink booze, much, huh?"

"I'm still on call."

Even though he really was on call, the bartender had it right. The truth was, Jim didn't actually drink booze very much; or at least not anymore. It seemed that every time Jim drank, some huge life-changing event occurred. It was these life-changing events that eventually put Jim Wekle on this damp muskeg-covered island in Alaska, alone and pissed off. It just made sense to Jim not to drink. Not that things could get much worse, but why risk it?

The coffee was still putrid. He had hoped that somehow, miraculously, the coffee might have changed, but no such luck. Flipping open the manila file folder, Jim went through all of the information that he had compiled on the murder case. The girl's name was Debbie Simms.

He had confirmed this through employment paperwork at the cannery. A home address was listed as Bellingham, Washington. She must have walked on the Alaska State Ferry in Bellingham and ridden through to Hollis on the east side of the island. Jim figured that she went to college in Bellingham, probably at Western Washington University. The Ketchikan Troopers Station was heading up the contacting of next of kin since the body had been transported to Ketchikan. Forensic resources were at a minimum in Craig, so it made sense that protocol was to move the body to a city with more technology and manpower available. Once an autopsy was approved by the family, the bullet could be removed and examined. Jim knew that this report would take some time. Ballistics would have to be farmed out to either Anchorage or Seattle.

A small news article had hit the Ketchikan and Juneau papers concerning the murder, and a short blurb was listed on a regional news website. For the most part, though, being so isolated meant that press coverage was at a minimum for this type of incident. The locals seemed to magically know everything that Jim knew concerning the girl. He wasn't sure if his partner, young Mr. Tavis, was blabbing or if news just traveled fast around the island by word of mouth. Probably a little of both, he suspected.

What he knew for sure was that the girl had been shot in the back while wearing a bikini. This happened sometime during the last few days of the month of May.

Somehow the body ended up in the saltwater. What he assumed was that the girl was using the hot tub at the Stockade, been shot for some reason and then dumped in the sea thinking that she would simply wash away with the current. Jim had no motive yet, nor did he have any suspects to speak of. He didn't have a murder scene, either. He only assumed the girl was in the Stockade hot tub, but had not even been able to confirm that. He hadn't found any blood evidence yet that suggested where she'd been shot. With the cannery's permission, he and Tavis had conducted formal interviews will the handful of current Stockade residents and nothing rang any alarms. There were some sketchy kids living there, and he wouldn't rule any of them out just yet, but he didn't have reason to suspect any of them of the murder.

To make matters worse, Jim didn't have a murder weapon. Without seeing the bullet that was lodged in the body and without any shell casing, he hadn't a clue of what kind of gun was used. The wound in Debbie Simms' body suggested a medium-caliber pistol at medium range, but nothing could be confirmed until autopsy and ballistic reports came in. When it came down to it, Lieutenant Jim Wekle didn't know much about this murder. He was completely stumped and he knew that had to change. It wouldn't be too long before answers were demanded, whether from the public or his superiors. Jim was new to his post and that would open him up to even more scrutiny by both entities.

"I think I read somewhere that rubbing your

temples was a sign of insanity. Either that or brilliance. I can't remember which."

Jim hadn't even realized he was rubbing his temples again. He looked up and standing in front of him was a strong-built man with sandy hair and chiseled facial features. The man wore a uniform almost identical to the State Troopers dress, with one exception: it was brown. Alaska State Fish and Game officers were actually under the same law enforcement umbrella as Alaska State Troopers. Fish and Game officers are mainly responsible for fishing and hunting law enforcement, but they carry a gun and badge all the same. Their training was similar and authorities similar in most capacities.

"You must be Gavin Donaldson. I was hoping to run into you soon."

"And you must be Jim Wekle. Welcome to Prince of Wales. You know, we actually had some nice weather last week."

"So I've heard." The two men shook hands.

Fish and Game officer Gavin Donaldson was stationed on the other side of the island in Hollis. The state brass figured it was a good idea to have at least one officer on each coastline. It was an hour-long drive on the highway from Hollis to Craig, but almost a whole day's boat ride around the island. As a result, the Fish and Game officials bought Officer Donaldson two aluminum twin-engine boats; one based out of Hollis and one based out of Craig. Any shoreline patrol or fishing regulation checks done on the west side of the island could be accomplished easier and more affordable by driving over the island to the second boat.

Gavin said, "I was checking licenses out on the water on this side today. Thought I might look you up and say hi." Gavin waved at the bartender, "Hey Shane, pour me a draft pint, okay?"

Jim said, "How was it out on the water today?"

"Rough. Wind and rain. Lots of lower-forty-eighters puking over the rails." Gavin sipped through the foam on his freshly poured beer. "Hey, I heard you caught a floater on your first day. Tough way to come into town."

"Yeah, more tough on that girl's family, though. Here, take a look."

Jim pushed the case file over to the Fish and Game officer. Gavin flipped through a few pages and asked, "No ballistics yet?"

"Might be a while on that one. I think the bullet's still in the body."

Gavin nodded, "I hear that. Most everything takes a while out here." Another sip on his beer, then, "Hey, you might see if there is any connection to the break-ins that happened last week."

Jim's eye twitched, "I don't know anything about break-ins."

"Yeah, ask Wonderboy about them."

"Who?"

Gavin chuckled and said, "Tavis, your number two. I call him Wonderboy. He hates it. The break-ins happened around town during the stretch of nice weather. Trooper Dan was on his way out and should have retired a long time ago if you ask me. Anyway, Tavis headed up the break-in cases. You should see if anything connects."

"Thanks, I'll do that." Jim snatched the case file back and wrote the words "Break-Ins" and "Tavis" on the inner flap.

Gavin finished his beer and shook Jim's hand again. Gavin asked, "Hey, you like float planes? I have a thing that I could use a little help on."

Jim hated float planes. "Sure, what day do you need me?"

"Not sure, yet. Soon. I'll give you a call. Maybe afterwards you can come over for dinner. My wife, Trish makes a mean lasagna."

Gavin started to head for the door when Jim hollered at him, "Hey Gavin, you know some guy that likes to play guitar in his boat after midnight? Long white hair?" Most of the locals at the bar began to laugh. Gavin smiled.

"Ah yes, I see you've met Kram."

"Who the hell is Kram?" More laughter.

"Well, Jim. When you figure that one out, be sure to let the rest of us know."

5

The call from the ECC came in shortly after one in the morning. A report came in of shots fired at a residence off Halibut Cheek Drive. It took Jim almost an hour to find the place since Halibut Cheek Drive didn't exist according to his computer. He had knocked on two incorrect doors before getting directions to the correct location. As soon as he turned into a driveway marked "Halibut Cheek Drive," Jim noticed that the house sat directly next door to the place he was summonsed to previously to deal with the so-called Kram.

Jim parked and knocked on the door. An elderly woman answered. She wore a nightgown that was open a little too far in the front, pink slippers with tube socks up to her knees and a Russian-style fur hat. She held a large rifle in one hand.

Jim's hand found the butt of his sidearm, "Ma'am, put down the weapon."

"Oh sure, otherwise you'll have to shoot me. Put me out of my misery, more like it. What the hell are you doing here anyway? Don't you know it's the middle of the friggin' night?" The woman laid the gun to rest against a cabinet that held four other rifles, three pistols, two cans of mace, a quarter stick of dynamite and what appeared to be a World War II hand grenade. Jim thought he even caught a glimpse of what looked like a ninja's throwing star.

"Ma'am, we had a report of shots fired from this address. Did you recently discharge your weapon?"

"Damn right I did. Just look at the mess. Little sluts!" She had chew spit beginning to drain from her lip onto her chin.

"What mess are you referring to?"

She pushed her way past the trooper and motioned for him to follow. Jim illuminated his flashlight. Around the corner, his beam displayed two garbage cans that had been toppled and trash strewn about the side of the house. Torn bags had been littered halfway into the thick trees.

"Damn slut bears. They wait till the cans are full, too. Always harder to clean up the mess. They do it just to spite me, I know it."

"We can't have you shooting at bears in the middle of the night. It is not safe and it is against the law." Jim bent down and started cleaning up the garbage mess.

"Well, trooper man, what would you suggest I do, then? Just let them have at it?"

"That's *Mister* trooper man, to you." Jim was securing the lids on top of the metal cans. He asked, "How about your garage?"

"What about my garage?"

"Well, you can keep the cans in the garage, and just move them out to the street the morning of your garbage pick-up day."

The woman turned and padded back toward her door. She was mumbling something about cops and sluts. Jim assumed she was done talking and had left him standing there, but a moment later, an electric garage door opener sprang to life. Still mumbling, she dragged both cans into the garage, spitting chew spit on her concrete floor.

She punched the button for the garage door and as it was closing she hollered, "You happy now?"

Jim hollered back, "Yes. What's your name?"

She yelled back, "Deloris. Now get the hell off my property before I start shooting at you."

Bill and Gladys Fetcherson held a small memorial service for their toy poodle, Snookums. They held the service, in the rain, at the end of a boat dock. The only other people in attendance were two drunk fishermen and the bagpipe player that they had hired. The bagpiper was also drunk and showed up with a saxophone instead of bagpipes. The only song that the guy knew how to play on sax was *The Heat is On* from the first Beverly Hills Cop movie. In between each reading of Snookum's life details, instead of *Oh Danny Boy* or *Amazing Grace* like they had planned, the musician belted out continuous repetitions of the same horn lick from the 1980's hit song. *Bah dah dee dee daht...bah dah dah dee daht* echoed off the cabins of various fishing boats.

The climax of the ceremony was to feature the Fetchersons singing in two-part harmony a song that they wrote while releasing a Polaroid of Snookums to live forever in the sea. The song was drowned out by an eagle that was perched in a nearby spruce tree. The bird thought the fishermen might be releasing another batch of old bait into the water and was squawking loudly in anticipation.

Instead of tossing bait into the water, the two fishermen were battling with the elements while trying to ignite a paper sailboat that was to carry Snookums' picture into oblivion. The constant rain had proven to be troublesome with regard to sailboat ignition. After squirting the paper boat with lighter fluid, Drunk Fisherman Number One accidentally sprayed Drunk Fisherman Number Two. Number Two happened to be holding a wind-proof lighter at the time. His clothes instantly burst into flames. Running frantically, Number Two ignored Number One's constant babbling about "Stop, Drop and Roll," and continued to flail flaming arms about the pier. Just as the Fetchersons hit the crescendo on the bridge of their song, fisherman Number One tackled Number Two and both went plummeting into the water. The Snookums photo gently sank to the bottom next to a rusted sewer pumping vessel. Gladys broke down sobbing, while Bill attempted to rescue the fishermen from the water. The sax player thought it was the appropriate time to rip into another chorus of *The Heat is On*.

Bah dah dee dee daht...bah dah dah dee daht reverberated through the trees as Bill secured the first fisherman onto the wooden planks. Seemingly on cue, the bald eagle took flight above the scene and let go with a chorus of eagle shrieks that Gladys interpreted as snide laughter from the raptor. With Gladys' wailing reaching a pinnacle, Bill suddenly discovered how much heavier Number Two was compared to the first fisherman. Attempting to pull Number Two onto the dock, Bill Fetcherson was launched head-first into the salty sound, only to be rescued minutes later by a drunk saxophonist.

Trooper Tavis Spurgeon reported the details of the late May break-ins. Two homes in Craig and the medical clinic in Klawock had been burglarized. In all three instances, a window was smashed in order for the intruder to gain entrance. In the first residence, nobody was home at the time of the break-in. The owner was south getting a medical procedure done. A few dollars were taken and the medicine cabinet had been gone through. Other than that, it appeared to be a fairly unobtrusive invasion.

The second home invasion occurred while the resident was in bed. The homeowner apparently scared off the burglar with a lot of shouting as nothing appeared to have been stolen.

"Did the resident get a look at the burglar?" Jim asked, his feet up on his desk.

Tavis leaned with his back against his boss's wall, picking his teeth with a toothpick. "No, he didn't. Old Mack is in a wheelchair. Takes him too long to get out of bed."

"How about the medical clinic?"

"That one was over before it started. Once the window was smashed, the alarm sounded and lights came on everywhere. There was no sign of the guy by the time I showed up. Nothing was missing. I don't think the guy even entered the building. My guess is the alarm system scared him off."

Jim rubbed his temples, focusing his thoughts. Shelly bounded in with a pot full of burnt coffee. Jim shook his head and she left. He longed for a good cup of quality coffee; fresh ground beans strained with the perfect temperature of water.

Tavis wrapped up his report, "I didn't have much to go on. The break-ins happened back on May 25th and 26th. Nothing since. Seems as though our burglar has decided to change his ways."

Jim took his legs off his desk and sat up. He said, "No, it seems as though our burglar has found his fix."

Tavis was confused, "Not sure what you mean, boss."

Jim elaborated, "A guy going in for a major medical procedure, a guy in a wheelchair, and a medical clinic. What do all of those have in common?"

A light bulb seemed to go on in the young trooper's head. "These were all about drugs, weren't they? Prescription meds? "

"More specifically, painkillers," remarked Jim. "And if our break-ins have suddenly stopped, then that means our criminal has found a source for his pills." Jim was fairly confident in his hypothesis. He had experience in dealing with perps addicted to painkillers in the past. Jim knew the addiction, in extreme cases, would lead one to break-ins, theft, forgery of prescriptions, and even worse.

"What source for pain meds do you think this guy might have found?"

Jim smiled and said, "I don't know, but that's what you are going to find out. This is your case, Tavis. Run with it."

"Where do I start?"

"How many pharmacies are there on the island?"

Tavis thought for a moment, "Two...no three, if you count the one in Hollis. I could go ask around, see if they have any painkillers missing. See if anyone in particular is putting in orders for more than usual."

"Bingo. That will get you started at least. Also, check with the medical clinic and see if any prescription pads have turned up missing. Let me know what you find out, okay?"

Tavis was half out the door, "You got it, boss."

6

The housing market in and around the town of Craig, Alaska was stagnant. There was basically no supply and virtually no demand for expanding the housing market. Pretty much every house was already taken by the time Jim Wekle arrived on the island. There were always rental houses available in the fall and winter, but once the king salmon started to run, all of these had become high-income vacation rentals for the charter fishing industry. Even if Jim had been able to rent one of these, it would only have been temporary. With the summer season just kicking in, all rentals would be booked for several months. The only other rental available was a room at the Stockade, but that just didn't seem to work for Jim. He would rather keep renting a room above Porty's than to house with a bunch of college kids.

He thought about possibly buying a home if the price was cheap and he could talk a bank into lending him the full amount. There were a total of two houses in the area that were for sale on the market. One of them had a giant hole in the roof that seemed to baffle the owner. The owner wasn't too sure how it got there, but claimed that it hadn't been much of an issue while he lived there. The owner recommended avoiding the room with the hole in the roof altogether and one could live quite happily.

The other place for sale was out the road a bit. It had over five-thousand square feet of living space, separate crew quarters, its own private dock and an indoor movie theater and exercise gym. It listed for just under two million.

Jim was desperately tired of living in a damp, cramped room above Porty's. The walls were thin, the bed uncomfortable and there was absolutely no room for his stuff. All of his belongings finally arrived on the barge, but the container still sat in the lot at Sea Tanks Marine Lines. Jim wanted to go pick up his stuff and move into a place, but he had few options. He had been in Craig for two weeks and had almost given up trying to find housing. That is, until an envelope suddenly slid under the door of his motel room.

Jim immediately opened the door and looked out to only see a flash of orange flying down the staircase. It was an odd behavior for sure, but odd behavior seemed the norm around there sometimes. Jim opened the envelope and unfolded a single piece of white paper. The following was written in blue crayon:

Heard you are looking for a place,

something to call home.

Look no further,

than Kram's portable dome.

The rent is cheap,

the spot is prime.

Come give me a ring,

when you're done fighting crime.

P.S. – Don't tell the damn tourists!

Jim was mildly intrigued, but what the hell was a portable dome? Jim was fairly certain that Kram was the guy in the boat with the midnight guitar concert. Kram seemed a bit unstable, and most of the locals believed the man to be completely bonkers, but Jim needed a place to live. It had to be better than the house with a hole in the roof.

The Trooper noticed that there wasn't a phone number listed on the paper. He doubted that "Kram" would be listed in the phone book, so he decided to head down to Porty's and ask the locals how he could get a hold of the weird dude. Jim flung open the door, took one step out of his room and fell face first over a crouched, orange-shirt-wearing man. Kram smiled with a sheepish grin and held up another envelope.

"Oops. Sorry about taking you out there." Kram still held his grin. Jim noticed a couple of teeth missing. "I

forgot to give you my number. I wrote it on this one."
Kram handed the envelope over to Jim, who was still laid
out on the covered walkway. Jim pulled himself to his
feet and opened the envelope. More blue crayon. It was
just a phone number this time.

Jim inquired, "If you have a place that I can rent, I
am definitely interested."

"Ah yes, a place to rent. Well, I wouldn't really use
the term *rent*, as much as I would say *earn*. I mean, don't
get me wrong, there's nothing illegal about the
arrangement, it's just that I need some help, per say. A
caretaker of sorts..." Kram's words tapered off and his
gaze seemed to drift to a far-off place.

"Kram? That is your name, right? You okay?" Jim
wondered if the long-haired kook had lost it. Jim snapped
his finger in front of Kram's face. It appeared to work as
Kram instantly switched back to reality; or at least his own
version of reality.

"A caretaker of sorts. Come, you'll see. Come,
follow me." Kram led Jim down the stairs into the gravel
parking lot of Porty's. The rain still drizzled, but it didn't
seem to bother the man. His long white hair still held in a
ponytail shed the water as if he had grown otter fur.
Kram's bright orange shirt held a picture and logo for the
old video game Frogger on its chest. His cut-off jean
shorts were ragged and stained with blood. Jim hoped it
was fish blood. His brown rubber Xtratuf boots splashed
through puddles without a care. Jim made a mental note.

He might have to get himself a pair of those boots. They seemed to be standard issue for most of the locals.

Kram hopped onto a small, one person motor scooter and donned a helmet. Kram said, "Only room for one. You must follow. I'll go slow. You won't lose me."

Jim started up his cruiser, a fairly new Ford Crown Victoria, fully decked out with all of the state-issued amenities, and he pulled onto the street behind his potential landlord. Kram turned his scooter to the south, and they headed out Port St. Nicholas Road. The road wove through trees, stealing views of the bay as it followed the shoreline around Port St. Nicholas Bay. Driveways to secluded homes popped up here and there, but population was very thin out in this area. At one point, the road turned sharply to the right, more than ninety degrees. Jim guessed that they had just gone around the head of the cove and were now driving on the opposite shoreline.

After a total of about ten miles of slow, curvy driving, Kram slowed his scooter and veered sharply to the right. Jim would have missed the turn if he wasn't following the scooter. There was no mailbox or markings of any kind; just a driveway that led down toward the water's edge. Cautiously, Jim made the turn and the gravel drive ended at a small parking lot surrounded by dense vegetation. There was no house, no "portable dome" or structure of any kind. Jim wondered what he had gotten himself into. He had followed an apparently crazed man into the Alaskan wilderness.

Kram parked his scooter and headed for a tiny break in the vegetation. He waved for Jim to follow. Nervously, Jim exited his vehicle and walked to the entrance of a small path. It was a very well built wooden walkway that led through a short patch of tall trees. The path opened up to the water with a view across the bay. Jim wished that the rain clouds weren't so low, as the view had to be spectacular on a clear day. A small, but well-built, floating dock was attached to the wooden path. The dock was secured to two tall pilings that plunged deep into the water. A curved ramp was bolted to shore and set on the dock with wheels on a steel track. The wheels allowed the ramp to move as the dock rose and fell with the tide.

The dock was only large enough to moor two small boats. One side was vacant, but on the other side of the dock, a craft was tethered to cleats bolted to a short rail. The boat was about fifteen feet in length, open to the elements with three bench seats and a medium-sized outboard engine hanging off the stern. Kram sat on the dock rail and threw both legs over into the Lund skiff and fired up the engine with a single crank.

"Kram, I thought you were showing me a rental property. I don't really want to go for a boat ride." Jim was not a big fan of boats, especially boats that small, and especially small boats piloted by a potentially crazy man. Kram kept waving him in. Motivated by his desire to vacate his room at Porty's as well as a nagging curiosity, Jim stepped into the boat, donned a wet life jacket, and held on to the gunwale.

The boat ride was short. A single small island protruded from the bay only about 300 yards from the edge of the Prince of Wales shoreline. Like all islands in the region, this one had a circle of jagged rocks on its shoreline and was thickly covered with evergreen trees. Kram guided the skiff with his right arm on the tiller, decelerated and tied up to a dock on the closest, most protected side of the island. The dock was almost identical to the one they left behind on Prince of Wales. As Kram secured the dock lines, Jim became more and more intrigued with the notion that this little island might hold the answer to his personal housing shortage. Kram was probably nuts, but at least he was guiding Jim on a little adventure.

An extensive and well-constructed trail system led Kram and Jim through the trees. The rain seemed to stop on the island as the drizzle had a hard time penetrating the dense tree limbs and mossy vegetation over their heads. The island couldn't have been more than about four acres in size. It was an almost perfectly round island with a little bit of a hump in the middle. Just inside of the hump, Jim spotted a tan colored rounded roof. They walked closer and a large yurt became visible.

"Ah, the portable dome. The one in your poem."

Kram grinned again, "I don't lie, Trooper Jim."

The yurt was constructed out of sturdy galvanized pipes that shot straight up from the ground and curved up to a center contact point in the middle of the roof. Wall and ceiling planks were secured to the pipes, and an industrial canvas stretched over the entire structure. A stovepipe exited the canvas at the apex of the yurt surrounded by a heat shielding protective fitting. A gutter system had been manufactured around the edge of the roof that sent water into a 4000-gallon holding tank positioned to the side of the building. A small, lean-to shed had been built next to the water tank. An expertly crafted boardwalk system surrounded the yurt and wood planked trails branched off in several directions. The air was moist and smelled fresh with a mix of saltwater and evergreen trees.

Kram opened the door to the lean-to shed and cranked up a Honda portable generator. It immediately hummed to life. Jim noticed a bank of battery cells next to the generator with clean, thick-gauge cables that ran from the cells into a conduit pipe. The conduit disappeared underneath the boardwalk in the direction of the yurt.

"Run this once or twice a day and you'll have all the juice you need," Kram said, pointing to his self-built power station. All of the boardwalks surrounding the yurt, the lean-to, water tank and electrical system appeared to have been built fairly recently. Everything was placed with precision and apparent expertise.

Jim asked, "Did you build all of this yourself?"

Kram winked and waved for Jim to follow him into

Brent Purvis

the yurt. A light switch illuminated a large and clean living space. Jim was surprised at how much room existed in the yurt.

"This looked much smaller from the outside," Jim remarked.

"All the comforts of home," replied Kram.

The floor was solid with plush carpet on top. The wall planks appeared clean and freshly painted. A small kitchen area with gas cook stove, refrigerator, cupboards and counter space curved along one of the walls. The bed and living area furniture looked brand new. A pellet stove was the centerpiece of the room and the exhaust pipe rose from the back of the stove through the roof of the yurt. Kram turned a knob and hit a button and the stove whooshed to life. Jim was surprised at how fast heat began filling the living space.

The interior of the yurt was all open and round with one exception. An enclosed bathroom with sink, toilet and shower was positioned along the curved wall opposite the kitchen. The makeshift bathroom walls had been crafted out of old boat hulls. Two different vessel names appeared sideways as the hull boards had been turned to a vertical position in order to stretch from floor to ceiling. Apparently, the *FV Raven's Breath* and the *MV Alieski* had given part of their sideboards for the yurt's bathroom walls.

Seeing that Jim was eyeing the boat names, Kram said, "Old shipwrecks from around the island. Figured I would put the wood panels to good use."

Jim sat down on the couch and water soaked through his pants. Kram said nervously, "Oh...uh, that got wet on the boat ride out here. Run the pellet stove for a day or so and it will dry out. Sorry about that. I would probably give the bed a day or two as well."

Jim thought the couch and bed looked a little out of place, like they weren't designed for a house. He figured it was probably just the way a yurt made things look, but there was something funny about the furniture. All of the furnishings seemed to match, following a tan and brown décor scheme and all with matching "C" logos on them. The drawers and cupboards were filled with clean plates and linens that seemed to match the décor as well. Other than the soggy bed and couch, this yurt was completely set up for immediate, comfortable living.

Jim thought about the ten-mile drive out a curvy road and the short boat ride. The isolation appealed to him. There was certainly a pain-in-the-butt factor with living this remote, but he was intrigued by the notion. Solitude actually appealed to him. The thought of not worrying about nosy neighbors, random drop-ins and loud vehicle traffic started to sound pretty good to the Trooper.

"How much are you charging for rent?"

Kram replied, "Nothing."

"I don't understand. You have to charge something

to live here, right?"

"Oh, don't worry. There is a bit of a catch. Follow me."

Again, the white-haired man was waving Jim to follow. They exited the yurt and walked on the boardwalk around the structure and up a short staircase. The steps took them to the apex of the small hill in the center of the island. Two wooden seats were positioned under an overhang. The seats were dry and comfortable. They had been perfectly placed atop the hill with views through the trees to almost every part of the island. A peek-a-boo break in the trees allowed a view across the bay toward Craig. It was late in the day, after nine o'clock, and although it was still light outside, Jim could see building and street lights from town in the distance.

Jim asked, "Okay, what's the catch?"

"Just sit. Sit and listen and watch. You'll see. Sit with me." Kram enjoyed rhyming. He wasn't the greatest poet Jim had ever heard, but at least the guy had a style of his own. Jim sat still and quiet, only moving to swat at the occasional bug. Several minutes of still silence went by. Jim shot Kram a questioning look, but Kram was lost in his own thoughts again. Kram stared blankly, lower lip falling. He seemed completely at peace. Or completely catatonic.

And then it happened. A movement and a sound to Jim's left. Then another behind him. The longer he sat, the more the island seemed to come alive. Movement on the ground, up a tree trunk, a splash in the water; there were creatures all over the island.

Jim whispered, "Kram, what the hell is all of this?"

"Magnificent, aren't they?"

Something furry scurried across the boardwalk, close to Jim's feet. It looked sort of like a long, skinny cat with a big, fluffy tail.

"What are these things? Weasels?"

"No, Trooper Jim, my new friend. These are minks!" Kram looked very pleased with himself. "And not just any minks. These are my own special blend." It was his island, amazingly handcrafted, and crawling with furry life forms. Kram was quite proud of himself.

"Minks? You mean, as in Mink coats?"

"Yes, Jim. The very same. Bet you didn't know that this is a natural habitat for these creatures." Kram took a long, full breath in through his hairy nostrils. "Magnificent, aren't they?"

"You already asked me that."

"You didn't answer."

Jim didn't know what to think. It was a strange sensation, watching the minks run amok.

He asked, "What are you doing with all of these suckers?"

"Selling their fur. What else? You said it best —

59

Brent Purvis

Mink Coats!" Kram snorted, "Hah, and nowhere else can
you get such a pure, jet-black mink coat than from these
little puppies. You see, I bred the standard American
mink with an obscure European variety and produced my
own line of mink. I call them the American Kram Mink.
What do you think of these beauties?"

I guess it made some sense to Jim. An island, what
better way than to keep the animals secure and to keep
the predators out. Jim still wasn't sure what the minks
had to do with him living on the island.

Jim asked, "So, assuming I agree to live here, what's
the catch?"

"I need someone to feed these critters. I have fifty
of the suckers living here, and more on the way, assuming
these guys start procreating. Keep the bears, wolves and
other such meat eaters away and toss these guys some
frozen fish every once in a while and you got yourself a
new home. Deal?"

Jim considered it for a moment. He asked, "How
often do the bears, wolves, and other such meat eaters
make their way out to the island?"

"No telling, yet. I just started this mink farm. You
do own a bigger gun than that sidearm, right?"

Ignoring the gun question, Jim asked, "How often
will you come out here?" That could be a deal breaker for
him. Jim really didn't want Kram as a roomy.

Kram laughed, "Don't worry. You'll rarely see me.

I'll drop off fish every other week or so. I've wired up a chest freezer in the lean-to for storing the food. Make sure you keep the battery cells charged and the shed shut up tight." Kram loudly blew his nose into the sleeve of his orange shirt and then continued, "I plan to trap and harvest fur a couple times a year. Other than that, I will leave you to your peace and quiet."

"I don't have a boat."

"The Lund skiff comes with the property. You pay for the boat and generator gas, the wood pellets for the heat stove and propane for the cook stove. I'll take care of the rest."

Jim stuck his hand out and said, "When can I move in?"

Kram shook Jim's hand vigorously, jumpy up and down, "Hot damn! I've got myself a trooper renter!"

On the boat ride back to Prince of Wales Island, Kram shouted above the engine noise, "Oh yeah, Trooper Jim?"

"Yeah?"

"I wouldn't leave the yurt door open. Those little minks are feisty suckers. They'll nibble on your toes at night."

7

A bald man wearing orange Stihl suspenders waited in the cab of his flatbed truck. A forklift set a pale green shipping container on the bed of the truck. Two men wearing raingear secured industrial straps over the container, firmly attaching it to the flatbed. Hauler Steve slammed the pedal down and plumes of diesel exhaust billowed upward. The truck bolted out of the Sea Tank Marine Lines loading lot and tore off up Highway 924. This main East-West island arterial, also known as the Hollis Highway, connected the towns of Craig and Hollis. It weaved close to thirty miles across a narrow stretch of the island, but felt much longer to drive as the road frequently changed direction and elevation.

On the west side of the island, Hollis, Alaska was originally founded as a mining community. The mine had long since been abandoned and only about one hundred people live in the community year round. The most significant event in Hollis was the daily ferry landing. Located on the east side of Prince of Wales, Hollis was the perfect locale for a ferry terminal as it easily connected the island with a half-day ferry ride to Ketchikan. In addition to the ferry terminal, a handful of residences, small shops, a float plane hangar, and a marina made up the rest of the town.

The Hollis highway left Craig to the north, passing through the native village of Klawock and then veered to the east. It ran past the seven-mile long Klawock Lake and then into a rainforest. The Hollis Highway did have some elevation changes, but for the most part, it ran in valleys between 3000-foot mountains. Due to the road conditions, most travelers spent about an hour making a one-way trip between Craig and Hollis. Hauler Steve usually tried to cut that time in half.

Jim rarely patrolled the Hollis Highway, feeling as though it was a job suited perfectly for Trooper Tavis, but every once in a while, Jim felt as though he should get his cruiser out and about. Jim clocked Hauler Steve doing close to 70 mph after flying around a corner and nearly swerving into an oncoming minivan. It took Jim longer than he expected to catch up to the speeding flatbed. Hauler Steve would really move on the straight-aways. Jim followed the truck at dangerously high speeds, lights flashing to no avail. Eventually, Jim had to blast the siren. This seemed to do the trick. Hauler Steve finally pulled over onto a small turnout next to a patch of skunk cabbage.

"They call you Hauler Steve, right? Saw you in Porty's a couple of times." Jim attempted to be friendly. Hauler Steve said nothing. He just stared forward, arms resting on the oversized steering wheel.

Jim tried again, "Think you might be in a little too big of a hurry there, Steve?"

No response.

"Let me see paperwork, okay? CDL included."

Hauler Steve grabbed the requested items and held them out the window, letting rain drizzle on them. The truck driver never once made eye contact with the trooper.

Jim noticed that his commercial license had expired. "Hey there, Steve. Looks like you need to update your license to haul. Look there, expired date."

No response.

Jim kicked at some moss on the ground. He thought about how best to handle the situation. Jim Wekle was not a believer in everything always being by the book. He believed that he was employed to keep the peace and to keep people safe. On a place like Prince of Wales Island, not all laws would necessarily be strictly enforced, but some more local-friendly handling of petty infractions might help Jim achieve the desired result. Jim felt as though he did have to find some way of getting Hauler Steve to slow down a bit, but shutting Steve down for lack of paperwork and slamming a huge fine on him probably wouldn't accomplish a positive result.

Jim handed back the paperwork and said, "You do me a favor, all right? Slow it down on this road and get your license updated within the next week. I don't see any reason to penalize you at this point, provided you do what I ask."

Hauler Steve took back the paperwork, and his pupils glanced to his left, almost making contact with the trooper's eyes. Jim took that as a "thank you."

Jim said, "I'll check back in with you next week.

Make sure you get that license updated, all right?"

Steve jammed the truck in gear and tore out of the pullout without much of a check for on-coming traffic. Jim hoped he had made the right decision by letting the trucker off easy.

Bill and Gladys Fetcherson had worn the same clothes for four days. They eagerly awaited the arrival of their RV in hopes that some of their belongings could be salvaged. They had hired a red-haired young man at Ross Land & Sea to extract their 2010 Luxury Coachman Plus from the distant logging road where they ran smack into a waterfall. Johnny Ross and his brother, Frankie, were too busy flying float planes to drive out and hookup the RV to their tow truck.

Bill Fetcherson made some calls around the island, but he soon found out that Ross Land and Sea was the only business connected to the road system that had a tow truck. An extra thousand was charged to the Fetcherson's premium MasterCard and, somehow, Johnny Ross found time to make the haul.

The Coachman was dropped off at the gravel parking lot next to Porty's. Gladys teared up when she saw how damaged the front end of the RV was. Bill opened the side door and Snookums' food bowl came rolling out onto the gravel. That was when Gladys lost complete control of her emotions.

Leaving his hysterical wife alone in the parking lot, Bill ventured inside the Coachman. The carpet was still soggy, but salvageable, he thought. But wait, something was missing.

The "Plus" part of Luxury Coachman Plus referred to the lavish cushions and upholstery that were added to the luxury couch and master bed. Each item was custom emblazed with a giant "C" logo and each sported the most advanced memory foam padding available in 2010. All linens, plates, silverware and other such furnishings had matched in color and style, and all were missing. Both the luxury couch and master bed were vacant as well. Torn away from the wall bolts, was more like it.

"My memory foam!" Now it was Bill's turn at hysterics.

8

The 1956 de Havilland DHC-2 Beaver, single-engine float plane piloted by the red-haired Frightening Frankie took off from Crab Bay at 8:30 in the morning. Gavin Donaldson sat in the copilot's seat next to Frankie Ross. Jim Wekle sat alone in the back with several boxes of cargo and two stuffed mailbags. The bush plane was built like an armored truck. Metal walls with visible rivets, thick and sturdy seats, sliding glass plate windows and an engine that rattled the ears. All three men wore headphones for both ear protection and communication. Jim listened to Frankie communicate with the seaplane base and taxi into position. Frankie gave himself plenty of room for takeoff and Jim soon found out why. It needed a rather long strip of clear water in order to take off. The Beaver seemed as though it was barely moving when it finally lifted from the water's surface. Jim was amazed at how something so bulky could suddenly evolve into something so elegant once it was floating in air. As the plane rose from the surface, small waves seemed to disappear into a shiny grey slate.

Shortly after takeoff, Frightening Frankie made a sharp bank to the right that made Jim's stomach curl. It appeared as though they were heading directly for one of the 3000-foot peaks, but Frankie banked again, nosing the

Beaver in a southeasterly heading between the mountainous crests. The weather was better, clouds still in the sky but no rain. Jim was pretty sure it was the first day without rain since he had arrived at the island. He almost forgot what it felt like to walk outside and not get damp.

Jim spoke loudly into his headset mic, "Hey, why do they call you Frightening Frankie?"

The red-headed Ross brother tossed his head back in laughter. "I guess it's because I make the mail run every morning. You know the slogan...something like; nor sleep, nor snow, nor easterly wind gusts, nor fifty-foot cloud ceilings shall stop the mail." Frankie Ross laughed again.

"Oh...Uh...Cool." Jim didn't think it was as funny as the pilot did. "Aren't these clouds a little low for flying into the mountains?"

Frankie said, "Naw, man. This is nothing. Way better than yesterday. Although you should have been here last month. Whew. Not a cloud in the sky..."

"So I've heard."

They were on their way to Lake Josephine, a high altitude lake only accessible by float plane. Gavin had received an interesting report from a pilot over in Thorne Bay that he felt was worth investigating. Gavin had invited Jim along as a welcome to Prince of Wales Island gesture. Nothing says "Welcome to Southeast Alaska" more than a float plane trip to an alpine lake.

The report filed by the Thorne Bay pilot was with regard to possible poaching taking place on the shores of Lake Josephine. The pilot had landed on the lake to do a little trout fishing off of his floats. He had his dog with him, and he let the dog off on shore to do whatever it is dogs do. After a few minutes, the pilot heard his dog yelping furiously. The pilot beached the plane and ran towards the sound of his dog. He eventually found his pet trapped in a beaver snare, half submerged in a stream that fed the lake. The pilot was able to rescue his dog and remove the snare, but reported the illegal trap to Fish and Game upon his return. Gavin decided that he had better investigate. Gavin also figured that it was a great chance to get to know Lieutenant Jim Wekle at the same time.

The float plane weaved its way between mountain peaks, and, much to Jim's relief, it seemed to fit perfectly between the cloud level and the ground. After about ten minutes, Gavin pointed through the windshield and Jim craned his neck around Frankie's head to spy a strikingly blue oval surrounded by lush evergreens. The plane flew over the complete length of the lake and then made a turn to nose into the wind. Banking hard to the left, Jim saw nothing but trees out his side window. For a brief moment, Jim felt as though he could reach out of the plane and touch the tips of the trees. Frankie leveled off and adjusted his speed and flaps and made a near perfect landing on the calm freshwater surface. The friction of the water on the floats was substantial as the float plane slowed to a chug in a matter of seconds.

Frankie's voice came through their earphones, "You can land these things on a small pond. The trick is to make sure that pond is big enough to take off from, otherwise, you might get stuck there for a bit."

"I take it this lake is big enough for takeoff?" Jim spoke into his headset mic.

Frankie replied, "Oh, no problem. Josephine here is over a mile long and a half-mile wide."

Gavin broke in, "And like almost all the lakes in the region, it is completely uninhabited. These lakes are only accessible by float plane. Total seclusion."

The plane slowly taxied over to a grassy spot on shore. Tall rock walls rose on either side of the pristine lake. There were no visible structures or signs of humans anywhere.

Frankie said, "I'll make my morning run to Ketchikan, finish a couple of errands there in town and be back to pick you guys up in a couple of hours. I'll try to have you back by lunchtime."

Jim handed Frankie two twenty dollar bills, "If you get to a store that sells good coffee, buy me a few pounds. Whole bean, dark roast if they have it."

Jim hopped off the float and sank down into the muskeg to the ankle line of his new Xtratuf boots. Money well spent, he thought. Gavin grabbed a backpack out of the cargo area, flung a shotgun over his shoulder, and latched the door closed. Frankie gave a thumbs-up after the two men pushed the plane back out into the lake. They watched the de Havilland aircraft roar to life and lift off with ease. The plane quickly disappeared between the mountains. Ninety seconds later, the sound of the engine had dissipated completely. Jim and Gavin were alone. There were no cell towers, no electrical lines, no roads, not even any trails in and out of the lake. A hundred feet into the thick woods would probably result in getting lost and disoriented. The feeling of true isolation swept over Jim, with almost an emotional response.

A few seconds into Jim's profound moment, Gavin unzipped his fly and took a leak on some devil's club. "Gosh, I love it out here," zipping his pants back up. "Jim, just look at this amazing scene. This defines tranquility."

Both men wore their uniforms with the exception of the brown rubber boots. The boots proved effective as they navigated a short distance along the shoreline of Lake Josephine.

"The stream is just up here in the northeastern corner of the lake. And don't worry..." Gavin patted the butt end of his shotgun. "Bear slugs. We shouldn't need it, but you can never be too careful."

Jim had plenty of experience dealing with bears. After serving four years at the Juneau Coast Guard Station and another eight years with the State Troopers in Anchorage, Jim had run into bears on many calls. He even had to put one down once. A grizzly wandered into a neighborhood outside of Anchorage and started munching on resident dogs. A simple relocation wouldn't do it. Protocol in that particular case called for shooting the bear as it was deemed an aggressive threat. Jim was first on scene, so the duty of dispatching the large animal fell on his shoulders. His training proved effective and he had the animal down with one clean shot.

Jim and Gavin worked through thick brush and squishy muskeg as they made their way along the shore. The two men located the stream and began sweeping the running waters with long branches of wood. Gavin's talents for beaver snare extraction were triumphant. He had located three snares before Jim found one. The snares were set up with large, looping zip-ties. The beaver would get hung up in the tie and the force of the running water would drown the animal. Trappers preferred this method to spiked traps as the pelts were never damaged by the snares. Trapping beaver was legal in Alaska with the correct permits, traps and marking indicators. It was obvious to both Gavin and Jim that this was not a legal operation.

Gavin said, "No animals in the traps. Means the poachers were here recently."

The men set the empty snares between them on a rock. Jim lit up a cigar and Gavin started rummaging through his backpack for snacks.

Jim asked, "Any way of identifying the poacher?"

"No, not really. I guess we could camp out here for a week and wait for their plane to land, but who's got time for that. Trish would kill me." Gavin offered Jim a cupcake, "Homemade. Trish is a great cook."

Jim accepted the offer. Jim offered Gavin a cigar. He accepted and said, "Don't tell my wife."

"Mum's the word."

After getting his stogie half lit, Gavin asked, "You ever been married, Jim?"

"Yeah, once. Ended not that long ago."

"Any kids?"

"No. Thankfully. I don't think I could handle living here alone without being able to see my kids." Jim puffed then crammed the remaining cupcake into his mouth. "How about you, Gavin. Any kids?"

Gavin said, "We raised a couple of kids. My boy runs charters out of Sitka in the summer and steelheading trips down in Oregon in the fall and spring. Comes home to help around the house during the winter." Gavin paused, staring blankly at the lake surface. "Our daughter died a couple of years ago."

Jim uncomfortably replied, "I'm so sorry, man."

"Bone cancer. She was just a teenager."

Jim considered what kind of nightmare the man must still be living. Words didn't seem to be appropriate. The two stayed silent for a bit, Jim puffing randomly on his cigar, and Gavin just letting his hang between two fingers.

Finally, Gavin tapped his ash and said, "But life goes on for the rest of us, doesn't it? Time to see if there are any hungry fish out there."

Gavin produced a collapsible fishing rod from his backpack and put it together. He strung line from a small silver reel through the loops and attached a Rooster Tail to the monofilament line. Gavin stood on a rock close to where the stream entered the lake and began casting out, cigar clenched in his teeth. On his third cast, a beautiful wild cutthroat trout bit hard and jumped out of the water. Gavin played it for a while then reeled him in. The fish was close to sixteen inches and fat from eating mosquitoes.

Gavin released the fish quickly back into the lake and asked, "You want to catch one?"

Jim wanted to say yes, but instead, he informed his friend that he didn't possess a state-issued freshwater license. "Wouldn't look too good, fishing without a license in front of the game warden."

Gavin handed him the pole and said, "I didn't see anything."

For the next hour, the men took turns reeling in fish. They placed a wager on who would catch the biggest. Jim knew the bet was futile, and sure enough, Gavin landed a twenty-incher. They had another hour or so to kill before Frankie was scheduled to return, so they decided to walk up the lake shore a bit. The trek wasn't easy, stepping over fallen trees, slippery rocks and soggy ground that came close to swallowing up their boots. Soon they found themselves on the northern shoreline of the lake.

Jim spotted something in the water floating next to a log. "What's that up there? Something green and blue."

They hiked a few more yards and it suddenly became apparent. Tied to a log sticking out from shore, was a green and blue canoe.

Gavin said, "That's a little odd. There shouldn't be any watercraft on this lake. Let's go have a look." Walking over to the canoe, they noticed a clearing underneath tall cedar trees. Jim stepped into the clearing and discovered a fully functioning camp; tent beneath a lean-to, fire smoldering inside a rock ring, a couple of camp chairs and a folding table with a camp stove on top.

Gavin nudged the trooper, pointing, "Look over there." Hung on a clothesline were four beaver pelts. "I think we found our poacher."

Jim asked, "You smell that?"

"What?"

"Stand over here and tell me what you smell." Gavin moved and instantly caught a whiff. They looked at each other and then stepped around the back side of the lean-to. Growing among the trees were dozens of marijuana plants. The plants were dispersed strategically in areas that would capture the long hours of daylight and be shielded from excess rainwater by the cedar overhang. It wasn't the ideal climate for pot growth, but the plants were surviving.

"Ever feel like you're being watched?" Jim asked the question while unsnapping the buckle on his Glock 22 forty caliber pistol. Gavin dropped his backpack and removed the shotgun from its sling. Jim motioned for Gavin to check the tent. While the Fish and Game officer stepped toward the shelter, Jim stood post and scanned the trees around the campsite. The tent door was unzipped. Gavin used the barrel of his gun to pull back the flap. As soon as the sleeping area was exposed, a body flashed out of the tent, grabbing Gavin's shotgun with two hands.

"Stop! Troopers," yelled Jim out of instinct. The man from the tent rolled into Gavin with full force, causing both of them to fall back against the trunk of a tree. Both Gavin and the man held tight onto the shotgun as they wrestled. Jim stepped back and attempted to train his gun on the unknown man, but Gavin and his attacker were inseparable. As the two rolled to the side the barrel of the shotgun suddenly became aimed at Jim. The trooper jumped quickly out of its path, knocking over the table and camp stove. A frying pan fell to the dirt at Jim's feet.

Gavin was starting to lose the wrestling match and

his grip on the weapon. Gavin was a strong guy, but his attacker was much younger and faster. The attacker rolled Gavin onto his back and straddled the officer's chest. Gavin couldn't keep his hold on the weapon any longer and the attacker yanked it from his grasp. Just then, a dull thud sounded. The attacker fell off from Gavin's chest and writhed in pain. Jim stood at Gavin's feet holding his gun in one hand and the frying pan in the other.

After taking quite a blow to the head from his own cooking pan, the attacker was easy to secure. Jim had him handcuffed and hogtied with the beaver pelt hanging line within seconds. Gavin had regained his composure and regained possession of the shotgun. The attacker looked young, not more than twenty years old. He had the black hair and tan skin of an Alaskan Native and wore jeans and a short sleeve, dark shirt.

Jim said, "Quite a little operation you have here. Beaver pelts, nice little campsite, a little weed growing in the trees."

There was no response from the kid. Jim tried again, "What's your name? How did you get out here?"

No response. Jim and Gavin exchanged shrugs.

Gavin spoke, "Okay, you can keep quiet. We've got you on assaulting an officer, possession with intent on the mary jane, poaching..."

"It's not mine," the kid said.

"What's not yours?"

"The pot, it's not mine. I trapped those beavers, but that's perfectly legal. I qualify for subsistence rules, you know." Native Alaskans can hunt, trap, and fish under subsistence guidelines in their homelands.

Gavin said, "He may be right on that one, Jim."

Jim said, "Fine, but what about all that weed? How many plants you got back there, anyway? Fifty? Sixty?"

"They're not mine. I was just told to watch them for a while. Make sure no one messed with them."

Gavin knelt down next to the boy, "What's your name, son?"

"Ben. Ben Nakit."

"And who is it that asked you to watch over these plants?"

"I don't know. I swear to you, I don't know." Tears started welling in the boy's eyes.

"And why, if you are so innocent, did you lunge at me when I opened your tent? That's a good way to get yourself shot, you know?"

The sound of the de Havilland Beaver was unmistakable. Frightening Frankie was circling inside the lake's mountainous interior setting up for a landing. Gavin went out to the lake to wave Frankie over while Jim went to destroy the growing operation. After taking pictures of everything with his phone, Jim pulled each plant out at the root and piled them up next to the lake. Gavin broke down the campsite and moved all of the gear into the back of the float plane. Frankie happened to have a machete on board and was given the task of whacking the pile of pot plants into oblivion. The remaining shreds of weed were thrown into the lake. Jim was fairly confident that none of the plants would survive Frankie's onslaught nor the drowning in the lake, however, no matter how many times they washed Frankie's machete, the smell of fresh marijuana emanated profusely.

The canoe was tied securely to the underbelly of the plane between the two floats. Ben Nakit was untied and placed in a seat behind the co-pilot and next to Trooper Jim. Nakit was still handcuffed, and he looked quite forlorn.

"Whoo-wee, you boys know how to throw a party," Frankie yelled into his mic as the float plane lifted off from the lake. The entire cockpit reeked of freshly cut pot.

9

Most of the vessels that docked in either of the two marinas in Craig were powerboats designed to catch fish. There were a few bigger live-a-boards and some commercial boats, but the majority of the crafts were in the twenty to thirty foot range, fiberglass or aluminum hulls and had rather large engines designed to get to the fishing grounds in a short amount of time.

Only four of the boats moored in Craig's southern marina were sailboats. The owners of the four sailboats were an eccentric and stubborn group of geezers known as the Torcadero Yacht Club. The eight members of the yacht club (four husbands and four wives) averaged sixty-four in age, and they met every Tuesday night seated at the long table in Porty's bar. The four men only drank imported German beer, specially barged in for their weekly meetings. The four ladies drank only white wine and usually polished off several bottles.

All eight members wore hats; nautical caps for the men and Kentucky Derby sunshades for the women. The irony of wearing a southern sunshade in an Alaskan rainforest seemed to escape the ladies' attention. All members wore dark blue jackets that had *Torcadero Yacht Club* embroidered on the lapel in gold stitching.

The primary goal of the club was to promote what they referred to as the art of sailing Prince of Wales. A secondary goal of the group seemed to be sourly scowling at all power boaters. The climax of the club's yearly activities was the Torc Regatta, a four-boat race that occurred on a Saturday each year in mid-August.

In protest against the snobby sailors, the regulars from Porty's came up with their own event that happened to coincide with the Torc Regatta. The festive Porty's Beer Swig and Humpy Festival was planned annually for the same mid-August Saturday, and the crowd it drew was significantly greater than the Regatta audience. The festival took place in two distinct segments. During the Beer Swig portion, Porty's bar always offered free beer for the day to anyone that would jump off the bar's dock into the harbor; free beer for a week if you did it naked. By the time the four sailboats would return to the finish line at the end of the race, the Porty's crowd was lubed up and primed to start the Humpy Festival portion of the event.

Like clockwork, on the afternoon of the Humpy Festival several of Porty's regulars would carry tubs over to the stream that trickled into Crab Bay and they would collect as many dead humpy carcasses as they could find. When salmon were done spawning, they died and usually just washed downstream, so it was easy to collect dozens of smelly, rotting fish. The tubs would be carried up to the roof of Porty's pub where four giant catapults had been constructed. As soon as the sailboats came into view, the Porty's crowd would initiate launch procedures. Flying humpy carcasses would fill the air as they fluttered toward the Torcadero Yacht Club vessels racing for the finish line.

Being that the Regatta date was only several weeks away, the Torcaderos had much planning to attend to at the long table in Porty's bar.

"I don't know why we always have to meet here. These people are our enemies," one of the wives asked.

DeAngelo Smuthers answered, "Same reason I told you last week. Because this is the only place on the island that will stock Heineken. Besides, they only hate us one day out of the year."

"One very important day," the oldest man at the table pointed out. He commenced with a coughing fit, something common after each sentence that he spoke.

The old man's wife chimed in, "We could move the Regatta. Change the date. Change the location. Let them hurl their dead fish at seagulls for a change." The other wives seemed to like the idea. They all nodded, which resulted in several of their hats almost falling from their heads.

Roger Greeley motioned for Maggie the bartender to bring out another round. Four beers in green bottles and a full, corked bottle of wine appeared quickly.

Roger said loudly, hoping guys at the bar would overhear, "Maybe we will change the date. I'm thinking

Christmas Eve." Then quietly to his group, "Let's see those bastards jump into the bay in December. Probably kill some of them off."

The eldest man attempted to holler, "Yeah, Christmas. Kill you bastards off." More coughing fits.

"No, no, no. The date's not changing. Now listen up." DeAngelo Smuthers pulled the group in close around the table. He spoke softly, but sternly, "I have an idea. Something that will make this year very memorable." DeAngelo confidently swallowed half of his beer. With a smirk on his face, he scanned the other seven faces at the table to make sure he had their attention.

DeAngelo began to lay out the details of his plan. "Now, we know where these guys are going to be, we know what they are going to be doing and we know when they are going to do it, right? That gives us a huge advantage." He certainly had the other seven members riding attentively on his every word. He turned to Greeley and asked, "Roger, do you still own that cannon?"

It had been a long day. By the time Jim processed the Ben Nakit arrest, stored all of the confiscated camp gear, printed evidence pictures from his phone, and turned over the beaver pelts to Gavin, he was ready for some peace and quiet. Jim assigned Tavis to be the on-call officer of the night, and there wasn't much Tavis could complain about. It was Tavis' first on-call assignment since Jim arrived at the station. After buying a few groceries and checking out of his motel room above Porty's, Jim made the drive out to his secret boat dock in just over fifteen minutes. Even though it was pushing nine o'clock at night, it was still as light as day out on Port St. Nicholas.

Turning into his private driveway and pulling down into the circular gravel parking lot, Jim was surprised at what he saw. A light green shipping container rested on the ground of the parking lot. The tail end of the container perfectly positioned to open up near the top of the ramp that led down to the dock. The bill of lading was attached to the outer door next to a padlock. The name "Jim Wekle" was displayed on the lading slip as both the "TO" and "FROM" clients. There was a note attached to the back door of the container:

Dear New Trooper Guy,

Thanks for the break yesterday...Hauler Steve

Jim used a key to open the Masterlock hanging from the door. He swung open the container and there was all of his stuff, just as he had loaded it up in Anchorage. His stereo, computer, dresser, boxes of clothes, French press coffee pot, cigar humidor and the rest of his personal items. He hadn't realized how much he had missed his things until that moment. Living in the dank small space above Porty's pub had impacted Jim's emotions more than he realized. Seeing his personal belongings sitting so close to his new home, the trooper was nearly overwhelmed with a relief. Jim grabbed the humidor and coffee pot and relocked the doors of the container. Priorities! He would deal with the rest of it later.

Jim's first night in the yurt was not as comfortable as he had hoped. For some reason, the bed mattress was still wet. It couldn't have gotten that soggy from a little rain drizzle. He figured the crazy old coot might have dropped it into the bay or something. He had to ride back over to retrieve a sleeping bag and pillow from his container so that he was able to crash on the carpeted floor of the yurt. With his head in contact with the floor, dozens of little mink feet became quite audible as they scurried beneath his new abode. Unfortunately for Jim, the mink on his little island happen to be quite nocturnal.

The next morning, Jim called the station at seven sharp hoping to talk to Tavis, but Shelly Gurtzen informed her boss that the young trooper hadn't yet made an appearance.

"Give him a call Shelly, and let him know that I am taking the morning off today."

"Everything okay, Jim? You aren't sick, are you? If so, I can whip up a nice batch of soup for you and..."

Interrupting, "I'm fine, Shelly. I just need a little time to move in. I finally found a place to live."

Shelly bubbled, "Oh, wonderful. You just let me

know what a good housewarming gift might be, and..."

"Okay, Shelly. Tell Tavis to call if anything big is up. I'll see you this afternoon."

Jim enjoyed a couple of granola bars and a really good pot of coffee, thanks to the beans that Frankie had brought back from Ketchikan. After propping up the mattress next to the pellet stove on full blast, Jim made the short boat ride to the big island. He unloaded everything from the container and set all of his possessions on the gravel parking lot. Two things resulted in the decision to do this: first, to Jim's disbelief it wasn't raining, and second, not everything in the container would fit in the yurt, let alone in the Lund skiff. Decisions had to be made.

His reclining chair was a must. It was going to the yurt no matter what. His golf clubs, back into the container. The autographed picture of Christie Brinkley standing in front of the Ferrari in *National Lampoon's Vacation* – heading to the yurt for sure. An unused bread maker that he thought might have been a wedding gift – destined for the container. And so it went until Jim had whittled down all of his possessions to a manageable number of boatloads.

It took four runs in the skiff before the moving-in process was complete. The yurt proved bigger than expected as all of his stuff seemed to fit. By the time he was done situating his home, he was starved. A grilled cheese and tomato sandwich was quickly whipped up on the gas stove. With a sandwich in one hand and a fresh cup of coffee in the other, Jim wandered out to the lookout chairs on the rock above the yurt. For the first time in just over two weeks, Jim Wekle saw the sun. He gazed out across the sound at the town of Craig and the clouds parted just enough for rays to come streaking through, seemingly dancing across the water's surface. What really caught Jim by surprise, it was the first time in long while that he didn't feel pissed off or depressed. Lookout Rock on Mink Island provided a calming peace for the man.

Two weeks. Jim snapped out of his peaceful moment. If he hadn't seen the sun in two weeks, that meant it had been a little more than two weeks since that girl had been murdered. How close was he to finding the killer? Not very close at all. Jim ate his sandwich and ran through some of the recent case details in his head. The girl's family had finally made it up to Ketchikan and I.D.'d the victim as Debbie Simms. That simply confirmed what he already knew. The family authorized an autopsy, and a bullet was removed from the rib cage. No word on ballistics yet. The bullet would eventually be sent to Seattle, and knowing how backed up they would be, he might not get the report for another couple of weeks. Blood toxin tests had also been ordered, but no word on that report yet either. Jim guessed that there would be alcohol and possibly some drug use in her system, but no one that he interviewed reported that she was over-indulging in anything.

What else did he know? Think, Jim. She was hot-tubbing, apparently alone. Or at least no one at the Stockade remembered going in the tub with her. After interviews at the cannery and the Stockade, Jim determined that she went missing from the hot tub the night of May 29th. That was a Wednesday. She had been last seen eating tacos in the Stockade kitchen at around eight-thirty that night, so it was probably a late night dip in the tub. No one reported hearing a gunshot that night, or any night around that date. There was no blood found in the tub, at the Stockade, or anywhere else. If she was shot in or around that hot tub, it would have been heard and blood trace would have been found. She wasn't shot there.

But where was she shot? Jim finished his sandwich, all but a tiny piece of crust. A brave mink with brown fur and a spot of white on its back ventured onto the boardwalk. Jim tossed the crust onto a floor plank. The furry animal quickly gobbled up the bite and scurried back into the trees.

She couldn't have gone far! She was in a bikini for crap's sake. No shoes, or sandals, no sweatshirt or jacket. Debbie Simms walked from the hot tub, or was taken from the hot tub, to wherever it was that the murder took place. Jim was betting she walked, and Jim needed to get back out to the Stockade for another look around.

10

Jim was halfway into town when his phone rang.

"Report of shots fired." It was Shelly. "I'll send Tavis, but I think you are closer to the address. Home on Halibut Cheek Drive. The specific address didn't come up on my computer, but I have an idea of where it is. You know where the old ship's anchor is off of Northland..."

"Shelly, I got it. I'm on my way."

Even though it was the middle of the afternoon, Deloris was wearing her nightgown and slippers. This time, instead of a Russian hat, she wore a coonskin cap, straight out of a Davey Crockett movie. A large caliber rifle rested against an old, rusted out Volkswagen van. As soon as Jim got out of the cruiser, Deloris launched a brown loogie from her lower lip. The chew spit landed firmly on the right toe of Jim's Xtratufs.

"Put the damn cans in the garage, huh, genius. Well just look at this place. Any other brilliant ideas? How about we plant those cans firmly in your ass?"

"Nice to see you, too, Deloris."

Jim followed Deloris around to the side of her garage. A bear-sized hole had been ripped into the side of the structure. Claw marks in the siding were evident around the hole and black fur was stuck in the tattered edge. Wallboards and framing studs had been ripped from their post in the side of the garage.

"You haven't seen nothing, yet. Wait here." Deloris disappeared back into her house and hit the electric garage door opener. Jim walked to the front of the garage and peered inside. Both garbage cans were completely destroyed, trash was thrown all about. A standup freezer had been opened and dozens of packages of frozen salmon and halibut had been ravaged by the bear. Remnants of the plastic freezer bags remained, but they were ripped to shreds.

"What are you going to do about this? I live off that food all year long. Mr. Smart Man Trooper with your lock the shit in the garage." Deloris spit again. This time it missed Jim's boot.

She was pissed off, and Jim had to admit, she had good reason to be. He called Tavis and told him to pick up a sheet of plywood a hammer and a pound of nails. Once Tavis arrived with the plywood hanging out the back window of the Jeep Cherokee, the two men got to work. The troopers spent the next two hours cleaning up the garage and temporarily patching the garage hole with the plywood sheet. Tavis questioned why garbage can cleanup should fall under his duties as an officer of the law, but Jim shot him a look that sent chills. Tavis decided to keep his mouth shut and do as he was told.

Jim called Gavin Donaldson and relayed the

information concerning the overly aggressive bear. He gave Deloris and Gavin their respective contact numbers and assured Deloris that the Fish and Game officer would deal with the problem bear.

"As for your food supply, I'm not sure yet, but I'll think of something." Jim was sincere in his tone. "And Deloris, be careful with those guns. I can't have you firing off shots every week. Your neighbor is getting nervous. He's the one that keeps calling 911, you know."

"Ah, screw that old man." Then Deloris emptied a mouthful of chew spit on Tavis' newly polished, academy issued Trooper shoes.

Lip Rings and Neck Tattoos were back in the hot tub, this time without the girls and without a joint in hand. Lip Rings was sipping on a bottle of Yukon Jack. Rancid music blasted from a boom box next to the tub. Neck Tattoos had seen better days. His eyes were red and swollen and a random facial tick seemed to have manifested itself.

"What happened to him?" the trooper asked.

"Too much cough syrup. Drank the whole bottle," Lip Rings responded. Neck Tattoos seemed unaware that they were talking about him. His face spasmed again.

Jim took a stance between the Stockade and the hot tub. He made a visual scan of the area, followed by a couple of pictures on his phone. The view was breathtaking. The clouds had completely given way to blue skies. From his elevated position, Jim gazed out to the saltwater in front of the town. Islands dotted the horizon before giving way to an open sea.

"Fish come into the cannery yet?"

Lip Rings took a pull on the bottle and then answered, "Slowly starting to pick up. I worked a six-hour shift today. Butthead, here, was supposed to work too, but, you know."

Butthead, or Neck Tattoos, or whoever the hell he was, began shivering. He seemed unaware that his teeth chattered in rhythm with his spastic facial deformations.

"How hot is that tub?" Jim asked.

"No one started the fire today. Thermometer says..." He fished around for a while and came up with a white tube. "...seventy nine. It's pretty refreshing after a hard day's work."

Butthead appeared close to total bodily shutdown. He shivered, spasmed again, and then drooled into the tub.

"He doesn't look too good. You might want to pull him out of there."

Jim helped pull the kid out of the tub, wrapped a towel around him and told him to go to bed. Lip Rings got out as well and toweled off.

"You find out who killed that girl yet?"

"Still working on it. You hear anything?"

Lip Rings lit a cigarette and said, "No. Wish I could help."

"Engineering major? Is that what you said?"

"Yeah, just finished my junior year. One more year of classes and then an internship. Hoping to go into industrial structure design. Big suckers. Factories, all automated, travel the world. It's a global market now. That's why I've studied three different languages so far."

"You think you could design a garbage can that could keep out bears, but still be easy enough for an old lady to use?"

"Piece of cake. Do you have access to a welding shop?"

"I'll get back to you on that."

Jim walked back down the stairs toward the cannery. He stopped halfway to get a better look at the waterfront buildings. On the east side of the cannery, Ross Land and Sea took up half a block. A headquarters building and two sheds were positioned next to the road. The wood plank parking lot held a variety of off-road vehicles and two tow trucks. The ramp down to the water was steep. Must be low tide. A hangar, gas pumps and a float plane dock floated at sea level.

On the west side of the cannery, Sea Tank Marine Lines sat protected behind a chain link fence. A large warehouse and several outbuildings sat next to a huge lot filled with containers similar to what Jim belongings had arrived in. Several forklifts and Hauler Steve's flatbed truck sat dormant for the night.

Up the street from Ross Land and Sea were a couple of other small docks, hangars and various other industrial marine businesses, followed by Porty's and the two marinas. The other direction, past Sea Tanks, the road curved around the point and disappeared into a residential area.

Where could she have been going? Jim was stumped. He wasn't getting anywhere and it was getting late. He decided to stop by his office on the way home. Two messages were taped to the edge of his desk. The first message from Shelly was neatly typed and printed in 14-point Times New Roman Font. Shelly was even overly wordy in her messages:

Gavin Donaldson called at 4:34pm.

You were out of the office, not sure where, though.

Says that he will place a bear relocation trap in the area you requested.

He's such a nice guy, isn't he?

Trap will be installed within a couple of days.

Ever had his wife's cooking?

Trish is great. You really should go over there for a visit.

Sincerely, Shelly

Jim tossed the handwritten note in the trash, but made a mental note to tell Deloris about the bear trap. He grabbed the second message. It was handwritten on a torn cheeseburger receipt in barely legible penmanship. The message was from Tavis:

Hey Boss,

Dead ends on the pharmacy inquiries.

No large quantities or strange orders of painkillers recently.

No thefts or suspicious behaviors.

Checked Craig, Klawock, Hollis.

Can give a call to Coffman Cove or Thorne Bay if you want,

but they are pretty far out there.

Tavis

Jim left that one taped to his desk so he would remember to touch base with the trooper. At least Tavis had been running with his break-in investigation, contacting pharmacies like he was supposed to. The kid was young, but he had potential.

After filing a few papers and catching up with departmental emails, Jim decided to call it a night. He locked up the station and headed for Mink Island.

The shakes set in around midnight. The man in the blue baseball cap swilled some Jack Daniels in hopes it would help. He was sweating as he paced back and forth. His hands, they wouldn't stop shaking. More Jack, but that just made him feel sick to his stomach. He ran to the bathroom and puked in the toilet. It was the third time in the last hour. More pacing, anxiety running high. Beads of sweat gathered along the ring of his hat, soaking through. His mouth felt like it was full of wool and his throat full of razor blades. He tried drinking from a glass of water, but his trembling hands prevented him from raising it to his mouth.

The man in the blue baseball cap was living in a personal hell that he knew all too well. He had lived this too many times in the recent past. He knew the solution, the only escape. The only way out was more of the same. It was a vicious cycle that he was caught in the middle of, but there was nothing that he could do now, but one inescapable action. He knew where he had to go. He grabbed all of the cash that he could find, mostly ones, and headed out into the night. He hoped it was enough money to accomplish his goal. If it wasn't, he feared what desperate acts he would become capable of.

11

The sound of the portable generator started shortly after five in the morning. Then came the banging, the power saws, and frequent swearing. Jim walked out of the yurt, blurry-eyed and confused. The sounds of construction were coming from his island. He followed a path that led through some trees around the hump in the island and discovered his landlord busy at work.

Pound, pound, "Hot damn!" Pound, pound, "Ouch, shit!" Kram was working furiously on some sort of shed. He had already leveled beams set on rock as a foundation and was working on framing in the walls. The shed looked as if it would end up being about ten feet long by fifteen feet in width.

"Morning, Kram. What'cha got going there?"

"Drum room." Kram didn't look up from his construction duties. The man's ponytail was tied back with a white zip-tie. He wore a blue Space Invaders t-shirt and the same cutoff jeans and bare feet. His clothes were sopping wet.

"Oh, of course. Drum room." Jim needed coffee. "How'd you get out here this morning? I didn't hear a boat."

98

"Swam."

"Ah, yes. Makes sense. Your clothes are wet." Jim returned to the yurt and fired up the French press. He made oatmeal, toast, and sliced up some apples. Lacking a serving tray, Jim used a cardboard box that he recently unpacked and brought the breakfast items out to where Kram was working.

"Hungry?"

Kram dropped his hammer, shut off the generator, and quickly began to devour a piece of toast. They sat on an old Sitka spruce that had fallen years ago. Thick, moist fog filled the air. Wind was nonexistent and the temperature cool. It was actually a pleasant morning on Jim's self-named Mink Island; however, Jim assumed it had to be a tad chilly for his barefoot and drenched landlord.

"Kram, do you have a job?"

Kram paused his chomping and considered the question. "Yeah, building a drum room."

"No, I mean a career. You know, working nine-to-five, briefcase, lunch breaks, union dues?"

Kram snorted and small pieces of toast flew from his lips. "Me? A corporate goon? Come home each night and ask the wife and kids how their days were, work for forty years only to have my pension embezzled by a limp-dick, hotshot Yale graduate that couldn't tie a bowline knot if his life depended on it?"

"I take that as a no." Jim sipped his coffee. It was perfectly strong in flavor. "So how do you live? How do you pay your bills?"

Kram finished another piece of toast and was tearing through the apple slices, "Jim-Khan, some people live on an island in Alaska for the scenery, some live out here for the fishing, and some people..." He bit into an apple slice and talked while he chewed, "...some people live out here to escape the nightmares. You dig?"

Jim understood. Maybe he would "dig" later. "Why did you call me *Jim-Khan?*"

The apples were gone, Kram embarked on the oatmeal, "Because..." Kram already had oats glued to his cheek. Strands from his ponytail were getting stuck in it. "You look like Khan. From *Star Trek II: The Wrath of Khan.* But I'm sure you hear that all the time."

Roger Greeley and DeAngelo Smuthers worked in shifts and covered the whole island. They hit up every grocery store, bait shop, or marine outlet connected to the road system. In an attempt to not draw attention to their plan, the two members of the Torcadero Yacht Club visited each store twice over several days. During the morning hours, Roger Greeley entered each vendor and purchased a quarter of the frozen herring packages. "You can never have enough bait," he said as the clerk inquired as to why he needed forty-six dozen herring. Again, during the evening hours, DeAngelo Smuthers made his rounds to all of the same shops. He bought about a third of the bait that remained. "My dog likes to eat bait," was DeAngelo's standard response to inquiries. The men waited two days before sending their wives in to buy up the rest. They would have sent the other male members of the Torcadero Yacht Club, but feared the guys were too old to carry fifty pounds of frozen fish trays without collapsing of a coronary.

Between the four households, two chest freezers and three top-shelf freezers had been stuffed to capacity with small, smelly fish. That left one small above-fridge freezer left to store the remaining food that had suddenly been vacated. In an effort to keep food from spoiling, the wives of the Torcadero Yacht Club suddenly found themselves preparing colossal smorgasbords of random cuisine. The club members discussed strategy while choosing food from an aluminum tray of lasagna, three Anthony's Frozen Pizza's, some crab legs that the Greeleys had caught last fall, a crock-pot full of sweet and sour meatballs, and four different varieties of Swanson's TV dinners. Ice cream bars for dessert were melting in the fridge.

"Did we forget about any bait shop on the island?" DeAngelo led the meeting while trying to stomach another piece of Anthony's Supreme.

"Someone check the store between the two marinas?" Cecil Wright, the eldest of the group, wheezed while choking back a coughing fit.

Roger Greeley said, "Ferny and I took care of that one. They are completely cleaned out." Roger's wife, Fern, smirked and stroked the sleeve of her husband's club jacket.

Blue-Jay Haverford, one-time college basketball legend, now three-hundred-pounder, pointed and said, "Pass over some more of those meatballs. Throw in a crab leg while you're at it."

DeAngelo asked, "How are the mounting brackets coming, Roger?"

"Grand. They should be ready to install on *The Cyclone* within the next few days."

"And the explosives?"

Wheezing through each word, Cecil Wright answered, "Firework sales in Klawock start up next week. I have a source that will sneak in a case of M-80's. They should do the trick."

Turning to Blue-Jay Haverford, "And the fuse igniter?"

Haverford answered while polishing off the rice pudding compartments from each of the TV dinners, "Timing sequence shouldn't be a problem. I may have to fire off a few test rounds before we run the cabling, but we should be ready to rock. Hey, hand over another slice of sausage and cheese. This dinner is awesome!"

DeAngelo Smuthers felt proud watching his master

plan take shape. His crew was proving as effective as the America's Cup team. He got up to fetch the ice cream bars before they completely melted into a puddle in the fridge.

"Ladies and gentlemen, look out for the Torcadero Yacht Club. Let the race begin."

12

Jim Wekle decided that it was in his best interest to swear off alcohol altogether. It wasn't that he was an alcoholic or even a mild abuser of liquor. He had actually only been drunk four times in his life. But those four benders, each separated by four years, proved to be very significant in determining Jim's life path.

Growing up in San Diego, California, Jim was accustomed to sunshine, warm water, sandy beaches, dense population, very little rain, and no snow. Moving to Alaska was the furthest thing in young Jim's mind as he went through his high school years. His main interests as a teenager were learning to surf, checking out girls in bikinis, and working as little as possible. As his senior year in high school loomed, Jim dreaded having to choose a career direction. He was a good kid, but like many teens, Jim Wekle had no idea which direction his life might take in the future.

Toward the end of Jim's senior year in high school, he got drunk for the first time. Several of his buddies threw a late night party on the beach. Girls were supposed to show up, so Jim decided that it was prudent for him be there as well. A strange and rare midnight fog rolled in, which must have scared the girls away, and Jim found himself sitting around a campfire with four other guys and a pony keg. The young boys, all seniors, were high from the alcohol and caught up in the moment on that beach during the last year of their childhood. Over multiple toasts and keg stands, they made a pact to stay as close to that beach as they could the rest of their lives. They would all join the U.S. Coast Guard. The next morning, still tipsy, Jim was the only one that enlisted.

At first, he wasn't sorry about joining the Coast Guard. The training was fairly easy for him and seemed to fly by. When it came time for his first posting, Jim had fantasies of tending buoys in Hawaii or rescuing stranded beauties off the Florida coast. Even if he was stationed in his hometown of San Diego, Jim would be happy. His heart sank when he read the words, "Juneau, Alaska" on his assignment papers.

The reality of rain and snow replaced the dream of sun and sand. Girls in Juneau wore rubber boots and rain gear instead of the flip-flops and bikinis he dreamed of from the warmer climates. The young enlistee was depressed. Jim went about his duties professionally, even receiving commendations and promotions from time to time, but he was not happy. Grumpy was more his standard mood. He would serve his time in the Coast Guard and move on to the career portion of his life, hopefully somewhere that could grow palm trees.

Jim's time in the Coast Guard steadily passed. For the four years that Jim served in Juneau, he pretty much kept his nose clean as far as alcohol was concerned. He would enjoy the off-duty beer with the guys every once in a while, but when they really started whooping it up, Jim always removed himself. The party scene didn't really appeal to him. Everyone seemed too happy, and he wanted no part of that.

Jim knew that an important decision loomed. As his fourth year serving in the Coast Guard quickly came to a close, he was left wondering what to do with his life. He could re-enlist; even make a career of the Guard. With that option, though, he was left to the mercy of his commanding officers as far as where he would be stationed. Jim really wanted out of Alaska. He could be discharged from the Guard and return to his hometown and look for work. He could head to college, but he really had no idea what he would study, or how he would pay for such a venture.

A month before his time was up, several of his buddies invited Jim to a poker game. The invitation was a ruse. When Jim showed up, fourteen of his Coast Guard shipmates and two scantily clad strippers yelled "Surprise!" Jim had almost forgotten that it was his birthday. Summoning the nerve for a lap dance, Jim accepted several shots of tequila, three of which came from the navel of a girl named *Essence*. Thoroughly enjoying himself and infatuated with Essence's belly button, Jim allowed himself to over-indulge.

Three days later, when the phone call can in, Jim honestly didn't remember a thing. Seeking information from his bunkmate, he learned the shocking news that occurred late during his birthday party and deep into the tequila shots. Apparently, his Coast Guard buddies put him up to it. He had agreed as long as Essence let him suck on one of her toes during the whole procedure. Essence agreed with a giggle and the application was submitted electronically. The person on the phone three days later informed Jim Wekle that the Alaska State Trooper Academy was pleased to have a new recruit come in from the Coast Guard with such an outstanding service record. His training would begin in six weeks. Jim began to question the merits of alcohol.

After completing his training at the academy, Jim's first post with the troopers was at the largest station in the State. His fellow trainees were jealous; such an assignment was considered fairly prestigious and meant great opportunity for diverse experience and advancement. To Jim, getting assigned to Anchorage meant more snow and longer winters than one could ever imagine. He tried to hide the bitterness as best as he could. For four years, he worked hard, learned a lot about being a trooper, and served the people in and around Anchorage well. He proved to be an honest trooper, not afraid to work extra hours, and always volunteered for some of the dirtier jobs. This impressed his captain, and just toward the end of his fourth year as a trooper, Jim was invited to a rather large social function at his captain's home.

Trooper Wekle accepted the party invitation. Jim hadn't had more than a handful of alcoholic drinks during his four-year tenure as an Anchorage trooper, but that

track record changed dramatically the evening of his
captain's gathering. While wanting to impress his boss
and sensing that a promotion was in his near future, Jim
accepted the martini offered to him by the captain. The
martinis rolled down a little too smooth and a little too
fast. Six months later, Jim married the captain's daughter.

The romance was a whirl-wind initiated by booze
and propelled by sheer animal attraction. They dated for
only six weeks before getting engaged. The wedding
present from his new father-in-law was a promotion to
sergeant and his own office at the station. The other
troopers at the station resented the promotion, but Jim
didn't care. Maybe his life wasn't turning out so bad after
all, he thought. His new wife was good looking and the
daughter of his boss. Jim figured that had to play well for
him.

Things were looking up until the honeymoon. Jim's
new bride turned out to be completely insane. Instead of
honeymooning on an island with palm trees and sandy
beaches like Jim had hoped, his wife insisted on climbing
Mt. McKinley. Even though he lacked the training,
stamina, and equipment to make such an epic climb, Jim
went along with it as the idea of sex in a tent sounded
kind of kinky. They were only two miles out of base camp
when Jim's stamina and tolerance for glacial ice gave way.
He decided that they had better head back to base camp
before someone got killed, so she threw her pickaxe at
him. Their marriage went downhill from there.

Jim's wife turned out to be a psychotic

kleptomaniac. He suspected something was amiss when she showed up wearing an eight thousand dollar dress to a community fundraiser that was aimed at ending poverty on the Anchorage city streets. Things continued to spiral throughout the first few years of their marriage. More evidence of thievery cropped up at various intervals and they seemed to occur more and more frequently. With each event that she donned stolen goods, her lustful behavior seemed to grow. Jim worried that his wife's stealing compulsion was so out of control, he actually talked to his captain about the situation. Jim recommended that they send her away for professional help; instead, Jim was promoted to Lieutenant and told to keep his mouth shut.

A week after his promotion, Jim got drunk for the fourth and final time. He was pissed off at his wife and depressed about the manner in which he had moved through the ranks at work, and as a result, he chose to drown his sorrows in a bottle. When the call came in, he was two-thirds of the way through a fifth of vodka. Jim was off-duty at the time, but the responding trooper had called him as a professional courtesy. The trooper had Jim's wife detained in the back room of a Wal-Mart on the outskirts of town. The officer reported to his new Lieutenant that, apparently, a Wal-Mart greeter had subdued his wife trying to run from the store with an unpaid cart full of charcoal briquettes, two pairs of women's yoga pants, a box of icy pops, and a fifty-foot garden hose. Being in his current state of inebriation, Jim answered quickly and curtly, "Throw the bitch in jail."

The divorce was almost as fast as his transfer papers. Jim's captain and ex-father-in-law was so pissed off at the arrest, he tried to send Jim to Point Barrow, a village on the northernmost tip of the continent. Luckily for Jim, the only opening for a Lieutenant was at the Craig station on Prince of Wales Island.

Although he felt that the resulting divorce and transfer was in everyone's best interest, Jim swore off alcohol completely. He only hoped that he would remember this pledge after four years. Any major life changes at that point, he hoped, would come as a result of conscious decisions and deep consideration, not an impulse brought on by a bender.

"So why don't you drink, Trooper Jim?" Maggie asked after setting a cup of bad, black coffee in front of him.

"It's a long story."

"I've found that, in here, most stories are long." Maggie smiled and walked away. Jim wasn't sure if the pretty young bartender was flirting with him or just working on her tip. It didn't matter. The last thing Jim wanted was to get caught up in some romantic tryst. She was too young for him anyway. Jim did happen to notice that she was nice to look at, however. Life certainly could be worse than having bad coffee served to you by an attractive young lady.

Porty's was busy. It was a Tuesday night, which meant that the Torcadero Yacht Club sat at the long table, drinking Heineken and white wine, squabbling about regatta details. For some reason, they showed up with seven trays of frozen taquitos, which they graciously shared with the rest of the bar. A retired couple that awaited the repair of their luxury RV sat at a table a little too close to a dart board. Nervously, they watched two red-headed bush pilots trade shots of Yukon Jack while whizzing darts past their ears. A blonde Norwegian man boasted loudly about how great the fishing was; limits on kings all week long, and he hadn't even run his boat into the rocks yet this season. Hauler Steve sat at the bar, sipping beer from a can, not talking, still wearing his orange suspenders. Next to Hauler Steve, Tank Spurgeon and his nephew, Tavis, sat with the elder informing the younger about how much a beer used to cost back in the seventies. Three kids, barely old enough to drink legally, took turns jamming bills into the jukebox and desperately searching for any music that had been recorded in the past decade. One of the kids had shaggy brown hair and dual lip rings, one had tattoos on both sides of his neck, and the other was a pretty girl of Asian descent, fresh off the ferry and eager to find a summer job.

With the bar brimming, Maggie had called her brother, Shane, in to help serve drinks. Maggie and Shane Ketah were siblings that grew up in Klawock and started working at Porty's as soon as they were old enough. Other than the cleaning lady and a couple of cooks, Maggie and Shane basically ran the whole operation. The owner of the business was rumored to live somewhere in the lower-forty-eight and, as long as the money kept getting deposited in the bank, didn't have much say in the day to day happenings.

"Another round, Shane." Johnny Ross waved at the bartender. "Double or nothing? This time you throw first." Johnny's brother, Frankie, threw a dart that bounced off the board and landed tip down in the middle of Gladys Fetcherson's salmon chowder.

"Oops. Sorry about that." The pilot extracted the submerged dart, licked it clean and threw it again; this time nailing triple-seventeen.

Disgustedly, Gladys moved her bowl of chowder to the opposite side of the table and asked her husband, "When did they say the repairs would be complete?"

Bill Fetcherson ducked as a dart flew a little too close, "They've ordered the parts. The parts have to come up on the barge. It may take another week or two."

"I don't know why we don't just fly back to Utah. This whole experience has been a disaster. We can stay with my sister until we figure out what to do."

The thought of living with his sister-in-law made Bill feel ill. It was either that or the nine taquitos that he had just scarfed down. "Honey, we're in this together and we'll see it through. We both decided to sell the townhouse, buy the Coachman, and travel the continent. When you embark on such an excursion, things are bound to happen."

"Bound to happen? William, you ran into a frigging

waterfall, 'scuse my French. Snookums was eaten by a bald eagle, and somebody stole our couch, bed, linens, pots, pans and utensils. Don't give me that line, 'bound to happen.'"

"You just need a diversion, something to put your mind at ease. We are on vacation in Alaska, and I say we make the most of it." Bill Fetcherson stood up from the table just as one of the pilots let rip with a dart. The tip grazed Fetcherson's earlobe and blood dripped into his wife's salmon chowder.

After patching his ear with a bar napkin and some duct tape, Bill Fetcherson walked over to the blonde Norwegian. The charter captain was multi-tasking; one hand on his wife's large butt, the other re-enacting the morning's battle with a twenty-seven pounder.

"Pardon, but I happened to hear that you take people fishing. I was wondering how much that might cost?"

To Bill Fetcherson's horror and surprise, the charter captain took his palm from his wife's butt and vigorously shook the potential client's hand. "Dan Pringle's the name. I run the boat, and I find the fish. This plump, hot piece of woman here is my wife, Alice. She makes sure that you're well fed, serves the beer, and filets up the day's catch for you. Don't worry about the money, just top off the old gas tank in my boat and we'll call it even." Still shaking hands, Pringle continued, "Why don't we head out tomorrow. I happen to have a cancelation in the morning!"

Bill Fetcherson agreed. He felt this might be the
perfect diversion for his distraught wife. Pleased, he
hurried back to share the news with Gladys, stopping at
the bar to change the dressing on his earlobe.

13

It was the kind of morning that almost made you forget all of the rainy days. The sun shined down through perfect, blue skies. The lush green forests followed mountain peaks to their apex, some of which still had snow at the top. Jim lounged back in the wooden chair atop Lookout Rock and sipped his perfectly brewed coffee. It was early in the morning, but not cold. Wind was scarce, which was a rarity for Southeast Alaska. The water was flat calm. Looking out over a smooth Port St. Nicholas, Jim felt as though he could skip a rock across the surface all the way into town.

Jim's friend on Mink Island, the one with brown fur and a white spot, sat on the edge of the boardwalk. The animal was gaining in confidence as it hoped for another handout. Jim was prepared. He reached into his shirt pocket and produced a saltine cracker. He broke it and tossed half toward the mink. The animal jumped on the cracker and devoured it quickly, then scurried back to its safe spot on the edge of the boardwalk. Jim reached down with the second half of the cracker, this time holding the edge between his thumb and finger. He held still, barely clutching the cracker. The animal took several quick steps and then froze. A few more steps. As it closed in on the cracker, the mink's eyes darted back and

forth and its bushy tail twitched. The little animal
nervously anticipated anything that could possibly be
interpreted as danger as it pondered the risks of grabbing
the cracker. Jim held still, even though the position of his
arm was very uncomfortable. The animal crawled to
within an inch of the cracker, sniffed with small jerks of its
nose, reached its small claw out...

 Bam, Bam, Boom-Boom, Bop!

 The mink disappeared in a flash, and Jim slipped out
of his chair, breaking the cracker into crumbs when it hit
the deck. The drumbeat echoed through the trees,
pulsing with a deep bass drum that drove an infectious
groove. With technical solo fills between measures of
funk rock, and crash cymbals brightly splashing accents,
the beat emanated from the other side of the small
island. Jim refilled his coffee cup from the French press
and made his way toward the newly finished drum shack.

 Kram sat behind a green Pearl six-piece drum set.
An array of four different cymbals floated even with the
drummer's chin. The shed had been constructed in a
manner that allowed Kram to open up three of the walls.
They were built on hinges that dropped the wall paneling
from halfway up the frame, opening the room to allow
the sound to escape. Kram wailed on the kit like a crazed
animal, a snarl on his lip, eyes closed and head bopping
back and forth. He played from his heart and soul and
held back nothing. Ten measures into a spastic solo on
the floor tom, Kram let forth a yell that even topped his
drumming decibel. He put the exclamation point on the

scream by hitting two cymbals simultaneously with the bass drum then held his pose while the sound dissipated through the trees and bounced across the water.

"Hot damn! Nothing like a drum solo to get the blood pumping." He wore a faded yellow t-shirt that displayed a screenshot and logo from the old video game, *Defender*. His clothes were soaking wet.

"How was the swim this morning?"

"Invigorating, Jim. Simply invigorating. Life is amazing, isn't it? You want to play?" Kram offered forth his drumsticks.

"No, but thanks."

Kram crawled out from the drum shed and started raising the wall boards back to their closed position. "I left you a cooler on the other side. Mink food for the next few days. Just a warning...it smells a little ripe this time."

"I'm sort of getting used to the smell of frozen herring. I think I can handle it."

Kram snorted, "Not herring this time. Couldn't find any. Haven't ever seen them sell out of bait before at all the shops. But no worries. The mink will love this stuff. I wouldn't leave it on the other side too long, though. The bears will love it even more." Kram held out his right palm toward Jim's face, "Here smell it. Noxious, isn't it."

"That's okay. I believe you."

"Swam over here and it still didn't wash the stink

off. Oh well, I guess that's what happens when you leave salmon entrails outside for a day or two."

Jim managed to finish his coffee without smelling any of Kram's body parts. He made the quick trip over to the dock to fetch the cooler, fed the minks and then went back again to head into work. Tavis surprised him by actually being early for his morning shift.

"Thanks for the note on those pharmacy calls. It was a long shot, but I appreciate you trying."

"You got it, boss. I haven't given up on the break-ins. I bet we'll get the guy someday." Tavis was grabbing a fresh batch of traffic violation slips and stuffing them into his flip writer.

Jim unloaded his standard Trooper issue, Glock 22, 40-caliber pistol. He checked the chamber and then began to take apart the gun for cleaning. "Tavis, you're a local boy. You've probably got your ear to the ground more than I do. Have you heard anything about the Debbie Simms murder? Anyone talking about it? Any tidbits of speculation or small town banter?"

Tavis restocked his shirt pocket with two fresh ink pens, "Nothing, boss. No one has said a word, outside of the normal local rumor mill."

"What's the rumor mill saying?"

"Oh, you know. Stupid kid from down south, probably drunk or high, wandered in on something she shouldn't have and got herself shot."

Jim squeezed a few drops of gun oil from a small bottle, "That much I get. She probably went for a walk after hot-tubbing. Who knows why? It was nice weather, she got overheated from the tub, maybe wanted a soda or a snack. What I can't seem to figure out, though, is what it might have been that she walked in on. What is going on around here that is heavy enough to get shot for?"

"Well, boss. Like my Uncle Tank always says. There are two types of people that live on Prince of Wales. One, the people that grew up here, and two, the people that are trying to escape from where they grew up. I guess what he means by that is, there are a lot of weird folks living in the trees around here.

"So I've noticed." Jim had already reassembled his weapon with the efficiency of a marksman. The station phone rang and Shelly answered it quickly. Several seconds later she stuck her head through Jim's office door.

"Emergency out on the water this morning. Coast Guard's bringing them in, no injuries, but apparently, there seems to be some sort of dispute and they've requested a State Trooper presence to aid with conflict resolution. Coast Guard's towing in the vessel, said they will pull up to the long dock at Ross Land and Sea."

Jim donned his Stetson and said, "Well, Tavis. Let's go meet some more of those weird folks, what do you say?" Tavis donned his Stetson and they both left the station.

Bill Fetcherson had woken up early and was overjoyed to see the sun shining. He hoped that an Alaskan fishing trip on a beautiful day would ease the grief and frustration he and his wife had recently endured. Their retirement trip was supposed to be a dream come true. Bill and Gladys had sold almost everything; the house, cars, most of their bulky possessions. They bought the nicest RV they could afford, fresh off the lot, brand new. Their plan was to spend the next two years traveling North America; summer months in Alaska, Canada and the northern states. Winter months would find them in Baja Mexico and the Gulf states. Fall and spring would include everything in between. Two years of traveling with their prized toy poodle to welcome in the golden years of their lives. They boarded an Alaska State Ferry and made Prince of Wales Island, the first dot on the map. On the third day of a two-year voyage, Bill Fetcherson crashed into a waterfall and Snookums became the lunch of an antagonistic bald eagle.

Yes, fishing would be the key. It would have to help heal some of the wounds. At the very least, he hoped, make his wife bearable to be with. She was beginning to blame him for everything. It was his fault an eagle ate Snookums, it was his fault that parts for a Luxury Coachman Plus took weeks to ship to an island in Alaska, and it was his fault someone stole everything that wasn't nailed down in the Coachman. She was even starting to blame her husband every time it rained. Maybe hooking into a king salmon or two would be the just the trick.

As planned, the Fetchersons met Dan Pringle and his wife, Alice, at the fuel dock next to the southern marina. They didn't have to bring anything except fishing licenses and a credit card for the fuel dock. Dan Pringle promised to take care of the rest. Fishing gear, raincoats, sunblock, lifejackets, food, snacks, water and other beverages would all be provided. The Pringles promised a grand excursion all for the simple price of a tank of gas. Alice hinted that a tip would be nice if they landed a couple of big ones.

Bill Fetcherson loaded his frail wife onto the back of a twenty-two foot Hewescraft Ocean Pro aluminum welded fishing boat. The vessel had a grey and red hull with a white cabin enclosure. Six heavy-duty salmon rods and a green net stuck up from pole holders that lined the top of the cabin. Dual 225-horsepower outboards hung from the transom, designed to propel the boat upwards of fifty miles-per-hour on calm water. On the aft wall, giant letters identified the boat as the "*Norwegian King*."

Despite being a beautiful day, Gladys Fetcherson donned a rain jacket followed by the largest life jacket she could find. Bill handed over his Platinum Visa to the dock hand at the fuel pump and jumped on board next to his wife. Eager to get a fishing rod in his hand, Bill felt as though they were sitting at the fuel dock for an extremely long time. Unbeknownst to him, Dan Pringle had custom installed a 125-gallon gas tank and the going rate at the local fuel dock was $5.26 per gallon. Between the exorbitant out of state fishing license fees, topping off with boat gas, and the nylon weaved hat that his wife insisted on buying, this little morning fishing excursion had already charged over eight hundred and fifty dollars to Bill's Visa card. He still felt that it would be worth it to watch his wife reel in a big one.

Bill overheard the blond-haired charter captain discussing with his wife something about running out of herring. While untying from the fuel dock, Dan Pringle said, "Can't hardly believe they're sold out of bait. No problem, we'll just troll plugs."

Pringle explained that the best place to troll plugs was quite a ways out there, but no worries, they had a fast boat. With a full tank of gas and flat calm waters, Dan Pringle hit the dual throttles hard. They flew up on step and began weaving their way between the smaller islands, heading toward open waters. In an attempt to reach the plug-trolling destination a little faster, the captain of the *Norwegian King* opted for a shortcut through Sisko Pass, a narrow cut of water between two islands. Reluctant to check a tide book, and confident that his "natural powers of nautical observation" would successfully navigate them through, the *Norwegian King's* dual props clipped a submerged rock doing close to forty knots. Both outboards flew into the air, ripping their grip from the aluminum transom. The intense jolt sent three of the people flying into the bow of the boat where several lifejackets and eight tuna fish sandwiches cushioned their bodies. The fourth person had been standing on the stern fishing platform, peering around the cabin at the time of the accident. As the rear end of the boat blasted up from the impact of the rock, Gladys Fetcherson was launched high into the air before landing in the chilled waters some thirty feet in front of the boat. Luckily for her, she was wearing the lifejacket as the hard water landing rendered Gladys unconscious.

When the Coast Guard forty-footer secured the *Norwegian King* to the dock at Ross Land and Sea and dropped off the four people that they had rescued, Jim Wekle could see that there had definitely been an incident that would require his intervention. One woman was drenched, shivering, and appeared traumatized as she stubbornly refused to take off the lifejacket even though she was safe on dry land. An older man that appeared to be her husband had a bandaged right hand. Jim would have thought the bandage was a result of the boat crash, but Dan Pringle's nose was covered in Coast Guard issue bandages and dried blood.

Alice Pringle was the only one of the four willing to talk and described a post-wreck scene that included the man from Utah demanding cash back immediately. When Alice's husband explained that he didn't have any cash on hand, the retired man from Utah punched her husband clean in the face. By the time the Coast Guard vessel reached the dock, both men had reached an epic boil. Bill

Fetcherson threatened to start throwing punches again if refund cash and trauma money wasn't immediately produced, while Dan Pringle ranted on about his personal injury lawyer slapping on a suit that would empty the old man's retirement account faster than he could blink.

Jim and Tavis separated the two men and made each sit on the short rail surrounding the Ross' wooden dock. After a few minutes of calm intervention, Jim finally got both men to agree on a solution. Dan Pringle would not press charges and would not sue for personal injury from the punch in the face. In return, Bill Fetcherson would call it even on the boat gas charge to his Visa card. Once it appeared that the services of the State Troopers were no longer needed, Jim sent Tavis out on patrol. Jim decided to hang around the dock for a while just to make sure the action had dissipated.

Jim watched a frail, wet older woman wearing an orange life preserver walk gingerly away from the scene toward Porty's. The woman's husband scurried along after, displaying a concern that was not acknowledged by his wife.

Alice Pringle yelled to the woman, "Hey, what about my lifejacket."

The retired woman from Utah said nothing in response, but as she hobbled away, a trembling middle finger slowly rose from her left arm. The Pringles decided to let her keep it.

MINK ISLAND

14

Jim returned to his office. He had some paperwork and emails to get caught up on. He asked Shelly to make a fresh pot of coffee, and to his surprise, she agreed without going into too much detail. Jim sat and rubbed his temples before embarking on the paperwork. For some reason, he felt that a good temple rub helped prepare him for the job.

After about ten minutes, Shelly entered the office with a hot cup and stern look on her face. "Here, have a sip."

He took the cup and completed the assigned task of sipping. Shelly continued to stand in the office, still a concerned look. "Shelly, what is it? You seem a little less bubbly than usual."

"Well, I got a call this morning. It was from that girl's father. The Debbie Simms girl. Well, the father, uh... he wants to come out here and meet with you." Shelly went on to explain that Mr. Simms had flown up to Ketchikan to identify the body and authorize the autopsy and bullet extraction. He wanted to fly over to Craig for a day and see where his daughter spent her last time on earth. He wanted to see where she was found and talk to the office in charge of her murder investigation.

Jim wasn't surprised. "Shelly, set up the meeting. I will certainly make time for Mr. Simms."

Shelly turned, her concerned face turning to sadness. Jim called her back, "Shelly. You've been here long enough to know that this is a part of our duty. It's not easy, but necessary."

"I know, boss. I just get sad when I think about a father losing a daughter."

Jim agreed, "Yeah, me too. I only wished that I had more information to share with him."

The dispatcher went back to work at the front window. Jim thought Shelly Gurtzen might be overly chatty at times, but she kept a clean and organized office. The filing system was professionally processed, computer desks had cables neatly tied and routed. The meeting room and single holding cell were sterile and polished. The front safety glass that separated the office from the general public was smudge free.

Busily typing on the dispatch computer, Shelly heard the beep that indicated the front doors opening. Three young people walked into the station. Two had a seat in the cramped waiting area and one walked up to the window. The boy at the window had bushy brown hair and two rings hanging from his lower lip. Shelly wondered how he ate corn on the cob.

Speaking into the audio device, Lip Rings said, "We need to see one of your officers. Tall guy, middle-aged."

Shelly said, "You mean Lieutenant Wekle, I'm sure. What is this concerning?"

Lip Rings motioned to the two that sat behind him. One guy who had tattoos on both sides of his neck looked to be in his mid to lower twenties. A girl wearing a flannel shirt, jeans and rubber boots rubbed the shoulder of Neck Tattoos. The girl couldn't have been more than nineteen. Shelly hoped that the shoulder rubbing wouldn't escalate into anything more intimate in the waiting room.

Lip Rings said, "My friend, over there, has some information that I think Trooper Wekle should hear. It's about that girl that died."

Shelly buzzed them through. She led them to the meeting room and asked them to sit at the table. A minute later, Jim walked into the room. The three kids reeked of dead salmon. The slime line must be in full swing. Jim figured he better get their names in case their information made his official report. Lip Rings and Neck Tattoos might seem a bit unprofessional when typed into an investigation log. Lip Rings' real name was Shawn Foster. He was twenty-three and from Seattle. Neck Tattoos' name was Skye McDoogle. Skye was twenty-one and was from a suburb of Portland, Oregon where he lived in his parent's basement. The girl was nineteen and only there to support her new boyfriend. Apparently, Skye needed a lot of shoulder rubbing in order to talk to a State Trooper.

Jim said, "Now that we all know each other, why

don't you tell me why you're here."

Shawn Foster, aka Lip Rings, spoke first, and it was obvious to Jim that Foster was the only one of the three kids that possessed measurable intelligence. "Once the cannery work really fired up, it forced Butthead here to sober up. Once his brain cleared from the haze of continuous chemical abuse, he started talking about the Simms girl. I think you need to hear what he has to say."

Jim turned his attention to Skye McDoogle, aka Neck Tattoos. The girl progressed to rubbing his back. Jim really wanted the rubbing to stop. Skye didn't speak; he just kept staring at Jim. Jim raised his eyebrows, cuing the stoner that it was his turn. Finally, Jim said, "Uh, Skye is it? Why don't you tell me about Debbie Simms?"

Skye McDoogle said, shaking his head, "Dude. There was this guy." Then nothing. Jim waited, but nothing came.

"What about this guy?"

"Sorry dude. I'm just nervous. You're wearing your policeman outfit and everything. Carrying your gun and handcuffs. Dude." The girl sensed the increased anxiety level and moved her rubbing to the lower back area.

The trooper said, "You are not in trouble, here. You came to me. I just want to hear a little more about this guy you mentioned."

Shawn Foster said, "Butthead, tell him what you told me. Go on, man."

Skye continued, "Well, it was like, two or three times, this guy knocks on the door and asks for Debbie. They would sometimes go in the hot tub for a while and then they would disappear. I figured, you know, they would go do the nasty, you know. Huuhuh." He laughed like a surfer dude that had smoked too much weed.

Jim made a few notes and said, "Tell me more about this guy. You know his name? Ever see him since we found the body?"

"Dude, no. I have no idea who this guy is."

"Can you describe him to me? Young, old, tall, short, what kind of clothes he wore?

"Black."

Jim raised his eyebrows, but no other information came forth. Jim asked, "Was this man an African-American?"

"No, man. Black hair. I remember that. When he got out of the hot tub, his hair was so black that it looked all oily. It was trippy, dude."

"Trippy, right." Jim decided to not write that adjective in his report. "How old do you think this guy is?"

"I don't know. Older than me, but younger than you."

Jim made more notes, "That helps. Do you have any idea where they would go when they left the hot tub?

Back into the Stockade?"

"No, man. They would head down the steps. That's all I know. Never would see them after that."

Jim tried to make eye contact with Skye. "If you saw this man again, would you recognize him?"

"Dude, I don't know." Neck Tattoos seemed to actually be thinking, which appeared to be a painful exercise. "Yeah, man, like, I think I would. I was pretty sto... or, uh, tired when that dude rolled around, but I think I would recognize him." His girlfriend was proud of him. The massaging dipped further south, bordering on his butt crack. Jim tried not to look.

The trooper handed each of the two boys his card, thanked them for coming in and saw them to the exit. He pulled Shawn aside and said, "I think I have a metal shop lined up. You still willing to help me with my bear can project? I'll pay you for your time."

Shawn nodded and said, "I'll get to work on the designs right away. I don't get a lot of time off right now, but between the chum opening and the pink run, I bet we can get the project done."

Just as the three kids were leaving the station, Jim hollered, "Hey Skye. A word of advice, dude. Lay off the drugs. What few brain cells you have left will thank you." The stoner launched into his surfer dude laugh again.

The man in the blue baseball cap was out of pills. Jack Daniels would work for only so long, and then the shakes and sweats would set in again. The shakes and sweats would soon give way to nausea and then, eventually, total despair. He had money to buy, but feared that there would be no supply to fill his demand. He feared that the supply would arrive too late, again past the point of complete desperation. He feared that he would be forced into desperate measures again.

The man in the blue baseball cap left his home, got in his car and drove down the road. About ten minutes later, he was knocking on a red metal door illuminated by a single hanging light bulb. It was the same door he always knocked on when he was desperate. No one answered, so the man continued to knock. After several minutes of persistence, the door cracked open.

A rough voice quietly spoke through the slit of the open door. "We're closed for business. Come back next week."

The man in the blue baseball cap pleaded, "You have to have something for me. Come on, just a little is all I need."

The voice, "I said, we are closed. And a word of advice. You'd best lay low for a few days. Stay indoors. Keep your nose clean. No more breaking through windows, or you'll be cut off for good. Understand?"

Blue baseball cap pleaded again, "Just a few to get me by. I promise, no more break-ins. But you gotta help me out a little. Come on."

The door closed and a deadbolt could be heard sliding into place. The man in the blue baseball cap had been denied what he needed. A few days, he hoped he could make it. He hoped the Jack Daniels would hold him through better this time. He returned to his home, locked his door, dimmed the lights, and poured himself a tall glass of brown liquid.

15

Jim saw the kid crossing the street between the cannery and the Stockade. He had straight black hair. Jim knew who this kid was, and he wasn't exactly a Boy Scout. Ben Nakit crossed the street and walked in front of the cannery. Jim expected him to enter the tall cannery doors, but the kid kept walking up the sidewalk. The pungent smell of fish slime hit Jim in the face through the open window of his cruiser. The trooper studied Ben Nakit as he walked up the street. The black hair fit, but his age didn't. Neck Tattoos had said that the man with Debbie Simms was between their two ages. Ben Nakit was twenty years old. Jim remembered his age from booking the kid for the marijuana growing operation. Nakit might have been twenty, but he looked a bit younger. Jim also had to consider the source of this information. Neck Tattoos could have been so stoned that age wasn't relevant.

The Trooper watched Ben Nakit take purposed strides up the sidewalk. The kid walked past the Sea Tank Marine Lines warehouse and turned into the lot filled with containers. Nakit disappeared inside a trailer marked with a sign that said *Receiving*, then reappeared a minute later wearing a hard hat and an orange vest. He walked over to a forklift, fired it up, and began moving containers around the lot.

Jim Wekle exited his cruiser and jogged across the street. He stepped through a door in the warehouse indicating that it led to the shipping office. The warehouse was fairly large, but cramped with crates and pallets that had been unloaded from the containers. A shrink-wrapped pallet of new flat screen TV's, ten boxes of Florida oranges, boat parts, a crate filled with fresh two-by-fours; all fresh off a barge and labeled with which local business would be coming to claim the freight. A few smaller forklifts buzzed inside the warehouse. A table filled with grease-covered invoices and random clipboards was positioned against a far wall. Hauler Steve was propped against the table, smoking a cigarette.

Jim approached, and asked, "You know where I can find Tank?"

Without turning his head and without speaking a sound, Hauler Steve used his thumb to point toward an office in the corner.

Jim started heading to the office, then turned around and said, "Oh, and, thanks for delivering my stuff." Hauler Steve made brief eye contact, his version of saying, "You're welcome."

The office was small, messy and smelled of smoke. A woman entered information into a computer from a stack of invoices. She had a cigarette dangling from her lips. A man updated a shipping schedule with black marker on a giant, wall-mounted dry erase board. Tank

Spurgeon was on his desk phone, gabbing away through a cigar clenched in his teeth. As soon as Jim opened the door of the office, a dog began to bark at him.

"Blitz, shut the hell up," Tank yelled at the dog over the phone receiver. A brown and white German Bulldog retreated to a cushion in the corner of the room. Tank Spurgeon wrapped up his phone conversation and hung up the receiver, turning his attention to the trooper.

"Lieutenant Jim Wekle, Prince of Wales Islands' newest law enforcement. How the hell are you?" Tank was a strong looking man with black and white hair covering his head and face. A brown shirt that advertised *Sea Tank Marine Lines* was pulled tight over a pot belly. He stuck his hand out.

Jim shook hands with the barge boss and said, "Can't complain. At least it's not raining."

"I hear that. Hell, last fall we had sixty-two days straight without a break from the rain. Gets a little depressing when that happens." Tank took a puff on the cigar that hadn't yet left his teeth, "You should have been here that last week of May. Whew, it was nice."

Jim scowled.

Tank asked, "My boy, Tavis, doing good work for you? You know, I raised that man from the time he was seven."

"I didn't know that. You did a fine job. He's a good guy and developing into a darn good trooper."

The office phone rang. Tank motioned to the whiteboard guy to answer it. "Don't mean to be rude, but things are hopping around here. Can I help you with anything?"

Jim said, "Ben Nakit. I noticed he just started working a shift for you out there. He work for you long?"

A look of understanding came across the bearded man's face. "Ah yes, young Mr. Nakit. I heard about that arrest. Saddens me, to think... Anyway, yes, Ben has worked for me off and on for the past couple of years. He takes to a forklift naturally. That kid can run containers around the lot better than most of the old guys."

"Off and on? If he's so good with the forklift, why not employ him fulltime?"

"Barge only comes in once a week. Hard to keep five yard workers on fulltime. A lot of the old guys, they've got families to support. Plus, they've worked here for years. I do have my loyalties, you know."

It made sense to Jim. He asked, "When did Ben get out of jail from the arrest?"

Tank said, "I heard he made bail. Showed up the other day to work his shift without missing a beat. I'm sure, Lieutenant, that you're capable of obtaining more information than I concerning Ben Nakit's release."

The man had a point. Jim would put Tavis in charge of researching the court documents. The phone rang again. Tank said, "If you don't mind, I have a barge traveling north that is hung up by tides in the Wrangell Narrows and an insurance claim to fill out on some RV parts that fell off half way up from Seattle."

Jim shook his hand again and thanked him for his time. On the way out the door, Jim turned and asked, "What kind of stogie do you smoke?"

"Nothing but the best," Tank grinned, cigar still clenched. "Swisher Sweets. Four bucks a pack."

Jim laughed and said, "I'll have to give you one of my Dominicans some time. Four bucks a smoke, but they don't taste like a cat crapped in your mouth."

"The cat turd aftertaste is the best part." As soon as the door closed, the bulldog barked again. "Blitz, shut the hell up!"

When it came down to it, Maggie Ketah pretty much ran the show at Porty's. The duties were supposed to be split evenly between her and her brother, Shane, but Maggie had long since accepted the fact that her brother could only be counted on to work a few shifts and occasionally make some of the needed repairs on the old building. Maggie hired and scheduled the other employees, ran the books which included monthly reports to the non-resident owner, tended the bar, cooked the after-hours menu for the late night customers, and even scrubbed the toilets three days a week. She tried to take at least one night off per week, but that was becoming more and more difficult. Her brother had health issues. She desperately wanted to reduce his salary in order to hire more help, but she didn't have it in her heart. Besides, she feared that Shane would freak out on her if she even mentioned the topic. Her brother's mood swings were becoming more and more volatile.

The joint was hopping again. Maggie could keep everyone's drink filled provided that the cook would serve the plates for her. She hired one of the Stockade girls to help bus tables and do dishes part-time, and luckily the kid was working that night. It was a Saturday night, which naturally had its fair share of barflies, but in addition, the perfect storm of a break in the commercial fishing opening and an impromptu gathering of the Torcadero Yacht Club had slammed the place. Stealing a moment in the kitchen, Maggie dialed a phone number and pleaded with her brother to come in to help tend bar, but Shane insisted that he wasn't well enough to get out of bed. Maggie sighed, wished him the best and flew back to the bar to open four fresh bottles of Heineken.

"Now, timing is crucial. Are you sure we don't need a test run?" DeAngelo Smuthers questioned, running the meeting like always did.

The portly Blue-Jay Haverford said, "Trip igniters cued by RF timing relays. Piece of cake, DeAngelo." After his stint playing college basketball, Blue-Jay trained and served as a demolitions expert with the U.S. Navy. "I can go through my qualifications again, if you really want me to."

"No, no, you're right. I'm sure you will have everything rigged correctly."

The ladies waved an empty bottle of wine at the bartender, Maggie. Seconds later, a freshly corked magnum was placed on the long table.

Turning his attention to Roger Greeley, DeAngelo asked, "How are our herring supplies? Are you certain we have enough to make the true desired impact?"

Old man, Cecil chimed in, "Enough? Every crevice of my ice chest is packed with the stupid sardines." A coughing fit ensued.

Roger Greeley replied, "I think we have enough for four, but you recently talked about doubling to eight. We'll need more herring if that's going to happen."

DeAngelo smirked and looked around the room filled with his sworn enemies. "Let's double the load. Just look at all these little peckers. They don't know what's about to hit 'em."

Roger said, "A new, emergency shipment of herring has been ordered and should arrive by float plane on Monday. I say we hit the mother lode there, before it gets distributed out to the stores."

"Oh, Roger. You're so fiendish, I love it," Ferny whispered at her husband through pursed lips.

DeAngelo adjusted his nautical hat. He liked the idea. "Folks, we need to plan a herring ambush."

MINK ISLAND

16

The mink were hungry. Jim could tell. They were more restless and more aggressive than usual. It had been a few days since Kram had delivered a tub full of salmon parts and, with the apparent herring shortage in town, Jim lacked the resources needed for satisfying the little critters. A few of the mink had gotten brave enough to venture into the waters surrounding the island, swimming in the shallows looking for anything alive to snack on. The rest seemed determined to enter the yurt, knowing that there had to be a food source of some sort in there. Jim accidentally left the door ajar for less than thirty seconds and in that short time, a loaf of bread seemed to mysteriously disappear from his kitchen counter.

Jim had tried calling Kram a couple of times, but his odd landlord wasn't answering. The outgoing message started with screaming, followed by some sort of screeching feedback caused by a guitar amplifier. Jim left messages, but he wasn't entirely sure they'd ever be heard.

For fear that the little-clawed suckers would eventually scratch their way through the canvas wall coverings of the yurt, Jim decided that the minks had to be fed. He picked up a forty pound bag of cat food on his way home from work and carted it down the boat ramp. Once docked at his Mink Island home, Jim carried the cat food to the side of the island furthest away from his yurt and tore open the bag on the steps of the drum shack. He called to the minks by whistling to them as if they were dogs and then left the bag there unattended in hopes the little varmints would become satiated.

Jim noticed his dinner on lookout point was fairly uninterrupted, with only his white spotted little friend begging for a handout.

"I think it's time we name you, friend. What would you like to be called?" Jim offered out a piece of his ham sandwich. The furry little guy was now used to Jim's daily feedings and would scurry up and snatch the food right from his hand.

After eating, Jim fired up a cigar. It wasn't raining, but the night sky looked as though the weather was changing soon. He puffed on his mail-ordered imported smoke and noticed that his mink friend had scurried up and taken a seat on the unoccupied wooden chair. Jim's cigar eventually reduced in size enough to cause Jim to remove the paper label band that circled his smoke. *Oscar Fernandez Dominican Delights* was his favorite brand. He muttered, "Oscar, that has a nice ring to it."

"So, Oscar, my little friend. What brings you to Mink Island?" Jim asked the weasel-like mammal. "Me, oh, I don't know. Some might say a string of good fortune. Some might blame a streak of bad luck."

Another puff on the cigar. Lookout Point was proving to be a place of solace for the trooper. When he sat on the wooden chairs, looking over the beauty of rocks, trees, water, float planes and fishing boats, Jim could peacefully contemplate. He didn't even need to rub his temples to achieve deep thought.

"What do you think, little Oscar? Could Ben Nakit be a killer? My gut says no. But he's the best lead I've got." The animal occasionally adjusted its position on the chair, but seemed far less twitchy and nervous than the rest the mink brotherhood. "Yes, it seems as though I need to pursue this lead. What's that you say? I need a copy of Ben Nakit's mug shot? Good idea there, Oscar. I'll put Shelly on digging up that picture in the morning. How does that sound? I agree, sounds like a plan."

Jim's cell phone began beeping and little Oscar leaped off of the chair and hid under the deck. The call was from the Emergency Call Center. There was an urgent call for assistance just off of Halibut Cheek Drive. Jim asked the ECC dispatch if shots had been fired. The operator informed of no report of shots, but the woman that made the call claimed she might shoot the guy if he didn't shut up soon.

After extinguishing his cigar, dressing back into his State Trooper blue uniform and making the boat ride back to shore, it took Jim about a half hour to reach the scene. The commotion was not hard to find. A few yards up the road from where Deloris lived, two people sat in lawn chairs next to a large metallic tube. One wore a World

War II fighter pilot's hat and pink slippers. The other person wore a purple shirt with the Asteroids video game logo on it. Both Deloris and Kram were sharing a bag of Doritos and pointing at a large metallic tube. A grey-haired man wearing plaid pajamas shook violently at a metal grate that enclosed one end of the tube. Jim immediately recognized the man as the person Kram had terrorized weeks earlier with his mid-night guitar playing boat ride.

"I want these two arrested, and get me the hell out of this thing." The grey-haired man was frothing as a result of his tirade.

Ignoring the trapped old man for a moment, Jim nodded at his landlord seated in a lawn chair and said, "Kram."

"Hey there, Trooper Jim. How's the island treating you?"

"I talk to mink, now. And I pretend that they talk back."

"Perfect."

The man shook the cage door vigorously and began to cuss. Jim turned to Deloris and said, "I take it, this is the neighbor that keeps calling 911 on you?"

She smiled widely and said, "Doesn't he look cute in there?" She spat brown chew juice on the ground next to the cage.

Jim asked, "Either of you happen to know how this guy ended up encaged inside this bear trap?"

"No, not a clue." Both looked about as innocent as a five-year-old with her hand in a cookie jar.

A Bearwise Model 210 live bear trap is constructed out of an eight foot long, six foot in diameter galvanized cylinder. The cylinder is positioned atop a two-wheeled trailer that can be easily towed, thus allowing for successful relocation of problem bears without having to put the animals down. At the deep end inside the cylinder, a smelly hunk of meat dangles from a cable. Once this meat is tampered with, it triggers a cage door to be released and locked into place, thus caging the animal.

"Sir. Settle down and explain to me what happened."

"What happened? You want to know what the hell happened here? Those two should be locked up. Look at me. They did this." He continued to shake the door, kicking at it as he spit words from twisted lips.

"Did either of you put him in the trap?" Jim asked. They both claimed to be playing a game of Boggle at Deloris' house when they heard the old man's hysterical screams. They rushed out and found him trapped in the bear cage, called 911 and waited for help to arrive.

"That is bullshit! You hear me. They are lying. I know it."

"Sir, tell me exactly what happened."

The old man stopped his thrashing, gathered his thoughts and reported, "I had just gotten ready for bed. I poured myself a nightcap and turned on the TV to watch my *Matlock* reruns like I always do. Next thing I know, I wake up inside this thing. I completely freaked out. Thought I had died and gone to hell at first. I'm not too proud to admit, I was so scared that I soiled myself."

Kram pinched his nose and said, "TMI, Carl. TMI."

Jim asked, "Kram, did you drug this man and remove him from his own house?"

"Naw, man, it's like we told you. Deloris was kicking butt at Boggle, and..."

"Damn right I was!" Deloris had spit starting to drain down her chin.

Kram continued, "...and we start hearing all this carrying on. Being the upstanding citizens that we are, we called for help immediately."

"Aaaaaah!" The grey-haired man had lost it. "Upstanding citizens? Aaaaah! They sat down in their camp chairs and watched me like I was some attraction at the zoo. They kept throwing corn chips at me."

"Thought he might have been hungry," Kram interjected.

Bears are impressively strong and amazingly adept at manipulating things like doors to cages. Once triggered shut, the Bearwise Model 210's portal is designed to only be opened with a special infrared remote that accesses the cage's release mechanism. It is designed this way so that once trapped, an angry and disoriented bear can be released into the woods from inside the safety of a motorized vehicle. The remote control for this bear trap happened to be sitting on Gavin's Donaldson's desk on the other side of the island. It took over three hours for Fish and Game Officer Donaldson to get there.

After his release, plaid pajama-wearing Carl was furious that Deloris and Kram were not being arrested, but Jim explained that there really wasn't any confirming evidence, not to mention, if it really was a prank, it was only borderline on criminal.

"Borderline criminal? Borderline? Those two are terrorists for shit's sake. Throw them in the cage." Carl was inconsolable and needed help returning to his home. Gavin reset the trap and escorted Carl back to the safety of his house. Halfway down a short trail through the trees, Gavin could swear that Carl smelled like poop.

As the day wore on, rain started to drizzle. Jim asked, "What do you have against this guy, anyway?"

Kram said, "Long story for another day."

Jim said, "Kram, where have you been lately? I had to feed the minks with a bag of cat food."

"Had to go south for a few days. You know, the fourth is right around..." Kram's gaze fixed into space, his train of thought completely on pause for a moment.

"...the corner."

"What does that mean? And where do you go when you pause like that?"

Kram started throwing sticks at the meat, seeing if he could trigger the cage door to slam shut. "Not a clue of what you're talking about, Jimbo. But you know, the fourth is coming up. The Fourth of July. I went south to pick up the guys."

"Stopping throwing sticks at the bait. What guys did you have to go pick up?"

Kram obeyed the command about the sticks and started scanning the ground for rocks. "The band, Jimmy, the band."

Deloris chimed in, "Kram throws a concert down on the docks just before the fireworks every year. It's a hoot. Can't wait. I'm buying a new hat just for the big dance."

Gavin appeared back at the bear trap site and said, "You know, I think that guy crapped his pants."

Kram nailed the raw meat with a two-inch jagged stone and the cage door slammed to the ground. "Hot damn!"

Gavin hit the remote button again and said, "Knock it off Kram. This thing isn't a toy."

Craning his head under the rising cage door to scrutinize the reset process of the trap, Kram said, "I hired Maggie to serve the hot dogs and beer this year. I hired her just for you, Trooper Jim."

Defensively, Jim said, "What the hell does that mean?"

Deloris spit into the bear trap and said, "Word is, she's got the hots for you. Not many chicks around here, you know. You better jump on that while you have the chance."

Gavin started to chuckle.

Jim said, "Not gonna happen. Last thing I need is a girl in my life. They tend to depress me. Besides, I'm probably five years older than she is."

Smiling, Gavin said, "Try more like ten, there, Jimbo."

17

The call came in the middle of a rainy afternoon. Trooper Tavis Spurgeon arrived first as he was already on patrol in the area. By the time Jim arrived, Tavis had taken statements, photographed the scene and had a good enough handle on the incident to make a full report to the Lieutenant.

"Broke in through the back door. He smashed the door's window with a rock, reached in, and unlocked it." Tavis was reviewing notes from his flipbook as he brought Jim up to date. "The thief knew what he was looking for. Went straight for the medicine cabinet. He passed up about five thousand dollars' worth of home entertainment equipment. This guy was after prescription drugs."

"Didn't even take my outboard, over there." Dan Pringle pointed to a brand new trolling engine propped up on a wooden sawhorse with a hose attached to it. "That thing retails at close to three grand."

Jim walked with Dan and Alice Pringle to the back of their house. Tavis' report seemed accurate; window smashed, ransacked medicine cabinet, nothing else in the house seemed disturbed. Jim asked, "Do you know when this happened?"

Dan Pringle stroked his blond hair back and answered, "We left to go meet an insurance adjuster at our boat, probably around ten this morning. Got back about two in the afternoon and found it like this."

Jim made a note and said, "Four-hour time window. Seems like the thief might have known you would be gone. What meds are missing?"

Alice said, "Oxycodone. Had a full bottle of them. I also had a bottle of valium next to the bed. That's gone, too."

"Oxy's. Those are a pretty strong narcotic. Why were you taking them?"

Alice put both hands on her bulging lower back. "When we clipped that rock the other morning, it sent us flying into the bow. My back's been killing me, could hardly walk into the medical clinic. Doc gave me scripts for the Oxy's and, wait..." Alice hobbled into the bathroom and searched the remaining pill bottles, most of which had been dropped into the sink by the burglar. "Yeah, he got those too."

"What did he take, hun?" Dan Pringle asked.

"Muscle relaxers. Those things work, too. Loosens up my back enough so that I can actually walk. Could use a couple right now, if I had 'em." The large woman walked painfully into her living room and sat down on a stuffed easy chair.

Jim turned his attention to the charter captain.

"Dan, who knew about the accident?"

"Hey, you know, it's Prince of Wales. Everyone knows what happened out there."

"Yeah, I'm sure of that. But what I meant was who knew about the specific accident to your wife's back. Did anyone besides your doctor and pharmacist know that she was on pain meds?"

Dan stroked his hair again out of habit. He thought about the question, and then, "Well, we told the gang down at Porty's the other night. Busy night, and I've been known to talk kind of loud."

Jim agreed. He asked, "Anyone seem particularly interested in the information on painkillers? Anyone ask you what kind she was taking or anything like that?"

Dan Pringle thought for a moment and then shook his head, "I can't think of anyone asking questions like that. I have no idea who might have done this."

Clutching her lower back, Alice said, "I feel so violated. Damn, this back is tensing up on me."

Jim walked back out the rear door where his subordinate was inspecting the broken glass. Jim was impressed with how Tavis handled the scene. When Jim arrived, all parties concerned were calm, a proper assessment had been made and a full report offered to the superior officer.

Jim said, "Nice work on this today."

Tavis was eyeing the rock that he suspected was used to smash the glass. "Thanks, Lieutenant. And did you notice?" Tavis pointed up towards his Stetson.

Jim smiled, "Ah nice. No shower cap. Maybe there's hope for you yet, Trooper Spurgeon."

"Wish we could fingerprint this rock."

"Not going to happen. Forensics is not something we excel at here on Prince of Wales. We'll have to solve this the old-fashioned way." Jim thought for a moment, and then asked, "Tavis, when did those break-ins happen last month?"

"Late May. I can look up the exact dates if you want." Tavis started to go through his flipbook.

Jim stopped him, "No, that's okay. What is the approximate date right now?"

Tavis said, "Late June."

"See a pattern? Did you have any break-ins that you can remember back towards the end of April, too? Maybe something that looked like they were going after pain meds?"

Tavis thought for a bit, and then something registered. "Nothing that I can think of in April, but I do remember Trooper Dan getting called to the pharmacy in town back around the third or fourth week of March. I think there was an attempted break-in. I'll have to look up Trooper Dan's notes. Shelly probably input them into the computer."

"That's good, Tavis. When we get back, look up the notes on that pharmacy and get back to me." Jim sat down on the steps next to the broken glass, rain dripping from the rim of his Stetson. "So here's my theory. We have someone local that is addicted to painkillers, and from what I've heard, serious addiction to these pills can lead one to become extremely desperate."

Tavis asked, "How do you know it's a local guy, not a slime liner or tourist?"

Jim answered, "If the deal back in March is related, then this person is local. No one visits the island in March, right? Besides, I think it might be someone that frequents Porty's. So this guy..." Jim caught himself assuming, "Or girl...this perp runs out of their stash each month. The new stash must not be available until the first of the following month, for some reason. The perp runs dry, gets all wigged out and desperate enough to smash windows in order to find more pills."

Tavis asked, "So what do we do? Stake out the home of someone we all know is prescribed Hydrocodone? Blue-Jay Haverford's knees are shot. He pops pills every day just to be able to walk down the street. We could camp out..."

Jim interrupted, "No, Tavis. Nice thought, but you've got to remember, this perp is set, now. Between the valium, Oxycodone and the muscle relaxers, I bet we won't have any more break-ins this month. No, what we need to do is find the supplier. Someone around here is importing illegal prescription drugs and distributing them around the beginning of each month. Our job is to figure out who's dealing, and in order to do that, we need to figure out how the pills are getting here. There are only so many ways you can smuggle pills onto Prince of Wales, and we are going to figure out how that is happening."

Back at the Trooper Station, Jim put Tavis in charge of digging up information on regular shipments of any type of cargo that came to the island at the end of each month. Jim wanted Tavis to look into float plane cargo, ferry boat passage, and to talk to his uncle Tank about monthly barge shipments. He also asked the young trooper to keep his ear tuned to any local gossip that might be pertinent. For all they knew, someone could be transporting pills in their own boat or private plane.

With Tavis gathering info on the illegal pill theory, Jim had an angle in the murder investigation that he wanted to run with. After a few clicks on her computer, Shelly produced a printed copy of Ben Nakit's mug shot and details of his release from jail. Since he wouldn't offer up any information on the growing operation, Ben Nakit was charged with one count of possession of a controlled substance with the intent to distribute and one count of resisting arrest for his attack on Gavin Donaldson. The District Court in Craig, with its sole judge presiding, had set bail at twelve thousand dollars. Ben

Nakit paid for his own release in cash. Jim wondered how a kid that young, who worked part-time on the shipping dock, had that kind of cash laying around.

After thanking Shelly for the mug shot printout and enduring four minutes of babble about blueberry muffins, Jim Wekle hopped in his cruiser and headed for the Stockade. Drizzle had turned to hard rain. The wind was picking up, too. During the short walk up the steps to the Stockade, the trooper's clothes became soaked through on one side. A Stetson didn't protect much from rain that blew sideways.

The Stockade was completely deserted. No one was in the hot tub. No one answered the door. No one appeared to be inside. Jim walked back down the stairs and crossed the street to the cannery. It was a large, rectangular building with corrugated metal siding. Steam blew out several galvanized ducts and fluorescent lights illuminated the complex inside and out. Workers wearing green rain gear and brown rubber Xtratuf boots busily carted bins around the side of the building. A large accordion door was half raised, allowing workers easy access to and from the slime line. Fish smell wafted from every crevice. All the workers seem oblivious to the stench. The odor seemed noxious at first, but Jim was surprised at how fast even he was getting used to it.

Upon entering the cannery, Jim had a hard time telling the employees apart. They all were covered head to toe in rubber. Identical raincoats, rain pants, rain hats and boots kept everyone in equal appearance. Jim couldn't tell the guys from the girls, the young from the old, or the bosses from the employees. Dead salmon moved quickly down a conveyer belt where an assembly line of workers slashed open bellies, removed guts, chopped off fins, tails and heads and slid the meaty carcass down a shiny trough into a holding tray filled with matching fish. Other workers grabbed the sliced-up salmon and sent them into a steam processing machine. Others waited on the opposite side where steamed meat was separated from scaly skin and sent into the canning machine. Other workers waited for cans to emerge and sent them on through the labeler, and eventually, all cans were directed through a mechanized boxer. Cases of canned salmon were then hauled via hand truck and stacked eight feet tall at the end of the building away from the slime and carnage. The entire process ran quick and smooth, noisy and smelly.

Jim grabbed the arm of a passing worker. It was a young Asian girl that had white earbuds dangling under her hat. She was pushing a tub of fish guts toward the opening that led to the end of the dock. "Hey, I'm looking for Skye McDoogle."

The girl shrugged. She couldn't hear what the trooper asked. Jim yanked on the white cord of one of the earbuds causing it to drop from the girl's ear. "Skye McDoogle. Where can I find him? Younger guy, about this height. Tattoos on both sides of his neck." The girl pointed toward a stack of fresh cases of canned pinks.

Raising gloved hands covered in slime, the girl said,

"Do you mind?"

"Oh, sure." Jim stuck the miniature speaker back into the girl's ear socket.

Jim watched as she rammed the cart into a short, hinged wall. She ran straps from the wall around the cart and then pushed a button located on a grey box sticking out from the edge of the dock. Hydraulic lifts sent the cart moving into the air, tipping it toward an opening in the side of the building. Once the cart reached its apex, a mess of salmon heads, tails, fins and guts slipped over the edge, splashing into the bay.

Walking over to the stacks of cases where the girl had pointed, Jim saw two people unloading hand trucks. One seemed to be working very fast and efficiently, reaching high atop stacks with heavy cases of processed fish. The other employee moved at about half that speed. Jim guessed correctly which one had to be Neck Tattoos.

"Skye McDoogle. I have a question for you." The kid stopped stacking and appeared shocked to see the trooper standing next to him. The kid's eyes were red and swollen, eyes dilated.

"Dude, you surprised me, there. Something up, officer?"

Jim took out the mug shot picture of Ben Nakit and handed it over. "Do you recognize him? Is this the guy that Debbie Simms would meet up with?"

Skye McDoogle shook his head, "No man, that's not

him."

"Are you sure?"

"Naw, dude. This kid's too young. And his skin's too dark. And the face is all wrong. I'm telling you. That's not him."

Jim took the picture back and thanked him for his time. It was possible that Skye McDoogle was too stoned to correctly identify the picture, but Jim doubted it. Ben Nakit wasn't Debbie Simms' mysterious caller. The black hair was the only thing that fit. McDoogle seemed certain that every other detail didn't match.

Jim headed out of the cannery and back to his cruiser. The wind was really starting to blow. Rain pelted him in the cheek as he jogged across the road. It looked as though Jim Wekle was about to see his first Prince of Wales Island storm.

18

The impact of selling out of frozen herring was felt all over the island. Sport and charter fishermen were forced to explore other means of enticing salmon to bite than trolling a five-inch dead fish with two hooks sticking out of it. Rubberized squids, elongated white flies, black wooden plugs and a variety of other lures were being used. Some methods offered moderate success, but the absence of bait in the heart of a multi-million dollar fishing season truly caused panic among the charter captains. Catches were not as abundant and thus, tips were not as fat. Some charter companies paid astronomical fees and had small batches flown in from area towns. The local Prince of Wales bait shops tried to buy in bulk from Ketchikan, but were refused as the amount requested would have drained their limited resources.

A few crafty entrepreneurs chased live herring populations around the islands and caught just enough to temporarily satisfy some of the larger fishing lodges, but the reality set in that Craig and the surrounding communities needed bait in a bad way. The local shops banded together in an attempt to rectify the issue. They contracted with a herring farmer outside of Anacortes, Washington to deep freeze and ship up on an Alaska

Airlines flight to Ketchikan, three pallet loads of the little suckers. The shops' new consortium was named *Sell Herring in Town*, a named that lacked a certain punch until a marina operator made t-shirts using the acronym, *SHiT*. A logo was printed on bright yellow t-shirts featuring a float plane with a giant herring used as the fuselage and the lettering, *SHiT*, printed in grand font across the shoulder blades. A huge box of shirts arrived on a chartered float plane and T-shirt sales started out like wildfire. All of the shirt proceeds were being donated to the *SHiT* effort and money was starting to amass until an insightful letter to the editor of the Craig Gazette soon put an end to the fundraiser. The author wrote a scathing rant complaining that it should have been several cases of herring being specially flown in on the charter flight rather than an oversized box of yellow t-shirts.

With full support from every bait seller connected to the road system, Ross Land and Sea was commissioned to fly over to Ketchikan and pick up the half-melted freight from Anacortes. Stores hung signs in their windows advertising the date and time in which herring would be available. *SHiT* day, as it was being called, quickly approached. Charter captains sent their deck-hands down to campout in the parking lots of local stores, ensuring that they would be among the first customers to buy their full quota. A reporter for the Craig Gazette wrote an editorial comparing the campout to that of a Rolling Stones concert ticket line. Anticipation swelled, the whole community seemed to turn out at the float plane docks to see off the Ross Land and Sea planes.

To handle the excessive load, both Frightening Frankie and his brother, Johnny, made the fifty-minute flight to Ketchikan in separate planes. After securing their planes at a dock close to the airport, the Ross brothers were a little surprised to have not been met by anyone or any boxes of fish. Strict instructions had been given as to when the bait would be picked up and the Ross boys were guaranteed that the freight would be waiting for them. After walking up to the Alaska Airlines airport freight desk, the brothers were horrified to learn that the pallets of herring had indeed been carted down to the dock as promised. In fact, the shipping agent was pleased to inform the brothers that the flight had arrived early and the freight had been waiting for them for the past twenty minutes. Baffled, Frankie and Johnny walked back to their planes and noticed three empty wooden pallet frames lying on the dock.

Over two hundred fishermen, store owners and various other folks had gathered on the Ross Land and Sea wooden lot. When the two red-haired brothers landed, they saw American flags being waved while a sax player played a song they recognized from an old Eddie Murphy movie. Taxiing up to his dock, Frightening Frankie got caught up in the emotion of the homecoming and stuck his fist out the plane's window while revving his props a few times. The crowd went wild. It wasn't until Johnny, the more sensible of the two Ross brothers, came out of his cockpit and announced to the masses that the herring had been pilfered, did the flag waving cease and the crowd reluctantly dispersed. When the news hit a few fights broke out in the store's campout line, but generally, life went back to normal fairly quickly. Bait shops suddenly saw a surge in wooden plug sales.

A twenty-eight foot, wood-hulled sailing vessel sat low in the water and moved slowly under engine power. The sailboat had just exited the Tongass Narrows north of Ketchikan and veered westerly across the expansive Behm Canal toward Prince of Wales Island. This was a return trip and the vessel was fully loaded. The prior trip across the Behm Canal went quicker than expected. *The Cyclone* had little cargo weight and cut quickly through the water as wind from a mid-summer storm kept the sails full. The return trip, however, was a little different. The wind still persisted, but it met the sailboat head-on. *The Cyclone's* skipper could have chosen to keep the sails up and to tack back and forth, but three pallets of packaged herring were quickly thawing in the cabin of the boat. The decision to fire up the engine was an easy one. *The Cyclone* needed to make port in a hurry or juice from forty-three thousand small marine animals would begin to drain all over its plush interior.

Roger Greeley had reluctantly agreed to use his boat for the hijack mission. Already concerned that *The Cyclone* had to endure the mounting of a cannon on its bow, the last thing he wanted to risk was being boarded by the Coast Guard after stealing twenty-five thousand dollars' worth of fish. DeAngelo assured him that if caught, he had the perfect excuse. They would claim that City Councilman Haverford had asked the men to transport the herring back to town for the *SHiT* effort. They would claim ignorance as to the float planes that had been chartered for the same task. "All you'd have to do is give ole Blue Jay a call and he'd verify the whole thing," Roger rehearsed while taking water over the bow from a massive wave.

Even with a foolproof excuse, the whole herring theft operation still made Roger uneasy. What they were doing was no longer a harmless retaliatory prank. It was grand theft. And to make matters worse, Roger now feared that his vessel was about to inherit a stink that would never go away. Once herring juice seeped into the lining of his Tunisian throw pillows, they would have to be tossed overboard for sure.

"Roger, you look pale." DeAngelo Smuthers was the boat's only other occupant.

"I just wish this fricken engine could go faster. This boat is ripe."

"Hey, bite your tongue. You do not need a faster engine. Don't you recall the Torcadero Yacht Club credo?"

Roger Greeley rolled his eyes. They both said in unison, "Damn the engine, damn the prop, without wind in your sails, may your boat flop."

Roger said, "That's a stupid credo."

"Hey, I made that up. You were there when I penned that great poem."

"Dumb-ass."

The return trip to Craig's marina lasted into the night. The crew was forced to navigate by radar and digital chart as *The Cyclone* didn't dock until close to three in morning. The cover of darkness proved effective for unloading the fish boxes, and they had old-man Cecil's truck packed to the max by daybreak. Blue Jay's lone assignment was to secure more freezer space; a task accomplished by purchasing three brand new chest freezers from the local hardware store. Just about the time the men had packed the new freezers to their limits, Blue Jay's circuit breaker tripped. Since every outlet in the man's house was wired to only two 15-amp breakers, the male contingency of the Torcedero Yacht club was forced to steal power from Blue Jay's neighbor. A string of several long extension cords patched together was stretched through the trees and attached to their neighbor Carl's outdoor electrical socket. Carl's wiring scheme apparently allowed for a greater amperage load, as the yacht club men found they could power all three freezers off of the single line.

19

Jim Wekle was in his mid-thirties. He had recently been through a divorce. He hadn't been on a date in years. And he still couldn't believe that he had been tricked into it. Maggie Ketah was a very pretty young lady, but Jim honestly had no interest in pursuing a romantic endeavor. The skids were mainly greased by, he assumed, Kram; although, it seemed that Shelly and Tavis were in on it as well.

Jim should have been suspicious when Tavis volunteered to be on call that night. Although showing signs of promise as a trooper, Tavis Spurgeon was usually quite eager to get off the clock. The timing of it all should have tipped him off, too. Tavis had asked for thirty minutes to "run errands" before he officially went on call. Not more than a minute after Tavis left the station did Shelly the dispatcher step into Jim's office.

"Just got a call. They need you down at the north marina," She said. She wouldn't even tell him the details of the call. Claiming that the call sounded peaceful but fairly urgent, Shelly insisted that Jim head straight out the door and over to the marina. Completely clueless to the whole ruse, Jim bought it hook, line, and down-rigger.

When he arrived at the north marina, his radar-like

senses finally kicked in. A paper sign hung at the top of the ramp with letters written in blue crayon, "*Trooper Jim, This Way.*" An arrow pointed down the ramp. Three more signs in blue crayon later, and Jim found himself standing in front of an immaculate pleasure craft. Soft acoustic guitar music emitted from the cabin and the most wonderful food scents touched his nose. Suddenly the guitar music stopped and a person emerged from the cabin.

"All aboard, Trooper Jim. The S.S. Crazy Love is about to disembark," Kram announced while standing on the back deck. He wore black tuxedo pants and a bright yellow t-shirt with the word *SHiT* written across the back.

Jim stepped over the boat rail and descended into a plush cabin area. Maggie Ketah sat on a bench seat next to a neatly made table. She smiled through a glass of red wine she was sipping on. Maggie wore a pleasant looking flowered dress and had her hair pinned back on both sides. She was definitely a sight, Jim had to admit.

"Gawl damn it, sauce is too thin." The foul sounding voice blared from the galley area where Deloris busily slaved over a gas stove. To Jim's surprise, Deloris actually had put on real clothes for the event, but she did wear a large hat that resembled what the guards wear at Buckingham Palace. Luckily, there was no chew spit dripping into the saucepans.

Jim removed his Stetson and asked, "Is this seat taken?"

Maggie smiled and said, "Please sit. But just so you know, I had nothing to do with this."

"That's okay. I think a little night out will do me good. You look amazing, by the way." Maggie smiled, white teeth spanned between her tan cheeks. Jim said, "I would have dressed a little more appropriate than my work uniform, had I known."

Maggie replied, "I doubt you would have come, had you known." Even though she was correct, Jim decided it would be polite to disagree.

A diesel engine rumbled to life, dock lines were thrown aboard and Kram piloted the boat safely from the slip and out past the breakwater. "A little evening cruise before dinner. You two sit back and just relax." Kram winked at Jim from his seat behind the wheel. Deloris served thin strips of meat that she identified as sea cucumber as an appetizer. They were amazing, tasting somewhere between a steamed clam and fried bacon. The boat slowly rumbled between islands. Jim slurped on a fantastic cup of black coffee, Maggie gently tasted her wine. The two even seemed to be enjoying getting to know each other. They chatted pleasantly while the boat chugged along.

After turning into a secluded cove lined with tall trees, Kram threw the boat in neutral and disappeared from the cabin. A rattling sound caused Jim to stand and glance out the window. Kram was lowering an anchor chain, waving frantically behind him.

Deloris calmly said, "He wants you to put the boat in reverse." Jim did as requested. After backing up a few yards, Kram gave the stop signal. They were securely anchored and swinging lightly on the chain.

With dinner, Kram sat in a corner chair and played beautifully on an old acoustic guitar. His musical skill surprisingly impressed Jim. Kram moved effortlessly between colorful chords and lyrical melodic lines up and down the guitar's fret-board. Deloris served multiple courses; poached halibut with a blueberry reduction sauce, reindeer sausage atop braised kale, crab cakes with fried leeks, and a dessert that featured crispy cookie crumbs on top of homemade vanilla ice cream. The meal was fantastic, probably the best that Jim had ever had.

"Deloris, you are an amazing chef," Jim said. "I was stuffed two courses ago, but I just can't stop eating. Where did you learn to cook like this?"

"That's a long story, Jimbo. Just sit back and relax. Now comes the really romantic stuff." Deloris took off her hat, slapped a piece chaw in her lower cheek. She took a seat next to Kram, who still held his old six-string. With Kram strumming chords gracefully, the two sang in perfect two-part harmony *The Chain* by Fleetwood Mac.

"Listen to the wind blow..." Their voices seemed to melt together. As they performed the duet, Jim was so enthralled that he barely noticed as Maggie laid her head on his shoulder. It was a tender moment, one that caught the trooper completely off his guard. The song only lasted just under four minutes, but time seemed to stand still during the performance. When Kram lowered his guitar, both Maggie and Jim erupted into applause.

During the boat ride back to the dock, Deloris cleaned up from dinner while Jim and Maggie sat in deck chairs under cover of the aft awning. Jim couldn't help but smile. He had really enjoyed the whole experience.

Jim said, "This was, uh, unexpected."

Maggie questioned, "Unexpected good, or unexpected bad?"

Turning and smiling at his date, Jim said, "Good. Definitely good."

"Good enough to try again sometime?"

"I think so." Jim wanted to ask a question but debated whether or not it would ruin the mood. Finally, he asked, "How old are you, Maggie?"

"Twenty-four."

"You know, I am a little older than you. And you should also know that I am recently divorced."

Maggie laughed, "You're not a very good salesman, Trooper Jim."

"Well, it's just that. If we do have a second date, I want to make sure everything is out there on the table first."

"Okay, fine. Let's get it all out there. How'd you

first meet your ex-wife?"

Jim replied frankly, "Got drunk."

"What led to your divorce?"

"Got drunk again."

Maggie turned to face Jim. "You're not drunk, now, are you?"

Jim met her glance. "Stone-cold sober."

They kissed as the boat slowly turned into the harbor.

20

Twenty-seven new engine parts, front hood, grill, fender, windshield, radiator, replacement driver and passenger airbags, headlights, blinker lights, new carpet, couch with matching cushions, bed with matching linens and a dozen or so required assembly kits for a 2010 Luxury Coachman Plus were ordered to be shipped via barge to Craig, Alaska. The RV owner that placed the order authorized a "rush shipment." For the extra thousand charged to the owner's Platinum Visa card, "rush shipment" got the pile of parts to the Seattle barge terminus with barely enough time to make that week's boat.

For safety and security, random shipments are usually placed inside a pale green iron container to ride out the week-long journey up the Inside Passage. When Bill and Gladys Fetcherson's repair order reached the Seattle waterfront, the barge was minutes from pulling away. A rather new employee, eager to please, decided that the shrink-wrapped pallet of auto parts label with "rush shipment" had better make that barge. After all, a rush shipment shouldn't sit in the yard for a whole week.

The newbie forklift operator placed the pallet on top of a container full of new salmon plugs and rubber squid lures, also marked with "rush shipment." The barge left on time without a hitch, and the new forklift employee left to get drunk with his fellow dock workers, proud after a full day's work.

Just north of the Canadian Border, a storm that was slowly heading up the coastline overcame the tug and barge. Ten-foot seas rocked them a bit, but nothing that the tugboat captain hadn't seen before. The barge tossed around, but the heavy iron containers stayed in position without moving an inch. The shrink-wrapped pallet of Coachman RV parts, however, launched after the first big wave hit. A member of the tugboat crew happened to see the pallet fly from its perch atop the barge and reported the loss. Unbeknownst to the crew, though, the memory-foam mattresses and couch cushions created enough buoyancy to keep the pallet of parts afloat. The tug and barge kept chugging north, leaving the Coachman parts bobbing along behind at the mercy of the waves, wind and current.

The music drifted in through the thin walls of the yurt starting at about daybreak. Jim had hoped to make it to at least six o'clock without a phone call, a crazed drum solo, a hungry mink scratching at his door, or some such other rude awakening. No such luck. The music sounded a little too distant to be coming from his island. It was good music; rock from several decades prior. Jim thought he even recognized the tune. Maybe someone had camped out over on shore and turned up their boom box a little too loud. He wasn't exactly sure, but it didn't matter now. Jim was wide awake.

The music continued through coffee, shower, and breakfast. As Jim boarded the Lund skiff, the tunes seemed to be coming in from directly across the small stretch of seawater. As Jim tied up the skiff, the music almost seemed as if it was blaring from his car. Walking up the boat ramp to the parking lot, it increased in decibel with each step. This wasn't a CD being played through a sound system. This was a live band, and a good one at that.

When Jim reached the top of the ramp, the music stopped. They were either in between songs or taking a break. Walking towards his car, Jim stopped and turned. Something wasn't quite right. The door to his pale-green container was wide open. The lock that he had placed on the door had been sliced through by bolt cutters. Jim placed his hand on the butt of his pistol and inched toward the open container. He could hear rustling, talking, and the sound of a beer can being opened. He propped his body firmly against the side of the large box and readied himself. Jim pulled his weapon from its holster, placing it in prone position. He took a deep breath and jumped around the corner into the open end.

"Freeze," Jim yelled, gun pointing into the container.

"Jimbo, good morning man. Glad you could join us." Kram smiled. He was truly happy to see Jim. "This place is killer, man. Why didn't you tell me you had all this great stuff?"

A man holding a bass in one hand and beer can in the other lounged back in Jim's wicker chair. A curly haired shirtless man was preparing eggs on Jim's camp stove. A guy wearing purple spandex and a George Washington wig tapped out a drumbeat on Jim's old bench press; each size of weight creating a different tone within the beat. Scattered about Jim's possessions inside the container were a drum set, bass amp, guitar amp and PA system. A string of light bulbs had been hung from the ceiling and several of Jim's sweatshirts had been hung on the walls, he guessed, for acoustical reasons. An extension cord ran out the door and plugged into the side of a brown utility box positioned next to the boat ramp.

Kram was elated. "This is the guy I've been telling you about," he announced to the band. "This is Trooper Jim. Trooper Jim, meet the band."

Jim holstered his gun and then waved to the band. "Kram, you broke into my storage container."

"Ah, I knew you wouldn't mind. You didn't tell me you had a classic Nintendo. I love old video games. You mind if I hook it up after our next couple of songs?"

Jim shook his head, "Knock yourself out."

"Hey, Trooper Jim." It was the bass player. He was holding one of Jim's high school yearbooks. "Did you really *keep it real* with Shannon from 5th period?"

The drummer had moved on to the collection of empty cigar boxes. They seemed to resonate better than the weight set.

"Eggs are ready," announced the shirtless guy.

Kram said, "No food yet. Let's play something for Jimbo, here." Kram excitedly leaped to his Marshall stack and turned up a knob. His electric guitar was a Gibson Les Paul with deep red edges and a yellow sunburst on the top. It looked a little worn, but Kram could really make it buzz.

"Jim, you ever hear the tune, *Shackles of Love*? I bet you'll love it." Kram counted them off and they kicked into the chorus with such force and precision, Jim couldn't help but be impressed. The shirtless guy...Jim could swear he had seen him somewhere before...was the lead singer. Kram sang backup vocals and played the hell out of the guitar. The bass player and drummer provided an infectious groove. They finished the tune with a massive guitar cadenza and a bombastic final chord followed by all four bowing their heads in unison.

Kram looked up brightly and asked, "How about that, Jimbo my man? I wrote that song about thirty years ago, but it still rocks today."

"I'm not much of a music critic, but you guys kick butt. Please try not to spill beer on my George Forman Grill."

Brent Purvis

21

Entering the station, Jim immediately knew the mood was serious. Shelly and Tavis both had the look of concern on their faces.

Shelly said, "He's in your office. Only been waiting for a half hour or so. I was going to call, but I knew you'd be in soon. Should I have called? I know I should have called."

"Shelly, its okay." When Jim entered his office, a man stood up and offered his hand. Jim shook it and identified himself.

The man said, "I'm Sheldon Simms. I appreciate you meeting with me this morning." Sheldon was a short man with serious eyes. He had a brown mustache centered on a long face that had seen better days. Mr. Simms wore tan slacks and a button-up grey shirt open at the collar. He wore brown loafers on his feet, definitely not dressed for Southeast Alaska.

"Mr. Simms, I am so sorry about your daughter."

"I appreciate the sentiment. Do you have a few minutes this morning to show me around, maybe answer a few questions that I have?"

"Absolutely. I am happy to share information, but

you should know up front that I cannot yet answer who killed your daughter, or why she was killed. I can assure you that the investigation is my top priority, though."

"Anything that you can share would help."

They spent the morning walking around Craig. Jim showed Sheldon Simms the Stockade, the hot tub, they walked through the cannery, and they even went for a walk on the docks looking at the various fishing boats. The man's feet and clothes were soaked from the rain, but he didn't appear to care. Mr. Simms said very little during the walking tour. He seemed to be taking it all in, Jim assumed, as a memory of his daughter's last living place on earth.

After being asked if he wanted to see the place where Debbie's body was found, Mr. Simms said that he would like to make a quick stop first. He purchased a tiny bouquet of flowers at the grocery store before stepping into Jim's cruiser. The flowers were slightly wilted, but that didn't seem to bother the man. The drive out to the point was quiet, the sound of the wipers interrupting moments of silence. The tide was fairly high when they reached the rock that overlooked the kelp bed. Only the top of the brown sea vegetation was visible, poking their bulbous heads out of cold, black water. Sheldon Simms appeared to whisper a prayer before placing the flowers on top of the rock. Jim knew that the tide would eventually wash the bouquet away, but figured that Mr. Simms wouldn't mind.

They left the rock and drove back into town. Jim bought Mr. Simms a halibut burger at Porty's for lunch. Maggie was working, but sensed that it wasn't the right time for a friendly flirt. Smart girl, that Maggie. After lunch, Jim drove the man out the road in the opposite way of the point where Debbie was found. The scenery didn't really help in understanding his daughter's death, but Mr. Simms still appreciated the tour. It just seemed as though Sheldon Simms gained some sort of peace by exploring the island where his daughter took her last breath.

During the drive, Jim asked, "Did your daughter ever mention a boy that she was seeing up here?"

Sheldon answered, "My daughter didn't mention anything to me after leaving for Alaska. The last time we spoke was the night before she left. I was unhappy with her decision to come up here, even forbade her to go. But she was a stubborn girl. She had no intention of listening to my babble." The man paused and cleared his throat. "The last thing I ever said to my only girl wasn't good. You see, her mother had passed away a few years ago. Debbie was an only child. And I didn't want to let go of her, now that she was growing up." Mr. Simms paused, cleared his throat and continued, "It angered me that she wanted to spend her summer gutting fish on some Alaskan island. I told her that if she left, she wouldn't have a home to return to. Can you believe that Lieutenant? I didn't even give my girl a hug goodbye." A tear ran down the man's long cheekbone.

Jim didn't really know what to say, so he decided to just say what he honestly felt. "Sir, I am so sorry about what you are going through. I know this may not offer much to ease your pain, but I will continue to do everything I can to find the answers surrounding your daughter's death."

They finished their car ride back at the float plane dock. Sheldon Simms was scheduled to fly back to Ketchikan that afternoon and then back to his home the following day. The grieving father shook Jim's hand and thanked him for his time. Jim wrote down the man's cell number and promised to be in touch.

Before driving back to the Trooper Station, Jim sat in the cab of his cruiser contemplating what his next move might be. He was motivated more than ever to find Debbie Simms' killer. He had to have missed something. There had to be some clue, something that could lead him to the truth. Rain continued to fall, but it didn't seem to bother him anymore. The cynical outlook on his life's path seemed suddenly insignificant. It was the first time in his career, in his life for that matter, that he felt the immense responsibility of rectifying such a wrongdoing. He had been a part of murder investigations before, but never in charge of them. There were always superiors that would meet with the tearful family; there was always someone else who shouldered the full burden. Now, Jim was it. He had the reins and he had the responsibility. Jim would find the answers and someone would pay for their crimes.

The man in the blue baseball cap knew that the shipment had arrived. It was the first of the month, the day that his pills were always available. He had money to buy, but not enough to get him through a whole month. It didn't matter, though, as long as he could score pills now. Narcotic painkiller addiction was a nasty habit. It wreaked havoc on one's mind as much as one's body. A person in the throes of an addiction was likely to lie, cheat, steal, and even kill for a supply. The man in the blue baseball cap had it bad and needed his monthly stockpile. Once he had pills to gobble, he could function again. He could come out of his house during the day, go back to his job, even smile and be friendly with others. That's all he wanted, was to be happy. He just needed a large sack of white pills in order to accomplish that goal.

It was a little after midnight. The sky had finally turned dark. He knocked twice on the red metal door illuminated by a single hanging bulb. The deadbolt turned and the building's side door opened a crack.

"Come on in." A rough voice said through the crack. The man entered a small room. Someone behind him closed the door and threw the deadbolt into place. There were two men in the room. The man in the blue baseball cap knew both of them well.

Rough Voice said, "I thought I told you to lay low. No more break-ins."

Baseball Cap sounded shaky, "I just needed

something to get me by. You don't know what it's like. It didn't hurt anything."

"I can't have that kind of attention around here. Someone keeps trying to steal out of medicine cabinets up and down the island? That doesn't look good. Maybe attract a little too much attention."

Pointing to the plastic bags full of pills that filled a long table, Baseball Cap said, "I've got money, here. Just give me a bag, please." He took a wad of cash out of his pocket and offered it out. The other man by the door took a couple steps toward Baseball Cap's back.

Rough Voice grabbed the cash and said, "I'll take your money. But there's something that I don't think you quite understand." The other man took another step closer. Baseball Cap nervously anticipated receiving the pill bag.

Rough Voice picked up a pill bag and said, "You see, these pills are really meant to help with one thing. You know what that is, Shane?"

Shane was trembling. He tried to answer the question, "Wh...What. What are they for?"

Rough Voice said, "Pain!"

A blunt object smashed into the back of his head, crushing his skull at the rim of the blue baseball cap. The man that had hit him from behind stepped close to the limp body that sprawled on the floor. He swung the metal pole again, this time cracking the cranium at the apex of his head. Shane Ketah lay in a pool of his own blood. His blue baseball cap turned upside down, soaking in the dark red liquid as it oozed from his scalp.

22

Johnny Ross was the one that spotted the body. He was leading a five-person caravan of four-wheelers across overgrown logging roads north of Klawock Lake. The "Land" part of Ross Land and Sea centered on what the Ross brothers liked to call Rainforest Adventure Rides. Tourists housed at some of the area fishing lodges sometimes liked to set the poles and bait aside for an afternoon and be led deep into the forest while straddling a 200cc quad ATV. Johnny usually led the expeditions as he knew some of the better side trails and key points of interest.

One of the highlights of the "Deep Woods Package" involved all members of the expedition disembarking their bikes and following Johnny, bear gun slung over his shoulder, in order to peer over a rock down on to what he liked to call, a "feeding bed." The bed was mashed into the muskeg and bark, full of black hair and littered with hundreds of individual deer bones. Although it was an authentic feeding area for a resident black bear, Johnny Ross embellished his stories of how bears would stalk and pounce on their prey, dragging it to this spot and licking its bones clean within an hour.

What Johnny Ross didn't expect to find, was Shane Ketah's naked body sprawled amidst the deer bones and black fur. After a VHF radio conversation with his brother back at the float plane dock, both State Troopers and the island's Fish and Game officer were dispatched to the scene. Johnny Ross had stayed with the body in case he had to ward off any bears wanting an easy meal, but he sent his tourists to backtrack down the logging roads and meet the officers at the bottom of the hill. Normal vehicles couldn't make the trip up, so Gavin Donaldson, Tavis Spurgeon and Jim Wekle strapped down their equipment onto three of the ATV's and made their way up the mountain. A quarter-mile up the rugged path, Jim noticed a sign that read, "This road to be paved, courtesy of the Rural Island Vitalization Act (RIVA 2005 – Senator C. Travors)." Jim hadn't a clue of what the outdated sign meant, but he couldn't imagine any reason why the old logging road would be paved.

"It's a body dump, plain and simple," Gavin Donaldson spoke first after peering down into the feeding bed. "Makes sense, really. Strip off all of the clothes and set the body in the most logical place that a hungry bear might roam. My bet is, this time tomorrow, all that would be left is a bunch of human bones that would blend in perfectly with the surrounding deer bones. Rain would wash away the blood. No clothes to identify that there was a human."

Tavis asked, "Wouldn't the skull give it away?"

"Not necessarily. I hate to say it so gruesomely, but a hungry bear likes to get access to all the, uh... meat. I've read reports of bears crushing skulls and rib cages in order to get at everything. You've seen a bear tear through a garbage can for food, right? Just think what it would do to a body that was dumped into its prime feeding spot."

Jim said, "Looks like he was beaten to death. Those blows to the head had to be fatal."

Tavis appeared a little squeamish, "Geez, Lieutenant. One month on the job and you already catch two murder scenes. What are the chances out here?"

"Unfortunately, I think the chances are pretty good. I think both murders are related." Jim took a few pictures with his phone.

"How can you say that, boss? The Simms girls was shot and thrown in the water. Shane, here, was knocked on the head and dumped deep into the woods."

Jim asked, "Tavis, how many murder investigations have there been in the past five years here?"

"I don't know. None since I arrived last summer."

Jim turned his attention, "Gavin?"

Gavin Donaldson thought for a moment, and then said, "Plenty of deaths around here. Plane crashes, boat accidents, hikers getting lost..."

"Murders, Gavin. How many?"

"Last one I remember was about seven years ago.

187

Two guys got into it on the deck of a fishing boat. They were punching each other until one of them got knocked overboard. Never found the body, swallowed up by the sea. Actually, I think that one got ruled as manslaughter."

Jim nodded, "Exactly. And now, two apparent murders within a month's time. I don't have evidence yet, but I'm betting these murders are connected."

Johnny walked up and interrupted the officers, "Poor Maggie. Her brother like this. It's going to be hard on that girl."

The truth of Johnny's statement hit Jim like a brick.

Tavis added, "Those two are so close, too. Working together, running Porty's."

They were right, and Jim knew it. Knowing how fast news traveled around the island, Jim would bet that Maggie had already found out. Between the tourists that Johnny sent back and the VHF call to Frightening Frankie, Jim was confident that all of Prince of Wales knew that Shane Ketah was dead.

Jim spotted her standing next to his car when the ATV he drove rounded a tree-lined corner. Maggie was intense, but stable. She had been waiting for them at the base of the mountain for a while. Her eyes became swollen when she saw the body bag strapped to the back of Gavin's ATV. Jim didn't think that his single date and single kiss required him to console her, but he offered her a hug anyway.

Maggie's voice was stern, "I know that he was messed up, but I really don't know much else."

Jim waited. When Maggie was ready, she continued, "Shane hasn't been himself for the past year or so. And it's been getting worse. Every few weeks, he would claim to get violently sick, missing anywhere from two days of work up to a whole week. I begged him to see a doctor, or to talk with someone, or even to just let me know what was going on, but he refused."

"Do you know what was causing this behavior?" Jim was pretty sure he knew the answer, but wanted Maggie to talk it out more.

"He was using, Jim. I'm sure of it; I just don't really know what drugs he was on. Shane drank a bit, too, typically more right before he would get sick. Seemed to be a pretty harsh pattern, and it wasn't getting any better."

Jim gingerly asked, "Do you know anyone that would want Shane dead?"

"Shane was a good guy, never hurt anyone...but himself, I guess. I can't imagine who could have done this."

Maggie asked if she could see the body. Jim cautioned her against it, but she said it was something she needed to do. After the body was moved from the ATV into the back of the all-island med-van, Jim brought Maggie over. He unzipped the top portion only, exposing the bloody, badly beaten head. Maggie stood frozen and silent. Fearing that the longer she stared, the deeper the emotional wound, Jim zipped the bag back up and instructed the med-van to head out. Maggie's eyes gave way to a stream of tears down each cheek.

Jim and Tavis searched the victim's house. Shane had lived alone in a one-bedroom trailer. It looked as though he hadn't used a weed whacker in months as vegetation was beginning to consume the perimeter of the single-wide. Scents of stale food and spilled whiskey filled the inside of the dank living area. Shane Ketah was not the cleanest bachelor in the world. Dirty clothes were lying on the couch and floor. Dishes hadn't been washed in a while. The kitchen linoleum was sticky. An uncapped Jack Daniels bottle sat, almost empty, on the coffee table in front of a television set that looked to be at least ten years old.

"Lieutenant, check this out." Tavis was searching a table between the kitchen and living room. Lifting up a frozen pizza box, Tavis saw several empty pill bottles rolling on their sides. He handed one over to Jim.

"Prescription reads, Alice Pringle."

Tavis said, "I think we just solved our burglary case."

"It appears so."

Jim and Tavis continued to search the trailer. Jim

found more empty pill bottles in the bathroom cabinet, and none of the prescription labels were for Shane Ketah. Some of the dates were from over a year ago. Jim figured that Shane had been stealing people's meds for quite some time. Jim also found several empty Ziplock bags with a white powdery residue inside. The empty baggies were found throughout several different locations inside the trailer, and Jim guessed they had each once been filled with pills.

Tavis walked into the bedroom where his boss was looking through a nightstand. Tavis announced, "I think I have a theory. It all makes sense."

Looking up, Jim said, "Okay, let's hear it."

"Well, you said that Debbie Simms had been seen with a guy with black hair a few times, right? Well, Shane Ketah had black hair. Let's say Shane gets all high one night, maybe Debbie's involved in the drugs somehow, or maybe she's not very eager to do, well, you know. Shane flips out and shoots her, and then he tosses her body into the ocean thinking she'll float far away." Tavis walked across the room, then continued, "Well, I would bet that young little Debbie Simms, she probably wrote home and told daddy all about Shane Ketah. I bet daddy didn't fly in to talk to you and get the grand tour. I bet Mr. Simms flew into town, bashed Shane Ketah in the noggin out of revenge for his daughter's death, and dumped him in the woods all before meeting with you. It all makes perfect sense to me."

Jim thought there were more gaping holes in that theory than the Titanic. He didn't want to squash the young trooper's enthusiasm too much, so he said, "Well, why don't you try to find the gun, then." Jim thought that task might keep Tavis busy for a while. Jim doubted there was any gun in the house. Shane Ketah was an addict. There was nothing of real value left in the house. No computer or electronics worth a dime, no boat, no ATV's, no expensive toys of any kind, and surely no guns. Shane and Maggie weren't rich, but they made enough money running Porty's for Shane to afford at least a few of the normal items that Alaskan bachelors enjoyed. Shane had sold off everything of value to support his habit, Jim was sure of it. Shane Ketah wasn't a violent man. He was a desperate addict.

There were other holes in Tavis' theory. When Jim dropped Mr. Simms off at the float plane dock, the man had no suitcase. He hadn't brought a change of clothes. How could he have brutally murdered a man, transported the body to a bear feeding bed known only to the heartiest of locals, and then calmly walk into the Trooper Station wearing business casual without a spot of blood? Besides, Sheldon Simms was sincere in every way. Jim seriously doubted that the man had just committed a major felony.

Trooper Spurgeon's grand theory didn't make any sense, and Jim was sure that the trooper wouldn't be able to find evidence to support his theory. But he let him run with it regardless. At least the guy was trying, at least he was thinking. Jim collected a few items of evidence from the trailer and left Tavis to rummage around.

Jim had his own theories about what was going on around town, but had a few holes of his own to fill in. Jim headed for his office. He had paperwork to fill out, emails to return, and a telephone call to make to his superior at the Ketchikan headquarters. It was time for Jim to do a little research, and then it was time for him to ruffle a few feathers around town. There might even be a little field trip in his future, and, who knows, maybe he could talk Kram into going with him.

23

The Alexander Archipelago is a three hundred and fifty-mile long group of over a thousand islands wedged between the Canadian coastline and the Pacific Ocean. The archipelago, generally referred to as Southeast Alaska, is serviced by a fleet of State-owned motor vessels known as the Alaska Marine Highway. Resident Alaskans and tourists alike use the Blue, Yellow and White boats of the Alaska Marine Highway system as travel vessels between cities dotted on islands throughout the archipelago. Traveling what is known as the Inside Passage, almost half a million passengers a year are treated to views of the region's rugged beauty and isolation as the ships weave around the islands.

An offshoot vessel of the Alaska Marine Highway that connects Prince of Wales to the more populated Ketchikan area makes daily runs, allowing travelers to either connect with other boats heading north or south, or do some quick shopping for a day or two. After their ill-fated fishing excursion, coupled with the news of losing their RV parts off the side of a barge, Bill and Gladys Fetcherson needed a brief escape from Craig, Alaska. They had purchased a round-trip ferry ticket into Ketchikan with hopes that they would be able to spend a couple of nights in a hotel that offered a little more comfort than Porty's. Gladys looked forward to ordering halibut at a restaurant without it being served from the deep fryer. Bill had high hopes of finding a beer on tap that wasn't brewed in the mid-west.

They boarded the *M.V. Baranoff* and claimed two moderately comfortable chairs in the forward observation lounge. Once the motor vessel disembarked from Hollis and started making its way through Kasaan Bay as it exited the maze of Prince of Wales Island's shoreline, Gladys fell asleep in her chair holding a romance novel open to page three. Bill was just fine with his wife's quick slumber, and didn't even feel moderately embarrassed by the drool that drained down her chin. Bill Fetcherson was almost able to feel at peace, gazing out the windows across the bow, keeping a keen eye out for whales and other such sights. Unfortunately for Bill, he happened to be keeping more of a watchful eye on the waters than the captain of the *M.V. Baranoff*.

Seconds before impact, Bill Fetcherson could have sworn he was seeing an apparition. Chalked up to the recent trauma he had endured, Bill swore that it could not have been possible that an iceberg bearing the Coachman "C" logo just disappeared below the bow of the boat. The boom was felt in vibrations that shook from forward to aft. Gladys Fetcherson had been experiencing a recurring nightmare that included moments of the accident aboard the *Norwegian King* and her Snookums flying in the clutches of an eagle. When the collision occurred, it jarred Gladys from her dream, and she woke up screaming.

The shrink-wrap surrounding the pallet of Coachman RV parts reflected the daylight such that it blended in almost perfectly with the seawater. From the captain's high perch, he completely missed noticing the obstacle that impaled itself into the starboard hull. The front bumper of a 2010 Luxury Coachman Plus punctured a melon-sized hole in the vessel. Luckily, the piercing occurred just above the water line and the boat was able to stay afloat.

Grabbing a walkie-talkie and tuning into the ship-wide intercom, the captain announced, "Ladies and gentlemen, do not be alarmed. We have collided with an object that did, in fact, pierce our hull, but be assured that the amount of water spilling into our bilge is quite manageable. As a precaution, we have decided to turn around and head back for the Hollis dock on Prince of Wales Island. Please remain calm, stay inside the cabin area, and make sure you don a life preserver. Thank you."

Gladys' screaming continued through the entire announcement and the ship's purser had to convince the captain to repeat the message as no one in the forward observation lounge was able to hear his first attempt. Bill Fetcherson left his distraught wife and went to the lounge where he immediately acquired a new taste for Alaskan Amber beer. After slamming down his third pint, he said to the bartender, "To hell with the lifejacket, and keep the pounders coming."

MINK ISLAND

24

For the town of Craig, the Fourth of July festivities could not have come at a better time. The mood around the island had been somber following Shane Ketah's memorial service. The community had said goodbye to one of their own. They had appropriately grieved as the town closed the book on a young man's life. But now, a day later, it was party time.

The Fourth started out cloudy, but by noon the overcast skies gave way to sun and a pleasant breeze out of the northeast. Basecamp for the festivities was located on the docks of Ross Land and Sea. A giant barbecue had been built by Johnny Ross in his metal shop and lump charcoal sizzled under a stainless steel hood. A covered stage was positioned next to the hangar building and columns of speaker cabinets were stationed on opposing sides. Multiple kegs of beer sat in garbage cans full of ice and a bouncy house had been inflated for the kids' amusement. A chainsaw carving contest was scheduled for one in the afternoon, followed by the salmon egg spitting contest that Deloris usually won. Frightening Frankie offered free float plane rides (tips accepted) and the teenagers were given special exemption and allowed to cruise around the city streets on the Ross Land and Sea ATV's for the afternoon. The event each year culminated with what the locals referred to as the "Drunk Parade," followed by Kram's rock concert, and the annual fireworks show.

As fun-filled as the day's activities were, for an Alaska State Trooper it usually meant a long day of herding stupid people. In light of recent events, Lieutenant Jim Wekle thought that the town could use a little release. After Tavis briefed him on the usual mode of operation on the Fourth, Jim decided that their goal would be no drownings and no drunk drivers, but other than that, he wanted the locals to cut loose a little bit. The Coast Guard agreed to patrol vigorously the waterfront, and Tavis was assigned to shuttle people, "no questions asked," in his cruiser wherever they needed to go. A car key collection bucket was set up next to the barbecue and Tavis' cell number was posted on a giant sign that read, "Need a Ride? Call a Trooper."

Shelly was given the day off to spend with family and Jim's number was given to the ECC for any emergency calls. Jim felt that his most strategic option for the day would be to wander on foot around the docks next to where the ATV's were being dispersed. That way he could help keep watch on the mass intoxication as well as remind the teenage four-wheelers that speed limits and helmet laws still applied.

Shortly after the chainsaws fired up, Jim wandered over to the barbecue pit. Maggie busily monitored two dozen hot dogs that were smoking on the grill while a couple of other young ladies served hungry patrons. They had an efficient system down that kept the line small and the crowd satiated.

Jim threw on an apron, grabbed a pair of tongs and started to turn a row of dogs. "This is quite a shin-dig."

Maggie answered, "You think this is a party, just wait for Beer Swig and Humpy Fest later this summer."

"So I've been warned." Jim released a jumbo dog, glanced at Maggie and asked, "How are you holding up?"

"Not bad. This is actually just what I needed; a little distraction, watching people have a good time." Maggie placed a couple of cooked hot dogs into buns on paper plates.

"It was a good service yesterday. A lot of people showed up."

"We grew up on this island. Makes sense that a lot of people knew Shane and wanted to say goodbye."

Jim unloaded a new package of dogs onto the grill and asked, "Porty's closed up today?"

"Yeah. Shane was supposed to cover the bar while I cooked hot dogs. It just made sense to close up for the day."

"If you need a little more time off, I'm sure we could find someone to cover for a bit." Jim served two little girls wearing red, white, and blue face paint. They smiled at the trooper after he dropped dogs on their plates. After the girls left, Jim scanned the crowd making sure all was under control.

Maggie said, "I don't think I need any more time off. I'll open the bar back up tomorrow. I will have to hire someone soon to take some shifts, though."

Jim thought he saw someone familiar walk through the crowd. He offered, "When you're ready, let me help you pack up Shane's house. I imagine you'll have a big job there."

"You're a nice guy, Trooper Jim. But my aunt and uncle are still here from Hoonah. They want to help in some way, so I already assigned them that task. It will be a big job for them. Shane didn't exactly keep a clean house."

Jim silently agreed with Maggie, and then he happened to spy the familiar face in the crowd again. It was a young man wearing a red hoodie. He was weaving through the gathering of chainsaw viewers, heading toward the beer line. Taking off his apron, Jim said, "I need to get back to my rounds here, but you have my cell number. Call if you need anything at all, okay?"

As Jim started to walk away, Maggie hollered, "Jim?"

He stopped and turned, "Yes?"

Maggie's face was cold. "You're going to figure out who killed my brother, right?"

Jim stepped back toward her and said sincerely, "I

give you my word."

Trooper Jim Wekle jogged away from the hot dog stand and caught up to the young man in the red hoodie. The line for beer was rather long, with most people trying to fill three or four cups per trip. Jim tapped on the guy's shoulder and Ben Nakit removed his hood as he turned to face the officer.

"Remember me?" Jim asked with a smile.

Ben Nakit turned his face and said, "Whatever you want, I didn't do it."

"Hey, I'm just stopping by to say hello. I'm not here to accost you in any way."

"Yeah, I remember how friendly cops usually are."

"Well, we usually don't like being attacked from a tent in the woods." Jim stepped slowly with the pace of the beer line. He said, "I saw the court documents. Twelve grand for bail. That's quite a bit of cash. Where did it come from?"

Holding out his cup to be filled from a keg, Ben asked, "Is it a crime to have a savings account?"

"No, but it is a crime for a twenty-year-old to drink beer. What do you think you're doing in this line?" On cue, the guy pouring from the keg spout asked for the kid's driver's license. After studying it for a bit, the beer man handed it over for Jim to inspect.

Ben Nakit said, "It's my birthday. I'm twenty-one

and perfectly legal."

Jim handed back his license and said, "Happy birthday. Let me buy you the beer." Jim handed a few bucks over to keg man. Ben grabbed his beer cup, turned, and started walking away from the crowd toward the edge of the dock. Jim followed. The large wooden lot of Ross Land and Sea was built up over the water on tall pilings. Looking over the edge, the two men could see the float plane dock below. It jutted out away from them, rising and falling with the tide. Frightening Frankie was dropping off a load of free passengers, fervently accepting tips.

Jim said, "Born on the Fourth of July, huh? Just like Louis Armstrong claimed."

Ben Nakit spit over the side of the pier, watching it drop several seconds before hitting the water. "Who?"

"Louis Armstrong, the trumpet player. You know, the guy who sang *What a Wonderful World*?" Jim growled out the song title with a gravelly voice.

"Never heard of him."

Shaking his head, "Today's youth." After waiting a bit, Jim said, "You know, Ben, you don't have to take the fall for that pot bust. I read what you told Borough Council. You're claiming to have been the sole person responsible for the plants, but that's not what you told me when I arrested you. You told me that you were just watching the camp for someone else."

Ben drank down half of his beer, and then spit again. Jim tried again, "Ben. You're a young adult, but still an adult. This goes down the way it looks now, and you could spend time in jail. Do you really want that to happen, man?"

Ben Nakit's dark eyes scanned the scattered islands on the horizon. Frankie was just departing with another load of passengers. The de Havilland Beaver taxied out into a clear path on the waterway and its loud engine roared to life. Jim knew that Nakit was protecting someone, and he guessed it was because he was scared. When Jim made the arrest, he saw fear in the kid's eyes. Trooper Wekle was fairly certain that Ben Nakit was not a pot farmer or drug dealer; rather just a kid that made a few bad choices and gotten pressured into an illegal situation. Maybe Jim was a big softy, but he would hate to see this kid sit in a jail cell for a year or two.

Jim handed Ben his card and said, "Keep this. If you ever feel like talking or need anything, give me a call." As the trooper was walking away, he said over his shoulder, "And I hope you have a happy birthday, Ben."

The party raged into the evening. Deloris triumphantly defended her title as queen of the salmon egg spitters. Appropriate for the holiday, she wore an Uncle Sam's hat. Inappropriately, her bathrobe sagged open at the chest.

Trooper Spurgeon pulled up in his cruiser and rolled down his window, "Puke!"

Jim wandered over to the cruiser, leaned in and said, "What?"

"Puke, Jim. That's what I just had to clean up out of the back of my cruiser. This is not a damn taxi cab, and this is not what I went through the academy for. To clean up puke?"

Jim said sternly, "Tavis, settle down. For one day, you can suck it up and give a few rides to some local partiers. Better than pulling them over and administering DUI tests all day long."

A crew of Tavis' old high school buddies walked up and started cheering. They hopped in the back of the cruiser and ordered their old friend to drive them over to "Chuckie's house cuz they wanted to scarf down some killer tacos before the band fired up...dude."

Tavis looked out at Jim and said, "This is humiliating."

Jim ordered, "This is serving your community. Now start heading for Chuckie's. I hear the tacos there are killer, dude." Jim tapped the top of the cruiser twice. Reluctantly, Tavis pulled away from the curb. Jim heard more cheering as the car rolled down the street.

The "Drunk Parade" lived up to its billing. Other than a crew of teenagers on four-wheelers and a bunch of kids on bicycles, pretty much an entire town of drunken people staggered down Main Street for several blocks singing the Alaska state song in three-part dissonance. Several of the men removed their shirts and hoisted ladies upon their shoulders. The parade snaked right on Third Street and then another right onto Water Street. While passing the barge company and the cannery, the belting of song morphed into a version of the Beastie Boys, *You Gotta Fight...For Your Right...To Paaaaaartaaaay!"* On cue, a crew of cannery workers began shooting spray hoses at the parade, resulting in crazed cheering and the annual chorus of *Singing in the Rain.*

After making a three block rectangle, the parade ended back at the Ross Land and Sea lot. To Jim, it seemed to be harmless fun, even bordering on impressive that all inhabitants of the island knew every verse of *Singing in the Rain.* The parade participants were inebriated, yet they were happy. It was a celebratory gesture that brightened the town's mood, and by the time the crowd hit the beer line again, they were primed for the main event.

Kram and his band took the stage with flair. A zip line had been attached from the deck of a house up on a hill above town. The drummer was the first to drop onto stage, still wearing purple spandex and the George Washington wig. He sat behind the kit on stage and banged out a groove that instantly got the crowd moving. The bass player came soaring down the zip line next. He had on a shirt that had been made from an American Flag and wore a Speedo that exposed just a little too much of the man's business. By the time the bass player began slapping out a line in sync with the drummer, it was Kram's turn to slide down the zip line. The crowd cheered as the man flew overhead, white hair flowing behind, screaming, "Hot daaaaaaaaamn!" After landing in front of his full Marshal stack, he donned his Les Paul and screeched out a distorted solo that echoed around the surrounding buildings.

The lead singer was the last to fly in. As the aging rocker zoomed down the zip line, Frightening Frankie took his cue and flew close overhead pulling a banner that advertised the band's name. In massive font, the words *Kiss My Halibutt* fluttered on a white canvass behind the float plane. The lead singer grabbed the mic and went straight into the chorus of a tune that everyone seemed to know.

Two lines into the song, it hit Jim. He knew that he had recognized the singer before, back at the rehearsal in his container. The song was titled *Hair of the Frog* and it was the biggest hit from a 1980's hair band that Jim's older brother used to listen to religiously. The singer was Ted Manson. It had to be him. This guy was a legend. He fronted one of the most popular rock bands of the eighties; a band that went by the name of Axe Attack.

As the band rocked into the evening, things started to make sense to Jim. Back at the rehearsal in his container, Kram had said that he wrote the tune that they played. Jim knew that song, *Shackles of Love*. His brother used to play every album that Axe Attack had ever made.

Shackles of Love wasn't their most popular song, but it was stuck smack in the middle of the B-side of the band's third album. Jim figured that Kram must really have written that song, and that it was really Ted Manson wailing away on that stage. At least it made sense why his eccentrically odd landlord didn't really need a day job. With six albums that went double platinum, two decades worth of world tours, and royalties that still had to trickle in through continued internet downloads and contemporary covers of the old songs, Kram probably had millions in the bank. And here they were, rocking like the old days on a wooden dock in Craig, Alaska, under the moniker *Kiss my Halibutt*. It was one of the most famous bands of Jim's youth performing as though they were on stage at the Hollywood Bowl. And it appeared that Jim's George Forman Grill was positioned next to a row of amplifiers. The bassist seemed to be cooking a steak.

As the concert endured into the night, the crowd swelled. Dusk finally arrived and the band kicked into their A-list material in anticipation of the imminent fireworks. Maggie had shut down the hot dog cooking station, the ATV's were returned for the night, Frankie had tied up his float plane for good and only the beer vendors continued to serve the populous. Jim continued his duties monitoring the dock, heightening his awareness in order to ensure a safe climax to the event. The band's final encore was a tune Jim knew all too well. He remembered cruising Harbor Drive in San Diego in the passenger seat of his brother's Camaro, stereo blasting with Axe Attack's biggest hit. Listening to the live version brought Jim back to his youth. As the hit song *Jump my Bones* transitioned into Kram's guitar solo, Jim closed his eyes and soaked in every note. Completely enthralled by the music, the trooper failed to see a guy staggering dangerously close to the high edge of the dock.

Skye McDoogle, aka Neck Tattoos, was all partied out. He had hit the beer line too much and could care less about the aging band playing on stage. He wanted to head back to the Stockade and pass out on the couch. Unfortunately, Skye McDoogle had no idea which direction he was heading when he fell off the end of the Ross Land and Sea dock. The stoner tumbled close to twenty-five feet as he dropped into the icy water. Luckily for him, Ben Nakit saw the whole thing.

Jim's cell phone buzzed in his pocket, waking him back to reality from his Axe Attack trance. Ben Nakit had already run down to the float plane dock by the time Jim arrived. The cold water had sobered the guy a bit, but Neck Tattoos splashed frantically from the shock of the fall. Jim used a long pole to drag the drunk kid over to the edge of the dock and Ben helped pull the guy out of the water. Shivering and completely disoriented, Neck Tattoos babbled incoherently. Ben and Jim were forced to each take a shoulder in order to escort the young cannery worker back to the Stockade. They threw Skye McDoogle in a warm shower, and then helped him put on some sweatpants and a t-shirt before leaving him snoring on the Stockade's living room couch. Just as they opened the door of the Stockade, the first loud boom echoed through town. A brilliant blue flowering mortar lit up the sky above the water in front of them.

Walking back toward the fireworks show, Jim said, "Thanks for the call, Ben. If you hadn't seen that idiot fall off the dock, he probably would have died." Ben Nakit didn't say anything in response. As the two men walked, mortars continued to be launched from a barge that was anchored out in the sound.

The two parted ways once they reached the crowd of people. The rest of the night was fairly uneventful. After the fireworks show, Jim helped Tavis cart people back to their homes. Kram and his crew tore down the stage while the Ross brothers cleaned up the rest of the mess. By two in the morning, the dock was clear and the town was quiet again, with one exception. A solitary elderly man, enraged by the dismantling of the beer vendor's station, stood alone in the middle of the empty lot. In a crazed tone, he made only two demands. One, that the keg of Alaskan Amber be reassembled, and two, that his memory foam Coachman Plus mattress be returned to him immediately.

25

In the year 2005, a bill crawled its way through the United States Congress spearheaded by a senator from Alaska and backed by deep-pocketed lobbyists. The Rural Island Vitalization Act, or RIVA as it became known, was passed with the promise of dumping millions of dollars' worth of federal aid into Southeast Alaskan communities that struggled to thrive in light of region-wide sawmill and logging camp closures. RIVA was hailed as a source of immediate jobs and long-term prosperity as it was commissioned to build roads and bridges, revamp schools and hospitals, replace aging docks and subsidize year-round resident fishermen.

Several months after RIVA passed, Senator Carl Travors went up for re-election. Being hailed as the "Savior of Southeast," Senator Travors was voted in for a seventh term by a landslide. Shortly after re-election, a scandalous series of closed-door handshakes with the lobbyists that backed the bill occurred, resulting in very little money reaching the rural communities to whom it was promised. The bulk of the aid money created by RIVA went into the remodeling of the U.S. Senate offices in both Juneau and Anchorage, several lavish fishing trips in the Bahamas, a vacation home on Prince of Wales Island, and a televised golf event in Las Vegas, Nevada. News of the scandal hit the airways about the time the Senator was propping up his ball at the eleventh tee in Vegas. Network footage of Senator Carl Travors being rushed from the golf course surrounded by a caravan of security golf carts became one of the most hit on internet searches of the late 2000's.

The resulting inquiry led to the resignation of the Senator, but no criminal charges could be filed as Travors proved to be a genius when it came to a paperwork trail that covered his ass. All of the Senator's assets were seized with the exception of his vacation home of Prince of Wales. It could never be proved that the Senator used embezzled taxpayer funds to purchase the home on Halibut Cheek Drive. As a result, Carl Travors retired from politics and lived a life of solitude in the home just outside of the town of Craig, Alaska.

It was the power bill that finally pushed the man off the deep end. Unbeknownst to Carl, the exterior outlet that powered his neighbor's three deep freeze chests pushed his electric bill to almost triple of what it normally would read. Not bothering to check his electrical outlets, Carl Travors assumed it was all part of the local conspiracy against him. Enraged about his power bill and lack of police support after being caged inside a bear trap, he decided that someone would have to pay. Travors figured what better person was there to be the scapegoat of his recent turmoil than the new State Trooper in town. The former senator still had connections in high places and decided it was high time he called in some favors. After all, the current State Legislature had him to thank for their four-star offices filled to the gills with plush furnishings.

At the recommendation of his friend Gavin, Jim Wekle purchased a fishing license, rod, and casting reel. As the daylight faded from another damp Alaskan day, Jim stood on the outermost point of Mink Island repeatedly casting out a silver and pink Pixie spoon. As the summer progressed, more and more humpback salmon made their way from the open ocean into their spawning beds of the Southeast Alaskan streams. Humpies got their name from the gnarly bulge that appeared on their spines as they readied themselves for the spawn. Of all the salmon, humpies are the least appealing to eat. Their slimy texture and fishy flavor cause most Alaskans to release the fish as soon as they were landed. Humpies, however, happened to be quite fun to catch on a light trout rod.

Jim hooked into his first humpy after about his twentieth cast. He found the experience to be almost as entertaining as Oscar the mink did. The furry creature sat perched on a stump next to the water and watched as Jim fought the salmon all the way into shore. Splashing in the shallows as Jim released it, the pink salmon startled the little mink. Oscar ran for cover beneath a moss-covered rock close to shore.

"It's okay Oscar. That scary fish is gone. He won't hurt you." Jim went back to casting out the spoon. Rain dampened his shoulders, but it seemed to not bother him as much anymore. Maybe he was getting used to the rain. Jim had to admit, it was all the rain that helped create some of the most beautiful scenery on the face of the earth. Every ounce of land within sight was covered in the color green. Tall evergreens seemed to grow straight up from rocks, and their tangled root systems were covered with moss. Ferns, skunk cabbage, and salmonberry bushes sprouted up through the moss, filling every crevice above sea level with lush foliage.

"Oscar, let's see if we can hook into another one of those humpy guys." The little mink had scurried back to its perch atop the stump. Oscar was the only mink that wasn't scared of Jim. Often the other minks would scamper out from hiding when they sensed it was close to feeding time, but for the most part, they wouldn't come within twenty feet of the man. But Oscar was different. Jim often shared food with the little guy right from the palm of his hand. He had even managed to stroke the fur on the back of the mink's head a couple of times. Oscar would follow Jim all over the island, even out to the edge of the boat dock when he was departing for work each morning.

With the motion of casting out and reeling back, Jim found another tranquil way of passing time on Mink Island. Fishing was proving to be very conducive of deep thought. Jim would select a spot, cast out and let his brain drift away as he retrieved the lure. His mind brought up Maggie Ketah. He felt sorry for the girl, losing her only brother. He thought about the kiss. Was he crazy, kissing some girl on a date that he hadn't even intended to go on? It was the whole scene that made him do it; the boat ride, the food, the music, the great view on that back deck. He had better just put that whole deal on the side burner. Maggie was grieving. Not to mention, he didn't even want a relationship in the first place. He was just starting to enjoy being single again. He decided to forget about the kiss and let the whole matter rest for a while.

Jim thought about his friend, Kram. What a kook, ha! But man, that guy really could play the guitar. Was he really the musical brains and drive behind the classic band, Axe Attack? Jim was pretty sure of it. The topic would have to be discussed with Kram at some point in the future. He was not sure how forthcoming Kram would be with information, though. Speaking of kooks, how about that Deloris? Jim was glad that he was friends with her and not enemies. What's with all those hats, anyway?

Another cast and another topic for thought. The murders. What would he do about the murders? Jim did have a plan. He was pretty sure that he knew what he needed to do next in his investigation. A little field trip, as Jim called it, was in order. He needed Kram to go along, too. Jim had his suspicions about what was going on under his nose on the island, but he needed some information that would help prove his suspicions. The problem was, obtaining that information around town came at a price. Everyone on the island talked to everyone else on the island. Word spread quickly on

Prince of Wales, and only a certain amount of snooping could be done locally before the whole community knew about it. Jim needed to get off the island for a short time. It would only take him a day or two. He could leave Tavis in charge. Wonderboy held down the fort for a whole week after Trooper Dan retired. Jim was fairly sure the kid could handle a couple of days alone at the station.

The pole tip bent sharply, and the reeled suddenly buzzed. Jim set the hook and the fish reacted by stripping line at a fast rate. In the light of dusk, he saw the silhouette of a large salmon leap from the water, shaking its head and tail vigorously. The fish landed with a splash and immediately darted to Jim's right.

"I don't think this is a humpy, Oscar." Oscar the mink darted back and forth nervously in response. After allowing the salmon to take line as it raced to the right, Jim suddenly felt his line go completely slack. The first thought was that the line had broken, but Jim saw the fish jump out of the water again, this time much closer to shore. Jim started reeling as fast as he could. Eventually, the line caught up with the fish and the pole tip bent back over toward the waterline. The fish was still hooked. It had just made a run straight in towards the shore.

As the salmon peeled line from the reel while it made another run straight out from where he stood, Jim had the sudden realization that he didn't have a net. Knowing that he might actually want to keep this fish, Jim concocted a strategy of how he might land his catch. Jim had to fight the fish through several runs, but after a few

216

minutes of back and forth, the salmon seemed to be tiring. Keeping his pole tip up, Jim eased the fish into shore. The salmon swirled its tail, frothing the water, but it was obvious that there wasn't a lot of fight left in it. Jim stepped down into the saltwater and carefully positioned himself on two submerged rocks. There was a small indentation in the shoreline that Jim guided the fish into. He wedged himself between the opening of the indentation, trapping the catch between his torso and the shore. The salmon twisted and thrashed, but it was captured. It had nowhere to go. Feeling along the side of the salmon, Jim was able to wedge a couple of fingers inside the salmon's right gill. He could then lift the fish out of the water and carefully pulled himself back onto dry land.

Jim's heart raced with adrenaline still in his veins. It was a beauty of a Coho, probably ten pounds Jim guessed. Even though light had faded, bright silvery scales shimmered. Feeling triumphant, Jim withdrew a pocket knife and gutted the Coho on a rock next to shore. He tossed the entrails into the trees and instantly he heard several little minks race toward their late night snack. Back at the yurt, he sliced the beautiful fish into thick steaks. He threw several chucks into Ziplocks for future enjoyment and grilled up the rest for his own late night snack. After enjoying the freshest seafood he had ever eaten, Jim set his plate on the ground and let Oscar clean up every remaining morsel.

The barge company was buzzing. Forklifts of varying size weaved in and out of aisles of pallets and shipping containers. People wearing yellow hardhats and orange vests with walkie-talkies clipped to their belts crisscrossed paths pushing hand trucks carrying shrink-wrapped boxes of supplies. Refrigerated containers had been switched from barge generators to shore power in order to keep food from spoiling. Several new trucks and boats were lifted off the barge with a large crane sporting massive looped straps that kept the undercarriages safe from damage. It was standard operating procedure for the mid-month shipment of supplies for Sea Tank Marine Lines; total chaos.

As soon as Jim Wekle enter the smoke-filled office cube, Blitz, the bulldog barked once, sniffed his leg, and then trotted to a padded dog bed behind a file cabinet. Phones rang, outdated computers clicked, whiteboards were being updated with shipping customer names and locations. There were five people crammed into the small space and four of them moved through their duties as if choreographed by a master of ballet. The fifth person stood over a desk made of plywood and sawhorses. Stacks of invoices lay out in front of him, and a cheap cigar in desperate need of being ashed hung from the corner of his lips.

Without looking up from his paperwork, Tank Spurgeon said gruffly, "You picked a hell of a time for a visit, Lieutenant Wekle. Just happens to be the busiest day of the month."

"I brought a gift for you. And I have a question for you. It won't take long, I promise."

Tank grabbed a walkie-talkie from the plywood desk, crammed his thumb into the button, and yelled into the speaker, "Get the grocery container delivered now. If that load of produce spoils in my lot, I'll take the ten grand out of your paycheck." Releasing the button on the com device, Tank turned his attention to the State Trooper and announced, "You've got thirty seconds. Go."

Jim removed from his blue shirt pocket, a single cellophane-wrapped, seven-inch-long cigar. He offered it out to Tank and said, "Hand rolled Dominican. Maduro wrapper. Fifty ring gauge. I would recommend it after eating spicy food."

Tank received the gift, examined the cigar label and replied, "Thanks. Little better quality than my gas station cigar here, huh?"

"Just a bit. How often do the barge shipments come in?"

"Barge docks every Wednesday morning."

Jim nodded and asked, "When do you unload and distribute shipments?"

"As fast as we damn well can. I don't make money by having cargo sit on my lot or in my warehouse." The phone rang. Tank said, "Your time is just about up."

"I have a request. I would like to see your records

of all clients that received shipments on the last
Wednesday of last month."

Tank snorted a quick laugh. Cigar ash tumbled
down his shirt. "Trooper. One thing you will learn after
you live on this rock for a while. Most people that take up
residence here enjoy their privacy. And most people that
live here are my customers."

"I just want to see a list of names. I won't tell if you
won't tell."

Tank Spurgeon slid the cellophane-wrapped cigar
into the pocket of his shirt, then removed the lit cigar
from his mouth, and said, "You come back with a court
order and I'll show you that list of names." He turned his
attention back to the stack of invoices and said, "Thanks
for the cigar. I've got work to do."

26

The city of Ketchikan, Alaska is located on a southern shoreline of a large, mostly uninhabited landmass named Revillagigedo Island. With just over eight thousand people living within its city limits, Ketchikan is Alaska's fifth largest city. It is the hub of southern Southeast Alaskan activity and boasts the largest shipyard, cruise ship dock, medical facility, and shopping venues of the region. It is also a city of many nicknames, including; *The Salmon Capital of the World*, *Alaska's First City*, and *The Rain City*. With mountainous terrain behind it, the city of Ketchikan is sprawled along the island's coastline. Across a thin strip of water called the Tongass Narrows, Gravina and Pennock Islands helped protect the Ketchikan waterfront, enabling it to be the perfect location to harbor a cast of boats and float planes. The busy waterfront typically buzzed with planes taking off and landing, fishing vessels passing through, ferry boats coming in to dock, barges being towed by tugs, and massive cruise ships that carried thousands of visitors from around the world, all wearing matching rain parkas and eager to spend their cash on tourist crap.

The float plane trip took a little less than an hour. The weather was fairly nice with a few high clouds, little wind and no rain. Jim Wekle sat alone in the back of the noisy de Havilland Beaver while Kram sat copilot next to Frightening Frankie. They traveled due east over the width of Prince of Wales, snaking between a few mountain peaks, and looking down on thick evergreen trees and shimmering blue lakes. Jim spotted the small community of Hollis out the right side of the plane and soon they were flying over the open waters of Clarence Strait with a view of Revillagigedo out the front windows of the plane.

Frankie Ross' voice came to life in Jim's headset, "Humpbacks down there. Let's go in for a closer look."

The plane banked sharply to the right and Jim looked straight out his window to the sea below. He saw several black bodies appear and submerge in the waters below, spewing white spray from their curved bodies when they reached their visible apex.

Kram said, "That's a big pod. Must be thirty or more whales."

They circled twice giving the three men amazing views of the humpback whales. Some larger than a Mack truck, the marine mammals took turns surfacing and then plunging back into the depths leaving their massive fantail to be the last sight in the air.

Frankie said, "Seen it a thousand times before, but never get tired of it."

The pilot guided the plane back to its easterly tack and soon they found themselves wedged between islands in the Tongass Narrows. After talking to someone on the radio about landing instructions, Frankie guided the plane into the breeze and began his approach. Jim looked across the aisle out the left side of the plane and saw two cruise ships already docked, with another one slowly approaching.

Kram also saw the same sight. Spying the large ocean liners full of thousands of people, Kram let loose with a guttural response.

"Aaahaak!"

Speaking into his headset microphone, Frankie said, "Easy there, champ. They're only tourists." Kram averted his eyes from the waterfront scene. Jim began wondering how wise it was to invite Kram along on this trip.

The plane set down with ease and maneuvered its way to a waterfront dock. Jim confirmed with Frankie that they would be picked up in the morning for the return trip to Craig. Jim wore his Troopers uniform and carried a small overnight bag up a steep ramp toward a street-level wood-planked landing. Kram followed up the ramp carrying nothing. He wore only his standard jean cutoffs, brown rubber Xtratufs, green *Frogger* t-shirt and hair pulled back into the usual ponytail.

"Meet you at noon. You'll be okay until then, right?" Jim asked, trying to gauge his partner's reasonable sanity.

Kram clicked together the heels of his brown boots

and saluted, "Aye, Aye, captain! Noon on Creek Street. You can count on me!" Kram dropped his salute and sprinted across the busy street next to the wooden landing. He disappeared up a staircase that ascended up and over a rock wall. Jim felt mildly worried, almost as if he had released a dangerous virus on the streets of Ketchikan. But he had more pressing concerns than that of Kram's escapades. Jim had been summoned to a meeting at the Ketchikan Trooper's station. His superior had authorized his trip to Ketchikan and insisted on meeting with him as soon as he landed. Several minutes passed before an Alaska State Trooper cruiser pulled into the lot and picked him up.

Tongass Avenue was the main road that stretched the length of the town of Ketchikan. On one side of Tongass, industrial shops, fish canneries, float plane hangars and other waterfront businesses sat perched on pilings over the saltwater. On the other side of the street, several side roads shot up in elevation away from the water's edge. The cruiser snaked along Tongass in stop and go traffic past the densely packed industrial district, past the barge lines and State ferry dock, and past a post office and a grocery store. Eventually, the city lined street gave way to trees and sparsely placed residences as the cruiser traveled northwest up the island.

The driver appeared young. Jim figured he was fresh out of the academy. The young recruit wasn't very talkative, and Jim was fine with that. A few miles out of town, the cruiser took a right turn next to a large sign that read, "Alaska State Troopers Detachment A Headquarters." After pulling through an open chain link fence gate, the cruiser parked in a gravel lot next to four identical Ford Crown Victoria's. The lineup of cruisers was positioned in front of a headquarters building that had to be quadruple in size as Jim's station back in Craig.

Behind the headquarters building, a maintenance shop buzzed with activity as mechanics worked on Trooper issued vehicles. A massive covered structure hung over a paved lot that housed a stash of rescue equipment, snowmobiles, four wheelers, and two large aluminum hulled boats sitting on trailers. Gunfire echoed off of a steep rock cliff next to the headquarters building, as two Troopers honed their marksmanship at a gun range positioned behind the maintenance shed. Jim was impressed with the resources and activity surrounding the Detachment Headquarters. It certainly was more impressive than the small force that he commanded back on Prince of Wales Island.

After being buzzed through to the office area of the headquarters building, Jim was asked to sit in a small waiting area. He poured himself a cup of burnt coffee and kicked back in a very uncomfortable metal chair. With his free hand, Jim rubbed his temples.

"Jim Wekle, it's about time you came to see me." A tall woman with brilliant, curly red hair stood in the doorway of the Captain's office. She wasn't an old woman but had slight wrinkles on her face. Jim guessed that she was in her mid to upper-fifties.

"Captain Reesa McEwen." The woman stuck her hand out. Jim stood and accepted the handshake. "Come on in and sit down. I know you came over to Ketchikan as part of your investigation, so I won't take too much of your time, but there are a couple of things we need to discuss."

The woman guided Jim into a sterile office with a large, clean desk that took up most of the room. Jim sat in the only chair that was placed opposite the desk. The room was hardly decorated, with only one picture hanging on the wall. The picture displayed the Captain shaking hands with a former Governor of the State of Alaska. The rest of the walls were painted white and completely clear and clean. The desk featured only a computer, a blank pad of paper and a nameplate that read, *Captain Reesa McEwen*.

The captain sat and glared at Jim. "I don't waste time with small talk, Jim. There has been a complaint filed concerning your performance as Lieutenant of the Craig Station."

Jim appeared surprised, "I wasn't aware of that."

"I know that. The complaint reached my desk just yesterday. I would have called, but I knew you were coming in today."

Jim was familiar with what it felt like to have a superior question his performance as an officer. He had just gone through the ordeal up in Anchorage that landed him the Craig position. What confused him, though, was

226

that he couldn't figure out who on Earth had filed the complaint or what it could be about.

The captain opened a desk drawer and removed a single piece of white printer paper. She appeared stoic as she read aloud:

"A pattern of incompetence has led me to believe that Lieutenant Jim Wekle is not fit to lead Alaska State Trooper operations on Prince of Wales Island. This pattern starts with the string of unsolved crimes that have occurred on his watch, and continues with negligence of duty surrounding a list of abhorrent behaviors tolerated by Trooper Wekle. Lack of follow through on complaints submitted by myself that include kidnapping and illegal administering of a controlled substance should be enough alone to incur disciplinary action. However, with the recent tolerance of lewd behavior by our local populous during our Independence Day celebration which led to a near-fatal waterfront accident, a mere disciplinary action would not suffice. It is my belief that Trooper Jim Wekle should be relieved of duty effective immediately. Sincerely, Senator Carl Travors, Craig, Alaska."

Immediately defensive, Jim contested, "Kidnapping? This guy is crazy. His neighbors pulled a little prank on him. And that near-fatal accident that he is talking about happened when a burned-out cannery worker..."

Captain McEwen interrupted Jim's retort, "Listen, a woman cop in Alaska doesn't get to be a Detachment Captain by letting some shit-weasel politician intimidate her. You see that picture?" She pointed to the sole picture on her wall. Jim nodded. "I was sent to the Governor's mansion to be honored after taking down a drug ring outside of Juneau. Ten minutes after that picture was taken, the bastard grabbed my ass. I had him hogtied face down on the floor of his office before his security team even realize what had hit him. I keep that picture on my wall to remind me to never let myself be intimidated."

Jim squirmed in his seat, "Yes sir...ma'am."

She continued, "Carl Travors is a prick! We all know that. I don't need you to address every complaint that halfwit concocted." Jim nodded again. McEwen continued, "I could care less about this stupid complaint, but for some reason, Travors still carries clout with the higher-ups."

She stood and turned to stare at the blank wall behind her desk. "I will make this very easy for you to understand, Jim. This is how it will work. The higher-ups tell me to investigate this complaint. You solve those two murder cases. I tell them to screw off. It's that simple."

"And if I can't solve the murder cases?"

"Then you might be scrubbing barnacles off the hull

of one of those boats you eyeballed on the way into the office. Are we clear?"

"Crystal." Jim stood up and started to walk out of the office.

"Wekle, one more thing."

Jim stopped and turned toward the fiery red-haired woman, "Yes, Captain?"

"I know resources are thin out there. What can I do to help?"

Jim didn't need much time to answer. "Captain, I need ballistics on the bullet that killed the Simms girl. It's been weeks and I still haven't heard anything."

Reesa McEwen nodded and said, "I will see what I can do."

27

Bill Fetcherson's recent string of bad luck seemed to manifest itself in the form of obsessive behavior. Between his newfound addiction to Alaskan Amber beer and his growing compulsion for restoring the Luxury Coachman Plus, Bill began to exhibit maniacal behaviors. With alcohol clouding his brain, a Holy Grail-like quest began to form with regard to the RV renovation. All Bill Fetcherson could think about was one day returning to the captain's chair of his beloved Coachman.

What started as a continental journey into their golden years, turned out to be a nightmare of getting stranded on an island in Alaska. As the obsession grew in her husband, Gladys couldn't stay by his side any longer. She had experienced enough trauma recently; her dog being eaten by an eagle, her body being launched into a kelp bed, and now her husband falling completely off the deep end. Gladys Fetcherson finally had enough. Her retirement years had started off in disaster, and she was a fragile creature.

When asked how long her husband insisted on staying in Craig, Bill's response only fed Gladys' fears. "As long as it takes," was not a satisfactory answer, so Gladys booked charter fare on the next flight off the island and made way for her sister's home back in Mt. Pleasant,

Utah. Within days of arriving, Gladys had already purchased a prized toy poodle and named it *Snookums Two* as a living monument to her beloved first dog. All travel and poodle expenses were charged against her husband's waning credit card balance.

With his nagging wife out of the picture, Bill Fetcherson permanently checked out from his room above Porty's and took up full-time residence inside the RV. Although the engine still wouldn't run and most of the interior furnishings were still missing, Bill was allowed to run an extension cord from the shop at Ross Land and Sea in order to power the refrigerator. Even in Alaska, Bill liked to keep his beer cold.

With the ever-present struggle to get special order items delivered to Prince of Wales, coupled with the declining available credit left on his Platinum Card, Bill Fetcherson gave up on the idea of matching décor with the Luxury Coachman Plus interior. His passion for a memory foam mattress embroidered with a giant "C" finally faded, and his elderly back couldn't take sleeping on the floor of the RV. As a result, Bill began fervently collecting boat cushions from every source imaginable. He quickly bought out all the stores of every life-saving throw cushion, vest preserver and flotation ring. Once the island's limited retail supply was drained, Bill was forced to resort to theft. He would walk the docks early every morning and late each night, sipping from bottles of amber while looking over his shoulder. When the coast was deemed clear, he would bolt onto a nearby boat and

collect all of the flotation cushions he could muster.
Within a few days, the entire interior of the Coachman
was littered with an abundance of orange, red and white
flotation pillows. It resembled a colorful version of the
padded cell block of a loony bin.

The noon hour in downtown Ketchikan during the
summer tourist months was complete bedlam. Twelve
thousand rain-parka wearing, camera wielding, crazed
foreigners rambled six small city blocks, completely
oblivious to any indigenous life or culture. MasterCards
were swiped continuously in stores that were crammed
full of trinkets promised to resemble life in the last
frontier. Snow globes that rained caribou turds,
miniature totem poles made out of plastic, corked vials
full of "real S.E. Alaskan rainwater," and ulu knives made
in China busted forth from shelves and bins that spilled
out onto covered sidewalks.

Enormous cruise ships would unload their throngs
onto docks that stretched the length of the downtown
area. Once unloaded, the tourists need only to cross
Tongass Avenue to reach the shops, restaurants, and bars.
Wearing brightly colored, ship-issued raincoats that
resembled giant condoms, hordes of people would step
out into oncoming traffic without even a second thought.
The allure of the tourist traps and bald eagle sightings
seemed to pull swarms of people into the road without
fear or consideration of moving vehicles. The rain parkas

were most likely colored so brightly as an intentional signaling device for oncoming traffic.

Jim Wekle had borrowed an unmarked cruiser from the Detachment Headquarters and proceeded down Tongass Avenue en route to his rendezvous with Kram. Unknowingly, Jim's chosen meeting place had been selected in the heart of tourist territory. Taking three times longer than anticipated, Jim was almost across town when several short women of Asian descent backed up into the street in front of his car. Luckily they all wore yellow parkas that immediately caught Jim's eye. After slamming on the brakes, he was amazed to watch the group of women pose directly in front of the nose of his Crown Victoria. Smiling at a man on the sidewalk, the group stood as statues while the man snapped several shots with his Nikon. Following the photo shoot, the cameraman joined the group as they stepped into the other lane of oncoming traffic. They continued across the road completely oblivious to the world around them. Feeling snarky, Jim rolled down his window and hollered, "Have a nice day!"

After finding a rare parking place close to Creek Street, Jim hopped out and made his way through the horde to the meeting place. He had already changed out of his Trooper uniform and wore blue jeans, white sneakers, a green flannel shirt and a San Diego Padres baseball cap. Although it was a fairly nice day, he was amazed at how most of the tourists continued to wear their rain parkas. The slippery, yellow jackets made it easy for Jim to weave in and out of the crowd of people that packed the sidewalks. About a block up the street, Jim crossed a bridge expanse, and then he turned left onto a wooden boardwalk labeled *Creek Street*.

Creek Street wasn't actually a street, but rather a wooden boardwalk that followed a short length of the historic Ketchikan Creek. Back in the old days, Creek Street was a red light district that was frequented by fishermen. The saying goes, "Ketchikan Creek was a famous spawning grounds for fish and fishermen alike." Now, historic buildings built on stilts hanging over the creek featured shops, restaurants and the famous Red Light Museum that attracted visitors daily.

Jim had heard reports that the Rain City Coffee Company served the best brew in town. It also happened to be located next to a cigar shop, so Jim had to make Creek Street one of his destinations. Ready for a good cup of coffee and a sandwich, Jim quickly swerved his way around the slow-moving tourists up the boardwalk. After passing a couple of curio shops, he heard several screams from up ahead. Jim jogged forward, quickly moving to join a crowd of people that blocked the expanse of the wooden walkway.

"There it goes!" Someone yelled and pointed. A different man yelled something in a language that Jim didn't recognize. A few shrieks by some of the women.

"I don't believe it," another person exclaimed.

Craning his neck to find an open view, Jim finally

was able to spy the cause of the commotion. A humpy salmon flopped its way across the wooden path and disappeared into the bushes next to the boardwalk. A few seconds later, another salmon came scurrying across the walkway. Each fish slid across the wooden planks on their sides, bumping into nail heads and other raised portions of the boardwalk. With each snag, the fish flip-flopped its way over the bump, giving it the appearance of life.

Jim let out an exhale as he calmly skirted the edge of the crowd. Without being seen by the masses, he slipped past some tree branches and snuck into the bushes where the salmon seemed to be disappearing. Kram sat cross-legged, surrounded by dead humpies and a rat's nest of monofilament fishing line. He grinned sheepishly at Jim.

"I have a couple left. Watch this one." Kram began tugging on a nearly invisible string and another fish appeared from across the other side of the boardwalk. More shrieks and comments exploded from the crowd of onlookers. Several Australian tourists snapped pictures with their smartphones. The dead fish entered the tree covered hiding place and slithered across Jim's sneakers.

"Hey, watch it. I don't want to smell like dead humpy all day."

"Too late for me. I'll probably reek for the rest of the week." Kram began tugging on his final string. This time, the scaly body of the fish got hung up on a rusty boardwalk screw head. Being soft from rot, the head portion of the salmon messily tore off and sling-shot straight into the wooden clearing, hitting Kram right in the chest. At the sight of a headless fish corpse still lying on the boardwalk floor, the crowd moaned and quickly dispersed.

"Are you done now?"

Kram grinned and said, "I can always torment the tourists another time."

Kram snipped clean the fishing line from each of the humpies and stuffed the rat's nest into his pocket. The two men stepped out of the brush and onto the walkway.

"You're just going to leave those fish corpses in the woods to rot?"

"Why not?"

"Won't that create an incredible stench?"

"I love the odor of rotting fish meat. You should embrace the stink, Jimbo." Kram was wiping fish slimed hands on the thighs of his jean cutoffs. "Besides, it will remind the tourists that they are truly getting the whole experience. Nothing says Alaska quite like dead humpy stink."

28

Lunch in the coffee shop was decent, but took longer than expected. The place was packed with parka-wearing Europeans. An elderly couple from Switzerland ordered the last piece of smoked salmon quiche. Jim was slightly miffed but settled on a turkey bagel with tomato and cream cheese. He ordered a triple shot Americano and a glass of ice water. Kram snacked on a packet of cellophane-wrapped saltines.

"So you basically need me to run recon for you while you make nice with the suits in the office?" Kram had cracker crumbs stuck to his chin.

"Basically, yes. I need to know who is scheduled to receive container shipments in Craig at the end of the month."

"And you can't just flash your badge for this information?" Kram tore into another packet of crackers.

"It's possible that would work, but I see two potential issues. One, they don't have to give me any information without a warrant. And two, the bigger stink that I create, the more likely it is that word will spread. I'm trying to maintain the status of covert operations here."

The waitress walked up with a plate that held Jim's

sandwich and a cup that held his very strong espresso.

Kram raised a finger and asked, "Can you bring me some more of these Feldman's Fine Saltines? They are simply divine." The waitress frowned and walked away.

"Do you think she heard me?"

"She heard you, Kram. It's just that those crackers are for customers that actually order food from the menu."

Kram's attention drifted as he gazed into the ceiling of the coffee shop. Jim assumed he was lost in thought over his cracker situation.

After a bite of his rather stale bagel, Jim asked, "So, you understand what I need?"

Snapping back to present time and place, Kram answered, "Sure. Piece of cake. Locate all shipping containers with 'Craig, Alaska' written on the lading sheet. I write down all names associated and bring it back to you. Like I said, piece of cake."

"And please, Kram. Be fairly discrete. I'm already in a little hot water with my boss."

"No worries, captain. I can be discrete. For all you know, I could've served in the special forces back in Nam." Kram's head snapped and his gaze momentarily fixed again on the same invisible spot on the shop's ceiling. Jim wondered briefly about the Vietnam reference, as it possibly added one more piece to the puzzle that is Kram.

Jim asked, "Do you have a paper and something to write with?"

"Check!" Kram extracted from the pocket of his jean shorts a crumpled up piece of notebook paper and an orange crayon.

Stuffing the paper back into his pocket, Kram asked, "So you think you can solve two murders just by seeing who in Craig is receiving a container shipment at the end of the month?"

"Maybe not directly."

"So what, murderers are being smuggled into town inside shipping containers. Jimbo, you may want to rethink that one."

"No, not murderers. Pills."

"Pills?" Kram seemed to be searching for his invisible spot of thought upon the ceiling tiles.

"Illegal pills and they are getting onto the island somehow. They seem to be showing up just before the first of every month."

Kram connected the dots, "And now, because the container shipments that sit in the Ketchikan lot will head out soon and end up on Prince of Wales close to the end of the month, you think your pills are stashed in there somewhere." Kram battled with a particularly stubborn cellophane cracker wrapper.

"You know, Kram. I'm not really supposed to discuss this stuff with you. Besides, you could be a suspect for all I know."

Kram leaned back in his chair and stroked his ponytail while he chuckled, "Yeah man, you had better keep an eye on me for sure." He snorted a laugh and almost fell straight back in his tilted chair.

Jim secretly agreed with the comment about keeping an eye on him. Jim said, "I am counting on your complete confidence on all this stuff. Let's just say that the info I need you to get is going to have to be obtained through non-official means. I asked Tank for his client list, but he refused. If I got caught jotting down names without Tank's permission, I could get into some pretty deep trouble. Thus, this trip to Ketchikan and me soliciting your help."

A Japanese couple walked up to Kram and Jim's table and held out a camera. Through sign language, they requested to have someone take their picture. Kram leaped to his feet and grabbed the camera away from the rain parka wearing man.

"Ah yes. A photo to commemorate your lunch in a café on a boardwalk where fishermen used to get laid. This is perfect. Over here." Kram waved the couple through the crowded coffee shop toward a bank of windows that overlooked Ketchikan Creek. "Right here. This will do nicely."

Kram positioned the Japanese couple so they were

perfectly framed by the center window. He asked a group of tourists that were snacking on salmon lox to vacate their table for the brief photo shoot.

"Everything must be perfect to commemorate this momentous occasion," he said as he waved patrons away from the posing couple. Kram flipped the camera on and began snapping pictures, twisting the camera into vertical, horizontal and even diagonal positions in front of his squinting eye.

"Bigger smiles, now. Work it, work it." More pictures snapped. Kram moved backward without looking and bumped into a table, almost spilling glasses of water. Café patrons seemed to spread out of his way like the wake of a speedboat.

"Now look serious. Mean faces. Like you are determined to conquer this obscure land called Alaska." More picture snaps. More moving the camera to different vantage points. Kram sprawled his body on the floor and took pictures backwards, facing up at a very confused pair of Japanese tourists.

"Just a couple more. We've almost got the money shot. Need better angles." Kram asked a lady from South Carolina to stand up. He grabbed her chair and positioned it in the center of the café. Standing on the chair with the camera up to his face, he began singing *America the Beautiful* while completely filling the memory card of the camera with multiple snapshots.

At the top of his lungs, "*And crown thy good with*

brotherhood..."

The confused Japanese couple realized that the song was closing to a crescendo and all eyes were on them. They stood tall and proud as Kram finished his anthem.

"...from sea to shining seeeeeeeeeeeea." Kram snapped his final picture, raised both arms almost touching the ceiling from his perch atop the chair and the entire coffee shop burst into applause. He took a sweeping bow, hopped off the chair and offered the camera back to the smiling, nodding couple.

Returning to his seat, Kram opened a fresh pack of crackers.

Jim asked, "Did you have fun."

"Just giving them some memories, Jimbo. You ready to head for the docks?"

"Absolutely. After one quick stop next door, of course."

"Ah, yes. The cigar shop. Imported, handmade stogies kept at a constant seventy-three percent humidity. You know, Southeast Alaska is probably the only place on the planet that uses a humidor to keep humidity out of their cigars."

"You're probably right. Let's go."

As the two stood to leave, Kram waved at the waitress and yelled across the room, "More Feldman

Crackers to go, please!"

Roger Greeley nervously sipped on a bottle of beer while he watched two of his counterparts work feverishly on the bow of *The Cyclone*. Roger had purchased his sailing vessel the week after retiring from a thirty-six-year career as a tax accountant. His boring life as a number cruncher had finally ended and the adventurous goal of sailing the islands of Southeast Alaska had finally become a reality.

When Roger Greeley wiped out most of his retirement savings by purchasing the sailboat for nearly two hundred grand, dreams of protected anchorages and leeward tacks filled his mind. His reverie included a vision of his wife preparing a simple lunch below deck in the galley, while he masterfully guided his ship from behind the wheel. Roger envisioned Orcas off his starboard bow while bald eagles circled above. He longed to weather a storm while anchored in the shelter of a tree-lined cove. For weeks leading up to his retirement, he monitored the VHF marine radio channels, learning to speak the nautical lingo. He purchased boating outfits that both looked classy and helped protect him from the harshness of island weather. At no point during his dreams of sailing the waters of America's last frontier, did Roger Greeley picture what he saw now; the exposed butt-crack of an overweight man installing a 70-caliber cannon on the bow of his sailboat.

"Aw dammit!" The expletive from Blue-Jay Haverford was preceded by a small splash just off the bow of the anchored *Cyclone*.

"Watch what you're doing, you idiot. That's the second wrench that you've dropped into the sea in the past half hour." DeAngelo Smuthers spat words at his partner on the bow of the boat. "If we run out of tools, that means we are heading back home without a test-fire. Plus, I'm making you buy me replacements for both of those wrenches you dropped overboard."

"Hand me another crescent wrench and stop criticizing. I don't see you bent over the railing trying to secure these mounting brackets."

DeAngelo offered the tool and said, "And pull up your shorts. We don't need to see your ass-crack."

Mounting a two hundred and fifty-pound steel cannon to the bow of a fiberglass sailboat was proving to be a challenge for the three men. With every hole drilled through the deck of *The Cyclone*, Roger Greeley emitted a squeamish, high pitched sound that seemed to project from his nostrils. DeAngelo Smuthers barked orders in between sips of bottled beer and Blue-Jay Haverford did most of the actual labor. Four mounting brackets had to be secured to the deck by extending long bolts into the ship's forward sleeping berth. Perched above where Roger and his wife would normally rest their heads when sleeping aboard, multiple nuts and washers had been secured on the threaded ends of the long bolts. The thought of smacking his head on one of the nuts after waking in the middle of the night made Roger Greeley cringe.

"I thought you were supposed to be a ballistics expert. How long should it take to mount a simple cannon?"

Blue-Jay farted and replied, "Sorry, but the military failed to train me in the fine art of sailboat weaponry. Now shut up and help me lift this thing into place."

It took the strength of all three men to awkwardly maneuver the heavy mortar across the bow of the sailboat. It was just the three of them working on the boat in secluded wilderness. Earlier, in a moment of self-claimed wisdom, DeAngelo had decided that the women and old man Cecil were best left at home. As he put it, "*The Cyclone* will be cramped enough as it is with Haverford's fat ass on board." However, once they began to lift the big gun into place, DeAngelo wished he had a few more sets of arms to help.

The boat rocked back and forth as the trio fought with the weight of the gun. Roger Greeley was almost knocked over the rail, but DeAngelo let go of the cannon and grabbed him just in time. Suddenly, holding up the weapon alone, Blue Jay Haverford found he was unable to support the weight with his two arms. The cannon dropped on his foot and he let forth with a stream of profanities that would have made his old college buddies proud.

They finally were able to maneuver cannon into place. With the measurements appearing to have been accurate, the cannon slipped perfectly over the mounting brackets. Blue-Jay finished off the job by securing the top bolts into the brackets and it was soon time to test fire their weapon. All three men stood anxiously next to the long silver barrel. Tilting it upright, Blue-Jay Haverford poured black powder into the firing chamber followed by some wadding and topped off with a golf ball.

Roger was concerned, "A golf ball? We don't want to kill anybody with this thing."

"Relax, Roger. The golf ball is just for the test fire. We aren't actually going to be firing projectiles from this cannon at a crowd of people."

Nervously, Roger Greeley retreated from the bow of his anchored vessel and sought refuge behind a ring-shaped flotation device. DeAngelo's excitement grew as he watched his ballistics partner install the fuse.

Giddy as a child, DeAngelo exclaimed, "This is going to be awesome."

The Cyclone was anchored in a small cove several miles south of the city of Craig. The wind was calm and the boat floated peacefully in the cove with the anchor chain sitting slack. Tall cedar trees lined the shoreline off to the starboard side. The island's elevation rose steadily behind the tall trees. They were surrounded on three sides of the cove by rock cliffs.

The volume of the explosion peaked at decibels exceeding the threshold of pain. Sound waves reverberated off the cliffs and seemed to dissipate over several long seconds. Wildlife scrambled through the trees and birds took flight. The voluminous eruption utterly destroyed the peaceful tranquility of the secluded cove.

The force of the blast immediately caused the bow of the sailboat to jerk quickly to its left side. After about a half second of propelling through the water in the opposite direction of the cannon's discharge, the anchor chain became taught and stopped the drift of the boat suddenly in place. Following in line with Newton's laws of physics, three deafened men were hurdled fanatically toward the deck rail of the sailboat. Given Blue-Jay Haverford's relative size, the impact on the boat's rail was similar to that of a buffalo herd. The rail gave way and all three men were launched off the side of the vessel into the cold saltwater.

On the shoreline opposite from where the men entered the water, a white golf ball sat firmly implanted four inches inside the trunk of a seventy-year-old cedar tree.

29

The industrial sector of the Ketchikan waterfront closely resembled Craig's waterfront, just on a grander scale. Instead of one float plane dock, there were several small airlines scattered up the length of Tongass Narrows. Instead of one fish cannery, there were three, all positioned in close proximity to each other. There were several small fishing boat docks and a major shipyard large enough to dry dock a small cruise ship. Three densely populated marinas were interspersed among a couple of tugboat businesses and a helicopter company. There was also an Alaska State Ferry terminal and several old buildings that looked as though they might fall off their pilings into the water. Ketchikan's industrial region was only a mile or two up the road from the downtown tourist center; however, the difference was like night and day. No one wore rain gear or carried cameras, and everyone wore brown rubber boots.

Positioned on the northwest side of the industrial sector were three barge lines. Two of these barge companies were main competitors in the distribution of goods from the "lower forty-eight" to the main ports of Alaska. These businesses both had loading docks on the south Seattle industrial waterfront and subsequent docks in Ketchikan, Juneau and Anchorage. Shipments were then dispersed from one of these three main ports to all outlying areas by land, air or sea, depending on how remote the final destination was. It was quite an integrated network that took quite a bit of distribution time. It simply was an Alaskan way of life; if you want a new car shipped up from Seattle, it can take anywhere from one week up to almost a month depending on how far removed you live.

A third, smaller barge company sat wedged between the two major competitors. Sea Tank Marine Lines received shipments and containers from the two major companies, loaded the goods onto their own barges and used their own tugboats to pull the load over to Prince of Wales Island. Cargo from one of the major barge lines would come into Ketchikan on Thursdays. The other major company would typically tie up to land sometime between midnight and four on Monday mornings. Containers were unloaded and transferred by forklift over to the large Sea Tank lot, where the cargo would wait to be loaded onto the barge bound for Prince of Wales.

The Sea Tank cargo barge would typically come into its Ketchikan port by late-afternoon on Monday, get unloaded, and then reloaded with fresh freight in a feverish frenzy of forklifts and cranes. Once the loading was complete, the Sea Tank barge would typically depart by nine at night for its slow journey across Behm Canal and around the southern cape of Prince of Wales Island. The barge would arrive in Craig at close to midnight and be ready for its unloading process early Wednesday morning.

It was the middle of a Monday afternoon when Jim Wekle walked into the Ketchikan office of Sea Tank Marine Lines. He tried to ask several workers if he could speak with the person in charge but was ignored three times. Jim was not used to being ignored, but he was dressed in street clothes and was not recognized as any kind of authority figure. Finally, he flagged down a large man driving a small yellow forklift. The forklift driver motioned for Jim to head into a small, single-wide trailer that sat on the edge of the cargo lot next to a small warehouse. As Jim walked across the lot he noticed that activity buzzed in a similar manner as the company's sister port in Craig, but the warehouse and storage facilities seemed to be much smaller. This was simply a transfer lot. Shipments that came into port were moved onto this lot and then reloaded on a new barge. Jim couldn't help but be impressed with how the entire operation seemed to move at an amazingly fast pace, with each entity knowing exactly what to do and when to do it.

The trailer had a door marked "Office" with painted black lettering. Jim walked through the door and found himself at an L-shaped counter looking at two ladies working a bank of phones, radios and computers with motions that resembled synchronized swimming. While cradling a phone receiver between her ear and shoulder, one of the ladies smiled at Jim. She was quite fit and had curly black hair that hung down to her shoulder blades. She wore tight Levi jeans and a green flannel shirt that was untucked. She appeared to be in her mid to late-thirties and was extremely pleasant looking. The other woman was a tad older, with straight black hair, and little heavier body set. She threw on an orange vest and a white hardhat and bolted past Jim out the door without even making eye contact. This left Jim alone in the tight office space with the nice looking, curly-haired woman.

"Found it... No, it looks like it missed this week's boat. Yeah... We'll get it out to you next week, okay. Alright, then. Bye." She hung up the phone and again smiled at Jim and said, "What can I do for you?"

"I am interested in some information about shipping cargo from Seattle to Craig."

The pretty lady said, "That's what we do. My name is Wanda and I help run this place. What kind of information are you looking for?"

Jim turned to gaze out a dirty window that was half obscured by Levolor blinds. Stacks of yellow containers sat perched across the lot outside the cramped office. The skies above the container stacks were grey and a light drizzle started to sprinkle in true Southeast Alaskan summer fashion.

Jim said, "Wanda, it's nice to meet you. My name is Doug." She stuck out her hand and Jim/Doug shook her hand with a toothy grin. "The freight would be monthly, and not more than about the size of an apple box. My question is, obviously you wouldn't just stick that box on an exposed part of the barge. So how would you get that shipped out to Craig safely?"

Wanda replied quickly, "To be honest with you, a box of that size would ship a lot quicker through the post office. The mail flies up on the airlines and then flies out to POW by float plane. It's not exactly cheap, but a heck of a lot more efficient than waiting for the barge."

"But let's just say I wanted to use the barge, and not the U.S. Post Office. What would it cost to get a box barged out there from Seattle?"

Wanda replied, "There are varying factors of size and weight. Tariffs apply, but an apple-sized box from Seattle to Craig? Total guess would be between a hundred and fifty to two hundred."

"What would you do with the box? Obviously, it couldn't just get tossed on the top of the barge."

"It would get stashed in a 'catch-all' and unloaded into the Sea Tank warehouse until somebody came to claim it."

"A catch-all?" Jim asked.

Wanda began sifting through a stack of invoices while she answered, "We sometimes designate one or two containers as catch-alls. We load them up with random items that come off the Seattle barges and include some of the shipments out of Ketchikan as well." Wanda stood pointed out the window toward an open container. "See, that is a catch-all right there."

An open container across the lot was being loaded with three television sets, two bed mattresses and a box of computer parts by a young man pushing a hand truck. Wanda continued, "Sometimes it takes an extra week to get a full load. We don't ship catch-all's each week. And sometimes the Seattle barge companies take a little extra time in unloading their catch-all's. I'm sorry to say, small items are not always given shipping priority in the barge business."

"When do you ship catch-all's into Craig?"

"Last shipment of the month. Like clockwork."

That made sense to Jim. The drugs had to be coming over on catch-alls on the last barge of every month.

Something caught Jim's eye on a stack of containers just beyond the open catch-all. A man wearing an orange vest, jean shorts with a ponytail squirting out underneath a white hardhat was scaling the outside of a stack of containers. The containers were stacked five high and together stood almost fifty feet off the ground. With spider-like dexterity, Kram used door hinges and latches to climb to the top row of the containers. While holding onto a latching pole with one hand, Kram pulled out his crinkled paper and pinned it to the side of the metal door with the forehead of his hard hat. He scribbled something in crayon on the paper before gripping both with his teeth while he scurried over to the next container door.

Nervously, Jim tried to draw Wanda's attention away from the window view, "Ah, what about customs checks? Don't your shipments go through Canadian waters?"

"The barges do travel through international shipping lanes, but we never land on Canadian soil. No customs checks required."

Jim quickly glanced out the window again. Kram hung from the outermost container door by one hand, letting his feet dangle while he pinned his notepaper with one fist against the metal door. Jim almost choked at the sight.

"Would my small cargo undergo any kind of inspection of any kind?" Jim asked while trying not to stare at his counterpart out the window.

Wanda set both of her elbows on the office counter and rested her chin on her palms. She replied, "Look, Doug is it? You get a box of whatever delivered to my lot, and I get it delivered to Craig. No questions, no inspections, nothing. As long as you pay, you get to pick it up. Between you and me, as long as you sign the shipping agreement that legally indemnifies us, we could care less what you transport."

Suddenly, the door swung open and the straight, black-haired lady burst into the office. She wedged herself in front of Jim, pointed out the window, and asked Wanda, "What the hell is that?"

Wanda looked out to see that a small crowd of dock workers had assembled in the lot. They were looking at the top row of the stacked containers as a ponytailed man in jean cutoffs shuffled sideways across a row of cargo doors.

Surprised at the sight, Wanda replied, "I have no idea who that is. You go talk him down, and I'll call the cops."

The straight-haired woman burst back out through the office door like a steam locomotive. Jim slipped out behind her and walked purposefully and unnoticed toward the open chain-link gate that led off the property.

Exiting the Sea Tank Marine Lines cargo lot, Jim heard a stern female voice yell, "Sir. Come down from there immediately before you fall and kill yourself. The police have been called. Come down now!"

Jim then heard a familiar voice yell in reply, "Hot damn!"

Outside on the sidewalk at the corner of the fenced in lot, Jim turned to watch the whole scene unfold. Kram had climbed to the apex of the highest container and stood atop the stack with both legs shoulder-width apart. He began to beat his chest like King Kong and emit a Tarzan-like guttural scream. Turning and sprinting across the top row of containers like a crazed lunatic, Kram amazed his audience below as he leaped off the horizontal edge of the top box. The drop was only about ten feet each time. Kram had planned his getaway as the rows of container boxes stair-stepped down progressively toward the fenced-in corner of the lot.

With each ten-foot leap, Kram let forth another "Hot damn!" bellow followed by the loud crashing sound of both feet landing atop a metal box. With the last container, only one story high, positioned next to the outer gate, Kram jumped high over the fence and tumbled onto the sidewalk next to where Jim stood watching.

Brushing small gravel pieces from his exposed knees, Kram rose and said, "We might want to go now. I think they called the cops on me." The two men jogged quickly across the busy Tongass Avenue and disappeared up a side street where Jim's borrowed vehicle was parallel parked. Still wearing his orange vest and white hard hat, Kram ducked into the back seat and stayed hidden from view as Jim fired up the ignition and snaked the unmarked cruiser through several side streets on their quick getaway.

30

A short, pudgy bald man with a high pitched voice argued with a flight attendant at the gate of an Alaska Airlines boarding terminal. The man was holding up a long boarding line in the Seattle-Tacoma International Airport. The very high-maintenance passenger grew angrier by the second as the gate attendant argued with the man over whether or not he would be allowed to carry on his suitcase. The angrier that the passenger got, the higher his voice pitched.

"I've been flying in and out of Seattle for years and have always been allowed to carry my luggage on the plane. You know how much you thieves are charging for checked bags these days?" The man squawked at a timbre that rivaled a skill saw.

"Sir, your suitcase is the size of a small bank vault. We can't fit that in any of the overhead bins." The stewardess was growing tired of the altercation, and she readied her thumb on the walkie-talkie button in case she needed backup.

"You can take my bag and store it below the plane, but I'm not paying a dime!" The lineup of travelers behind the plump man with the chrome dome grew impatient.

A teenage boy with black eyeshadow and multiple piercings yelled, "Kick him off the plane. Don't put up with this shit!"

The fat man turned to flip off the teenager with black eyeshadow.

In order to ease tensions and expedite the end of the confrontation, the flight attendant finally offered a fifty percent discount on the checked baggage fee and boarded the passenger without further incident. Taking his seat just over the right side wing, the pudgy traveler watched a man wearing blue coveralls and yellow ear protectors hurl his massive suitcase from the top of the terminal steps. His suitcase hit the pavement with a thud, breaking one of the latches and allowing the man's fruit of the looms to hang out the side. After a second coveralled worker tossed his coffin-sized trunk into the cargo hold, the plane was sealed up and departed on time from SeaTac International Airport en route for Southeast Alaska.

Upon returning to the Craig waterfront, Jim headed straight to his office at the station. During the float plane trip home, Jim had studied the list of crayon-written names that Kram had procured from the Ketchikan barge lot. Two names listed on one particular shipment stood out and glaringly waved red flags at Jim. He needed to act quickly if he was to intercept this container before it was unloaded and emptied. He needed Tavis' help as well, as a court order, and he only had the better part of a day to put it all together.

As soon as he walked through the door of the Trooper Station, Jim heard shouting. Former U.S. Senator Travors' voice was reaching epic decibels as young Trooper Tavis Spurgeon took notes on a pad, seemingly writing down every word uttered by the irate politician. As Tavis continued his note taking, Shelly was pouring coffee into a mug in hopes to ease the former Senator's mood.

Another cacophonous racket caught the attention of Jim's ear. From down the hallway where the interrogation rooms and holding cells existed, a metallic clanging sound mixed with a string of profanities that would make a professional wrestler blush floated abrasively to Jim's ears. The scene was more than Jim could take.

"Quiet please!" Jim shouted. This got the attention of everyone in the station room, but the commotion from down the hall continued.

"I'll be right back. You stay quiet," Jim said pointing at Carl Travors. Seconds after disappearing down the hallway, the clanging and cursing subsided.

Jim quickly walked back into the station room and asked, "Would someone like to tell me why Deloris is in a holding cell?"

Both Travors and Tavis began talking

simultaneously. Shelly scampered about pouring more cups of coffee. Travors waved his arms like a televangelist, and Trooper Tavis read aloud from his notepad.

"Stop!" Jim rubbed his temples, grabbed a cup of coffee from Shelly and took a long sip. "Carl. Tell me what you are doing here."

"That's Senator Travors to you, Lieutenant."

"Former Senator Travors, start talking."

Travors put his hands on his hips and indignantly said, "She blew the head off my bear."

Jim glanced at Tavis, who nodded slightly. Jim remembered the menacing stuffed grizzly that sat perched outside the former Senator's front door.

Jim asked, "Why would she blow the head off of your mounted brown bear?"

"She's insane, and she's a criminal. Plus, she's been stealing from me."

Clanging echoed from the hallway followed by Deloris' crass voice, "That shit-for-brains scandalous camel-testicle politician's excuse for a pile of whale puke is lying through his teeth. I haven't stolen anything from him!"

Jim hollered, "Deloris. Quiet." Then calmly to Travors, "What did you accuse her of stealing?"

The aging man produced a document from his inside jacket pocket. He opened the tri-folded paper and acidly pounded it on the counter in front of him.

"This is my power bill for the past month. Eight hundred and forty-six dollars. Doesn't that seem a bit steep for one month's worth of electricity? She had to have been siphoning off from one of my outside outlets, probably for that ponytailed fool to play his infantile guitar."

Jim hollered down the hallway toward Deloris' cell, "Deloris. Have you been stealing power from Carl?" Travors frowned at the use of his first name.

"Hell no, I ain't been stealing power from that some-bitch."

"Deloris. Did you blow the head off Carl's stuffed grizzly bear?"

Cackling laughter reverberated down the tile and cinder block hallway.

Jim said, "I take that as a yes." Turning toward Travors, Jim said, "I will cite her for the property damage, but as far as electricity theft, you're on your own there, Carl."

"Citation? Do you know how expensive that bear mount was? Plus, she could have killed me."

From the hallway, "If I wanted to kill you, you bastard, I would have replaced that sorry-ass stuffed bear with your lifeless corpse posed naked and bent over!"

"Deloris. Shut it!" Jim turned back to Travors, "If you want to pursue civil litigation, small claims court convenes the third Tuesday of every month. In the meantime, stop accusing your neighbors of stealing and maybe buy a welcome mat instead of posing a menacing bear outside your front door."

"I'll have your badge for this!"

"Shelly, kindly show the former Senator out the front door." As Travors was escorted out of the station in a huff, Jim Wekle turned toward his young Trooper Tavis and said, "Wait ten minutes, then release Deloris. You and I have some serious work to do."

31

After being cut off from gin and tonics during the ninety-minute flight from Seattle, a high-voiced bald man waited for his checked bag at the Ketchikan Airport luggage turnstile. After the fourth suitcase emerged from the black flaps above the conveyor belt, plus-sized boxer shorts and other such personal items began appearing interspersed in between bags. After several of these items drifted by, the short, pudgy man realized that these were his belongings. Amid much laughter from the other travelers, the short man chirped curse words as he pushed his way through the small crowd in an attempt to collect each undergarment. After amassing a pile of laundry, toothpaste and hair-growth tonic on the floor of the baggage arena, an accordion door next to the conveyor belt had to be lifted in order to produce an empty oversized suitcase with broken hinges that was too large to fit through the conventional luggage claim door.

The last traveler to exit the terminal, a half-drunk man clumsily dragged his massive trunk down a rain-soaked walkway onto a floating dock in front of the airport. An aluminum boat with a small enclosed cabin sat waiting for the man with its engine running.

"What the hell took you so long? I almost left without you when I saw the other passengers leave."

Unamused by the question, the fat man heaved his suitcase onto the back deck of the boat and took a seat inside the cabin opposite of the captain's wheel. The boat's skipper untied from the dock and pushed off.

Once up on step and heading northwest up Tongass Narrows for the Behm Canal, the boat captain said, "I still don't think it's a good idea for you to be here. As the saying goes, 'It's a small island, and keeping you hidden will be next to impossible.'"

"Well, if you local boys haven't screwed the pooch on this whole thing, maybe I wouldn't have to come and clean up the mess."

"What mess? Things are operating smoothly on the island."

The man's voice squeaked to a new high frequency, "What mess? Smoothly? I don't recall two dead bodies being included in the master plan."

The boat captain made a short turn to avoid a float plane coming in for a landing. Once clear of the waterfront activity near Ketchikan, the throttle was jammed forward and the boat planed out at a cool forty miles per hour. After passing Vallener Point and Guard Island, the captain veered sharply to the left and made a beeline across the open Behm Canal for Kasaan Bay on Prince of Wales Island.

"When's the next shipment arriving?" the passenger asked.

"They unload the barge in the morning. But there's a little catch this time."

"What kind of catch?" the fat man asked in high pitch.

From behind the wheel of the Alaska Fish and Game boat, Gavin Donaldson took a long inhale through his nostrils and replied, "There's a little situation we need to deal with before the barge unloads. Don't worry, though. We have it completely under control."

For thirty-seven years, William C. Fetcherson monitored pressure gauges, ph levels, flow valves, and noxious release fumes at the sewage treatment plant on the outskirts of Mt. Pleasant, Utah. His meager salary and biannual cost of living adjustments had been supplemented by his wife's earnings as an office manager at a local community college. They certainly were not wealthy, but had stocked enough money into retirement accounts over the years to achieve a little freedom following the close of their respective careers. With only one of their two children expressing any interest in post-secondary studies and Gladys Fetcherson's connection to their local community college; they got off relatively scot-free with regard to their children's education. All details were aligned and in full swing for Bill to retire two years prior to his sixtieth birthday - until the "great sewage shower incident" occurred.

Bill had always had a bit of a weakness when it

came to micro-brewed beer, and one fateful graveyard shift three months before his scheduled last day on the job, his hankering for finely crafted malted hops bit him firmly in the ass. After drawing the short straw during a scheduling meeting, Bill was assigned a week's worth of graveyard shifts in early April. As an avid fan of watching golf on satellite television, Bill attended his neighbor's Masters party for an entire afternoon of watching the world's greatest hit the links at Augusta National. Things really perked up for Bill when his neighbor brought out a pony keg of home-brewed cream ale. Feeling as though the solo duty of watching dials and computer readouts from midnight until seven in the morning was a task fit for a chimpanzee, Bill imbibed with his golf cohorts all the way through the donning of the Green Jacket. By three o'clock in the morning, Bill Fetcherson was asleep and drooling on the exact console that happened to be reading a severe pressure buildup in east city waste pipe. By the time the alarm sounded and woke Bill up from his dream of drinking Red Hooks with Phil Mickelson, it was too late. A top-side pressure release valve located next to a neighborhood 7-11 had blown a gasket and sprayed raw sewage all over a family from Des Moines gassing up for their long car ride home.

Although it was never proven that Bill Fetcherson had been drunk on the job, the Mt. Pleasant Sewage Company held him financially responsible for the mishap. Between the Haz-Mat crew mobilization and subsequent lawsuit that funded construction of a new chain of Des Moines Laundromats, the financial burden postponed Bill and Gladys' retirement by a few years.

After leaving him alone on an island in Alaska and returning to her home in Mt. Pleasant, Utah, Gladys froze what little money was left in their retirement accounts. Being stranded to live in an unfurnished Luxury Coachman Plus that didn't run, with very little cash and a waning credit limit on a Visa Platinum Card, Bill Fetcherson was forced to look for work. Given his recent kleptomaniac developments and an uprising in his micro-brew addiction, Bill sought out the only job on the island that left him alone and unmonitored during the night hours. In lieu of a local city police force and reports of recent flotation device thefts, the Craig City Council employed Bill to walk the city streets and docks several times per night as a security officer. If he encountered anything beyond suspicious, he had been instructed to call 911 and seek safe hiding until the State Troopers arrived.

Bill was ecstatic. He could hide out in his RV, drinking bottle after bottle of Alaskan Amber, only to emerge every so often to wander the docks in complete solitude. He could sleep in until noon, dink around all afternoon with various spare parts that the Ross boys sold him in hopes of rebuilding his Coachman engine and never once hear the nagging screech of his wife's voice or wretched yip of her new stupid toy poodle. Maybe his recent string of bad luck was a blessing in disguise. Maybe the shit-storm of unfortunate events was actually just the stars aligning in Bill's favor. Maybe this was his true retirement paradise.

As Bill staggered down the middle of a quiet, empty street at two-thirty in the morning early on a Wednesday, he continued to count his newfound blessings as he sipped openly at a brown beer bottle. Sometimes there was activity at this hour. Sometimes the cannery employed workers around the clock. Sometimes fishing boats departed for openings at all hours of the night. But this particular night was as calm and quiet as could be. Bill felt completely alone, and he found happiness in that solitude.

As he tottered along, Bill sang a melody that he had recently composed. The lyrics included references to "snookums" and "eagle bait" and the chorus followed a similar melodic strain to the 80's tune, *The Heat is On*. The refrain was always followed by hearty and sincere laughter. Ambling up the street past a deserted cannery, Bill drained the final drops from his beer. He tossed the bottle in the bed of a Ford pickup after searching the vehicle for random life preservers. Up the road a little further and he found himself in line with the chain link fence that surrounded Sea Tank Marine Lines. Continuing on past the barge line's encaged lot, the happy drunk plodded on his way. In his euphoric state, the City of Craig's night watchman failed to notice the illicit activities taking place only a few feet inside the fenced barge lot. Even had Bill Fetcherson noticed the three men attempting to sneak onto a recently docked and fully-loaded barge, chances are he wouldn't have performed any act entrusted of his duties. He was plowed. On he staggered with only one thing on his lubricated mind: one more stroll of the marinas in search of newly purchased life vests before retiring to the comfort of his well-padded and quite buoyant Luxury Coachman Plus interior.

32

It had taken Jim Wekle the better part of Tuesday afternoon to obtain a court order from the sole Borough Judge on duty. Jim's evidence was less than circumstantial, bordering on a simple hunch, but since it was Lieutenant Wekle's first request for a search warrant and the request was accompanied by a hand-rolled Dominican, the judge went ahead and signed off on it.

After jumping through the hoops of obtaining the court order, Jim headed back to his office in order to have a rather delicate conversation with his young subordinate. Afternoon had given way to evening, and the station's coffee pot smelled old and burnt. Jim asked Shelly to put on a fresh pot before she left for the day. Coming off highway patrol, Tavis entered the station just as Shelly was leaving. They exchanged "good nights" and Shelly let Tavis know that his boss wanted to see him.

Two quick knocks on the office window and Tavis was waved in and offered a seat and a fresh cup.

"Two creams, two sugars, right?" Jim asked as he handed the mug over.

"Thanks, boss. What's on your mind?"

Jim sipped at his pure black liquid and figured that it

was best to not drag things out. "Tavis, I have a theory about our painkiller drug smugglers, and my theory involves your Uncle Tank."

Tavis was solemn, yet silent. Jim continued, "I'll lay it all out for you, Tavis. But understand one thing. I am going to need your help on this one, and if this truly does involve your Uncle, well... It could be very difficult for you."

Both men took a sip at their mugs. Tavis said, "Okay. Tell me your theory and tell me the plan. I can handle it." Jim looked hard into the young Trooper's eyes. The kid was acting strong, and Jim admired that.

Jim began, "You and I both believe that Shane Ketah was the one responsible for our rash of break-ins around here. He was a drug addict, that's no secret, and we found evidence to suggest that his burglaries were motivated solely to feed that addiction. What's most interesting about the break-ins, to me, was the timing of it all. Always late in the month. So we've established this working theory that illegal pain meds are hitting the island around the first of each month and being distributed throughout most of the month until the supply runs dry. You with me so far?"

Tavis nodded and said, "And our working theory is that Shane Ketah's murder is somehow related, right?"

"Right. I have my theories regarding that murder as well, but first things first. The drugs." Jim stood from his desk and stretched his back. He set down the coffee cup and turned to look at a light drizzle that persisted outside of his office window.

Jim asked, "You confirmed with the Ross boys that no unusual packages were flown over like clockwork only at the end of each month, right?"

"Right."

"And the Post Office isn't worth much, since the Ross boys fly in the mail, right?"

"That, and who would be crazy enough to smuggle drugs through the federal monitoring systems in place by the United States Post Office. They will x-ray packages at will looking for that kind of stuff."

Jim was impressed, "Right again. So that leaves only three possible means of transporting drugs onto the island. One, the State Ferry. Two, personal boat or aircraft. And three, the barge lines."

"Sounds like this is where my Uncle Tank comes into play."

Jim sat back down at his desk and rubbed his temples to help clear his thoughts. Jim finished his self-administered massage and continued to lay out his theory.

"The timing is too regular for the ferry system. The ferries land at varying time intervals, but the drug shipments seem too habitual. And personally flying or boating the drugs in seems way too expensive. Drug trafficking is about making money. I seriously doubt that pill sales on Prince of Wales Island are profitable enough to merit its own charter system. The drugs have got to be coming in on the barge."

Tavis stated, "Just because the drugs are coming in on the barge, that doesn't mean my Uncle Tank is the one responsible."

"True, but I have a little more information that points me in his direction. I happen to know that a container is being barged over as we speak that is labeled a 'catch-all.' This basically means that the contents of the container belong to various people and it's all small enough to fit inside one shipping box. By law, the bill of lading on the outside of each container must list all names involved with all shipments. This particular catch-all includes a box that is being shipping from a Dan P. in Seattle, Washington to a Tank S. in Craig, Alaska. I believe this is our drug box and we are going to take a look inside early tomorrow morning."

"What makes you so sure this is the drug box?"

"Think about it, Tavis. Dan P. That has to be Dan Pringle. Dan Pringle was the last victim of Shane Ketah's burglaries. If Shane knew that the Pringles were involved in smuggling in his pill of choice, it makes perfect sense that he would break into the Pringles home in search of his fix. And it also makes sense the Ketah would have been killed for knowing this information and committing the burglary. Think about it, the last thing drug dealers want is attention from the cops, right?"

"I guess that makes sense. So we need to get a look at this box." Tavis sipped his coffee then asked another question, "And how do you plan to look inside this box? I don't believe my Uncle is a drug smuggler, but I still doubt that he would simply give you free access to start looking in containers and personal shipments. He could lose customers for that."

Jim produced a folded piece of paper from his desk and said, "That's what this little court order is for. Tomorrow morning, I want you to head out to the Pringles first thing. Pick up Dan and his wife and meet me at the Sea Tank Marine Lines lot by five AM."

Startled, Tavis exclaimed, "Five in the morning? That seems a bit early to me, boss."

"Deal with it. We have to get there before they start unloading, or this court order is a complete waste."

"Aye, aye, skipper. Five AM it is." Tavis stood and started to exit the office before turning back and asking, "So how does the Debbie Simms murder fit into all of this? You still think that is related somehow?"

"Trooper Spurgeon, that is the million dollar question. Still working on that one."

"And how did you come up with the information that this box is even being shipped over tonight?"

"Probably best that you don't know that one."

MINK ISLAND

33

Jim hadn't slept much. He had fed the minks, cleaned his gun, and eaten a light supper before trying to rest his eyes and brain. He knew that he was reaching with his theory, and he knew that if his search proved fruitless that it would piss off a lot of locals. But he had to do something. He was being pressured by his superior and bullied by a former United States Senator, and he felt as though he would quickly lose the respect of his local population unless he acted on the murders in some fashion. Reaching or not, Jim Wekle was going to exercise his search and hopefully resolve some of the local criminal activity that was taking place on his watch.

After a very restless attempt at sleep, Jim hit the boat dock at four o'clock in the morning. It was still dark out, and he wasn't the greatest at maneuvering the skiff in the dark. So he went slowly across the water. After tying up to the dock without incident, he walked up the ramp and through the short brush covered path. Just as he was about to hit the unlock button on the cruiser, the thick trees to his right seemed to move and crack with great force.

Startled, Jim put his hand on his holster and hollered, "Kram. Is that you?" It would be just like that nut to be sneaking through the trees before sunup. Tree limbs not more than ten feet from where Jim stood began to snap. Jim illuminated his long, black Trooper issue flashlight and scanned the tree trucks, but thick strands of salmonberry bushes were all that he could see. More twigs snapped. Jim's heart raced. He drew his pistol and lined the barrel with the stem of the flashlight.

"I am an Alaska State Trooper, and I am armed," Jim yelled into the trees. A silence fell over the parking lot. There wasn't a single gust of wind, drop of rain, chirp of a bird, or rustle of a tree branch. Jim could hear his own breathing and feel his own heartbeat. He took one step at a time toward the grouping of trees that had produced the ruckus. Peeling back barbed strands of berry bushes, he found an opening into the woods. Jim put one leg through, dipped his head under the vegetation and pulled his whole body through. He was surrounded by trees and slowly began turning his body with the beam of the flashlight scanning for life.

It happened in an instant. The bear seemed to explode out of nowhere. Crashing through the trees not more than a few feet from where Jim stood, a massive black bear bolted across Jim's path. Scared out of his mind, Jim fell back onto his butt landing on a very moist sponge of moss. Jim dropped his flashlight, but maintained his grip on the pistol. If the bear was going to attack, Jim wouldn't go down without a fight. Posed on his back in the utter darkness of the thick forest, the trooper clutched his gun and prepared for the worst. But the worst never came.

The crashing through the trees was loud and violent, but the sounds were moving away. The bear must have been just as startled as Jim was as it tore a new path in the woods at breakneck speeds. Jim exhaled, located his flashlight, holstered his gun, and pulled himself to his feet. His entire backside was soaked through with brown-stained muskeg water.

"Just great," he muttered under his breath.

Despite taking quite a fall in the woods, the only thing that Jim hurt was his pride. The seat of his trousers was wet and brown, and even though it appeared as if he had soiled himself, Jim had no time to return to the yurt and change uniforms. He made the drive into town without passing a single car on the road. The city streets were vacant of all activity. Even the cannery hadn't opened its doors yet. Just past the cannery, finally, there were a few signs of life. Just as light was beginning to appear above morning clouds, dock workers were reporting for a busy day of unloading the Wednesday morning barge at Sea Tank Marine Lines. The main gate was just being unlocked as Jim parked his cruiser, donned his Stetson and walked toward the small gathering.

"Isn't it a bit early to be patrolling the city streets, Lieutenant Wekle?" Tank Spurgeon was just fixing a padlock onto the recently opened chain link gate.

"Morning, Tank. I have a little issue to discuss with

you." Just then, Tavis Spurgeon drove up in the Jeep Cherokee with Dan and Alice Pringle in the back seat. Tavis looked extraordinarily sleepy and the Pringles looked pissed off.

When Jim turned toward the approaching vehicle, Tank spied his backside. "What did you do this morning, Wekle? Crap your pants?"

"Good one. I need you to set down your catch-all container and open its door for me."

Tavis opened the rear passenger door and Dan Pringle exited in mid-rant. "Lieutenant. Why the hell did you send your boy here to fetch us? We meet our morning charter in less than an hour. I really don't have a clue of what we are doing here and..."

Jim interrupted, "This won't take long." They all walked through the gate and into a fairly empty lot. The containers still sat on a long barge that had been tied up to the Sea Tank pier roughly five hours earlier.

Tank stepped in front of the Trooper and said in a low, rough voice, "I can't imagine why you want to see inside my catch-all, but I already told you that I don't make a practice out of just letting the cops have free roam over my business. You have no legal right to even be standing on my lot."

"This says differently." Jim slapped the court order on Tank's flannel-covered chest. After inspecting the document, Tank ordered his crane operator to locate the catch-all and set it down on ground level. Being slightly buried, it took close to a half hour before enough of the stacked containers were unloaded giving access to the catch-all. With each passing minute, Dan and Alice Pringle's whining escalated, Tank huffed under his breath, Jim longed for a cup of coffee, and Tavis continued to yawn. Eventually, the container was unstrapped from the crane and Ben Nakit picked it up with a forklift. Nakit drove quickly with the heavy load and dropped it with precision at a secluded corner of the lot close to where the small group of people waited.

Jim walked up to the metal door and located the bill of lading. A list of shippers, receivers and cargo weights had been scribbled on a piece of paper and secured under a protective plastic sheet. Jim scanned the names.

"Wait. Something's wrong." Jim scanned the list of names again. It was missing. Jim took out Kram's wrinkled crayon scribbling and compared it to the bill of lading. He located every other name on the list except the ones he came for.

"Tank, is this the only catch-all container that you have on this shipment?"

"Absolutely. You can look around if you don't believe me."

Jim intended on looking, but he knew that it wouldn't be there. Someone had changed the lading slip.

"Open it up," Jim ordered.

Tank had already sent one of his employees to retrieve a set of padlock keys. He turned the lock, moved two large handles attached to the locking hinges, and swung the doors open.

Alice Pringle pleaded, "Can I please go? I need to ready the bait bucket and tie on some new leaders."

"Not yet." Jim clicked on his flashlight and stepped inside. There were mattresses, flat screen televisions and several boxes of varying size stacked along the walls, but by no means was the storage box crowded. Jim snatched the lading slip from the outside door and began checking off the cargo. Every box on the list was accounted for.

"Nice job," Jim said appearing back in the doorway to the container.

Tank sneered, "What's a nice job?"

"There was supposed to be a box from Seattle in this container. The sender was listed as Dan P. and the receiver was Tank S."

Tank replied, "I have no idea what the hell you are talking about. And being that you have a habit of bothering me on my busiest days of the week, I've got work to get to. You can take that search warrant and shove it down your soiled pants." Tank turned abruptly and stormed off toward the warehouse.

Tavis asked his boss, "What happened to your pants?"

"Don't want to talk about it." Then Jim turned and asked, "Pringle, do you have anything to say?"

"Yeah. How could I have sent anything to Tank from Seattle if I've been fishing off the Prince of Wales western shoreline every day? Let's go, Alice. Our clients are probably waiting for us." Dan Pringle turned and started walking for the gate of the barge lot. He was through the gate and part of the way down the sidewalk before he noticed that his wife had not followed.

Alice Pringle moved her wide body close to Jim's and spoke softly, "You know, my husband's not the only Dan P. with ties to this island. And I'm pretty sure the other Dan P. that I know just happens to live in Seattle now."

Jim's face turned from disappointment to interest. He asked, "You wouldn't mind filling me in on just who that might be, would you?"

34

"I didn't realize you were such a good cook," Maggie stated with a hint of sarcasm as Jim spooned marshmallow dip from a small, white plastic tub into a ceramic bowl.

Jim winked and said, "You just wait. This is a treat fit for royalty."

Maggie stood next to Jim at the curved kitchen counter of the yurt while he prepared the snack. On top of the marshmallow dip, Jim plopped an entire brick of cream cheese that he had warmed to room temperature and instructed Maggie to stir the two white substances, thoroughly mixing them together.

"I had no idea you lived alone on this small island."

"There wasn't much else available."

"Does it get lonely out here?"

Jim started chopping apples into narrow slices. "Not much. My landlord stops in every once in a while. His visits usually offer enough entertainment to last me a while."

Maggie chuckled and replied, "I bet. Well, I'm glad you invited me out for a little snack; although, I feel a little guilty closing down Porty's for the afternoon."

"Everybody needs a little time off every once in a while. Besides, the boys can always slurp beer and throw darts on a rainy day. It's beautiful out and they should soak up a little sunshine." Jim finished the apple slices and dumped them onto a small plate. "I'll carry the apples and the dip; you get the sodas and let's go. I know just the place for our little snack."

"I'll follow you," she said with a gorgeous smile.

Jim led the way out of the yurt and up the boardwalk path. They climbed the short incline and took seats atop the lookout. The afternoon was stunning. Blue skies and sunshine offered sparkling views across the bay. Enough of a breeze drifted in from the north to create small white-capped waves on the water. Ravens were dive bombing at an eagle that drifted majestically above the bay. Two pleasure crafts were trolling for salmon close by and several purse seiners were heading off in the distance readying for another commercial opening. It was another one of those scenes that seemed to make up for all of the blustery, damp days that Southeast Alaskans had to endure.

"Here, try one." Jim picked up an apple slice, dipped it in the white concoction and handed it towards his date. Without taking the slice in her hands, Maggie leaned over and bit the apple treat out from his fingers.

"That tastes like candy. Wow, I'm impressed."

"I know. Who would have thought something so fancy could taste so good." They both smiled and laughed lightly.

Maggie ate another dipped apple and said, "I didn't think you were going to ask me out for a second date. I was worried that you didn't enjoy the first one."

Jim felt a little embarrassed, "I, uh, wanted to play hard to get, I guess."

"Well, I'm glad you finally asked. This is nice."

Jim smiled at the beautiful young lady and replied, "Yes. This is nice."

As they continued snacking on the apples, small talk turned into life stories. Jim enjoyed listening to Maggie detail her high school friends, stories of her family, and how she came to work at Porty's. Even though it was sad, Jim enjoyed listening to Maggie talk about her brother's tragic and short life. It seemed to him that she was dealing with Shane's death well, even though she still didn't have the answers he had promised regarding the murder. Jim didn't enjoy as much the sharing of his life story, but he talked anyway. He told of growing up on the sandy shores of Southern California and how he came to enlist in the Coast Guard. Jim reluctantly told stories of his marriage and subsequent divorce. Maggie laughed heartily at the story of his wife's arrest and his forced relocation to Prince of Wales. It was the perfect second date. They enjoyed each other immensely, laughed, learned about each other and never let the mood get too serious. They finished their apples and sodas and the stories were just winding down.

POP!! The sudden sound shocked both Jim and Maggie.

"What was that?" Maggie asked.

POP!! It echoed through the trees.

Jim stood up and said, "Stay down. I think that's gunfire." The intermittent sounds of a small caliber weapon were close by. Too close, Jim thought as he estimated the gunfire to be occurring on his island. With full police training kicking in, Jim quickly moved toward his yurt in a crouched position. Maggie followed close by, even though Jim unsuccessfully tried to convince her to stay hidden. Jim disappeared inside the yurt and reappeared on the boardwalk within seconds holding a shotgun loaded with bear slugs.

POP!! The gunfire continued to sound off every ninety seconds or so.

"I don't suppose I could convince you to stay here?"

Maggie replied, "Hell no. I'm sticking close to the man holding the shotgun."

With Maggie close behind, Jim hopped off the boardwalk onto the spongy muskeg and carefully weaved his way around tree trunks and moss-covered stumps. Jim moved quickly and quietly. He was impressed with Maggie's ability to do the same. They maneuvered around the drum shed structure and crept close to the far end of the small island.

"Stop," Jim whispered while holding up his hand. He could see movement ahead through a batch of blueberry plants. The foliage was just thick enough to obstruct a good view. Jim started to move again, this time quietly skirting the edge of the berry bushes. He could make out the outline of a man moving about in a clearing opposite the blueberries. As the berry plants began to thin, Jim decided to make his move. With the palm of his hand, he signaled Maggie to stay put. Jim gripped the shotgun strongly with both hands and charged through the thinned edge of the bushes.

"Freeze!" Jim yelled in his deep, guttural cop voice. Caught by surprise, a man stood still with both arms in the air. The man's back was facing Jim. He had a dark green rubber apron tied in knots behind his back. One had held open and high in the air as he stood frozen, but his left hand held something dark, limp and fuzzy. The man's ponytail hung across the top row of apron straps, almost reaching the belt line of his jean cutoff shorts.

"Kram, what the hell are you doing?"

Kram turned, sporting a goofy grin on his face. As he turned, the lifeless furry object in his left hand exposed a face with dark red blood oozing from a hole just below a limp, hairy ear. The front of Kram's green apron was splattered with blood. Kram tossed the mink corpse he held onto the top of a pile of five other comatose furry creatures.

Shrugging, Kram said, "It's harvest time."

Jim scanned the ground surrounding the makeshift butcher shop. Several large cages baited with salmon heads had been placed throughout the area. Six of the mink traps were empty and had been reset. Four cages sported live animals that twisted and turned as they attempted to find a way out of the trap.

"Haven't gotten to those little guys yet," Kram said as he motioned toward the live traps that sported the doomed mustelids.

Maggie emerged from behind the blueberry patch with a disgusted look on her face. Kram grinned and shrugged again and said, "What, you didn't think I was raising these things to become pets, did you?"

A sudden, horrific thought shot through Jim's mind. "Oscar!" Jim tore over to the pile of mink bodies and began lifting them off one by one, looking for an animal with brown fur and a distinctive white spot on its back. Next, he inspected the four caged minks.

"He's not here," Jim said with a breath of relief.

"Who's not here?" Maggie asked.

"Kram, is this your first batch of harvested animals?"

"You bet, Jimbo. Six down, forty-four to go. You see, I only trap ten at a time, pop them behind the ear with my twenty-two pistol here, and process the hides over on shore while the traps refill."

"You mean, forty-THREE to go." Jim stared straight at his landlord.

Kram said, "I didn't miscount, Jim."

"You are NOT popping Oscar behind the ear with your twenty-two pistol."

Maggie asked, "Oscar?"

Jim answered, "Yes, Oscar. Little guy with brown fur. He's the only one I've seen that has a white spot between his shoulder blades and he's the only one that will eat a peanut butter sandwich out of the palm of my hand."

Kram laughed. "I think Lieutenant Jimbo has a pet."

"Damn right. And if you kill my pet, I will lock you up for discharging a firearm on private property."

Confused, Kram said, "But this is my private property."

Jim, still gripping the shotgun tightly, moved to within an inch of Kram's face, "Do not kill Oscar. Got it?"

Understanding perfectly, Kram said, "Got it."

Grabbing Maggie by the hand, Jim turned to walk away while saying over his shoulder, "And wait until we are clear before popping another one behind the ear."

When the couple reached the corner of the drum shack, Kram hollered, "I assume you will be paying me what I would normally get for Oscar's mink pelt."

Grumpily, Jim yelled back, "Add it to my rent."

35

Shawn Foster, also known as Lip Rings, worked on the side project only on his off days from cannery duty. In the heart of the commercial Southeast Alaskan fishing season, there weren't many days off from a slime line job. But every once in a while, when certain fisheries were closed, cannery workers would find themselves with several days' worth of free time.

Lieutenant Wekle had funded the project and set up time for Shawn in the Ross Land and Sea metal shop. Shawn Foster's engineering training proved fruitful as his bear-proof garbage can design came together quickly. Johnny Ross had loaned a small flatbed truck for delivery and Lip Rings, Neck Tattoos, Kram and Jim were busy installing the custom-made cans outside of Deloris' home.

Deloris was inspecting the whole operation in a nightgown that exposed a little too much of her backside. She wore army issued combat boots, a red, square mortarboard graduation cap with a hanging tassel, and sported brown tobacco stains on her lower lip.

Deloris cackled, "You sure these tin boxes will keep out those punk-ass bears?"

"I would stake my engineering degree on it," answered Shawn Foster.

Jim asked, "I didn't think you had your degree yet."

"Future degree. The box will hold. I'm sure of it."

"Hopefully it's a little stronger than the side of Deloris' garage," Jim chuckled.

The design was really quite ingenious. Twin metal boxes were bolted onto iron flats that had been secured into the ground with a cubic yard of concrete. The boxes hung at a slant for ease of access to the holding chamber. To access the empty chamber, a small opening in the metal lid, just large enough for a human hand, gave way to a release button that caused the top of the boxes to pop open. The opening mechanism was not only too small for a bear paw, but required one to be adept with finger placement in order to hit the release mechanism. Once open, the twin chambers were large enough to carry two household sized rubber garbage cans. After placing trash inside the cans, the metal lid would snap back into place, securing it from any wildlife in search of a midnight snack. The structure was incredibly sturdy, yet easy enough for a cranky elderly woman to use daily.

It had taken the strength of all four men to lift the new garbage box off of the flatbed truck and place it between the iron flats. Kram and Neck Tattoos held the box in place while Jim and Lip Rings worked socket wrenches.

Jim said, "This is really a cool design, Shawn. You know, you might think of obtaining a patent. There might be quite a few folks in these parts interested in investing in bear-proof garbage boxes like these."

Shawn answered, "Would I have to split the profits with you since you funded the prototype?"

"I'll have my lawyer contact your lawyer to draw up the papers." They both laughed.

While holding the box steady, Kram began to study the tattoo that ran up the right side of Skye McDoogle's neck. Leaning into his stare, Kram asked, "Would you be willing to take off your shirt?"

Once the bolts were secured, the box was released and stood on its own. Jim and Shawn Foster began a thorough test run of the new box with Deloris critically following their every move. Kram and Skye McDoogle moved off to the side.

Kram moved to within inches of the tattooed neck. "What is that?"

"You just wait, dude. It will blow your mind." The young kid took off his sweatshirt and t-shirt, exposing a string of multicolored descriptive pictures. The neck told the end of a story that began just below the bellybutton. The entire closing episode of the Star Wars saga was depicted across the upper body of the young stoner. Han Solo's escape from the clutches of Jabba the Hut rested below the belly. The tragic death of Yoda came diagonally up the rib cage. The left nipple was utilized as the face of an Ewok. Luke Skywalker's epic struggle between good and evil was portrayed from the base of the neck up to just under the ear.

Completely fixated on the impressive illustrations, Kram exhaled a classic, "Duuuude!"

Skye McDoogle replied, "I know, right? Duuuuuude."

The two strange individuals, separated in age by decades, seemed to bond in an unspoken, cosmic sort of way. Kram's eyes were wide, fixated on the inked designs. He kept scanning the upper body of the kid who proudly stood, hands on hips, displaying his body as if he stood atop a mountain peak.

"Kirk to Enterprise. Sorry to break up the chest viewing, but I think our work here is done," Jim said.

"Wrong movie, Jimbo."

"Don't care. Help load up the tools."

Robert Jerome Haverford the Third grew up privileged in a wealthy Catholic family in a suburb of Omaha, Nebraska. As a youth, he achieved only nominal grades, but displayed promise in his ability to hit three-point jumpers. With his father's connections at the hometown Jesuit school of Creighton University, Robert Haverford was welcomed into the basketball program with open arms. Normally, a C+ high school grade point average wouldn't cut the mustard at such an institution, but the team's perennial lack of an outside threat coupled with funding for new locker rooms from the Haverford trust, allowed Robert to make the starting lineup by his sophomore year.

As his skill for draining twenty-three footers increased proportionally with his lust for corn-fed beef, Robert's senior year earned him the reputation of being the fattest shooting guard in NCAA Division I basketball. After breaking the school record for three-point shots, Robert's first name was forever replaced by the college's mascot. Before his last game as a collegiate athlete, a heated battle between Creighton and their rival Southern Illinois for a chance to go to the NCAA tournament, Blue Jay Haverford downed an entire rack of beef ribs in an effort to satiate his appetite for Nebraska styled whiskey-infused barbeque sauce. With sauce stains evident on his jersey, Blue Jay went up for a jumper early in the first half and came down awkwardly on both legs. The force of his swelled girth caused both of his knees to simultaneously pop, thus ending his basketball career forever.

Being mortified by his son's obesity-induced, nationally-televised injury, Blue Jay's father forced his induction into the United States Navy, ensuring that his son would be stationed as far away from Omaha, Nebraska as humanly possible. Left partially immobile and with barely any skill other than competitive eating, Blue Jay's father feared that his son would end up scrubbing the latrines of battleships. His father bribed the naval officer in charge of Blue Jay Haverford's enlistment and "demolition's expert" magically became the highlight of his official military file.

After unsuccessfully discharging a series of submarine mines in the Indian Ocean, Blue Jay was up for a dishonorable discharge before his father once again swooped in with a large chunk of cash. A campaign donation was made to the chairman of the Senate Naval Appropriations Committee and Blue Jay was transferred to a small underwater testing facility in the chairman's home state. Senator Carl Travors purchased a new indoor swimming pool, and Blue Jay Haverford was stationed at a nuke sub base in rural Southeast Alaska. Even though he was unofficially never again allowed to come within two nautical miles of military explosives, the moniker of demolitions expert followed in his doctored paperwork while he served a quiet, modest career documenting blips on a radar screen.

Accessing the necessary information required to set off radio-controlled fuses that would ignite firework stand explosives required appetite inducing exhaustive internet research. Blue Jay had already polished off a platter of frozen burritos before test firing the first homemade bomb. The only thing explosive about the first several attempts at setting off the charges was the gas that exited the former basketball player's rear end.

"For the love of Pete. You smell like a dead camel." DeAngelo Smuthers had already grown tired of futilely plugging his ears and ducking for cover every time Blue jay yelled, "Fire in the hole." The gaseous discharge finally reached old man Cecil's nostrils, and the geezer began to wheeze uncontrollably.

"I can't believe that one didn't fire. Pull up Google again, and this time do a search on 'triggering a homemade bomb with an RF switch.'" Blue Jay was stumped. "Maybe I forgot to match the send and receive frequencies again." He plucked a fresh bean burrito from a tray that Cecil's wife had recently delivered and started recalibrating his radio detonating trigger.

Roger Greeley slammed close the lid of his laptop computer and barked, "You want to get the FBI, ATF, CIA, and IRS for that matter, breathing down my throat. First, it's public knowledge that you mounted a starboard firing cannon on the bow of my boat, now you're using my computer to research homemade bomb making. Why not mail a threatening letter to White House while you're at it."

The four men had been trying to trigger the test fires all afternoon the in gravel pit behind Cecil Wright's house. The Wright's nearest neighbor lived a half mile down the road, so the Torcadero Yacht Club's first ever attempt at pyrotechnics was assigned the perfect locale. Bean burritos and internet access just happened to be an added bonus. The women sat inside, making fun of their husbands and drinking wine. The mood in the backyard was growing more and more tense with each failed attempt.

DeAngelo said, "Roger, relax. I think government agencies have better criminals to investigate than a retired mattress salesman from Fairbanks."

Roger retorted, "I was a tax accountant. Cecil was the mattress salesman."

"Whatever." Handing a pair of wire strippers to Blue Jay, DeAngelo ordered, "Re-check your fuse connections, put a butt plug in and try it again."

Four failed attempts later, DeAngelo had given up on covering his ears. The resounding announcement of "Fire in the Hole" had become so anticlimactic; he had resorted to cynically rolling his eyes while taking a swig of his Heineken each time that Blue Jay jammed his thumb on the button.

The explosion was deafening, earth-shaking, and completely unexpected. After growing tired of his failure to ignite the equivalent of a quarter stick of dynamite, Blue Jay Haverford wired three more M80's to the radio controlled fuse with the thought that more had to be better. In the process, he unknowingly happened to bump the positive wiring terminal just enough for it to make a clean contact with the fuse igniter, which was the only problem all along. With the increase in explosive quantity, and the fact that the M80's sat on the ground surrounded by loose rocks, gravel splintered and went flying in a three hundred and sixty-degree mushroom pattern. A boulder the size of a small watermelon shot straight past old man Cecil, missing the man's left ear by a millimeter. The shock of the whole event seemed to temporarily cure Cecil Wright of his wheezing fit and brought the women streaming out of the kitchen in order to inspect the gaping hole in the side wall of the house just next to where the old man was seated.

With ears ringing a high-pitched hum at chainsaw decibels, Blue Jay Haverford and DeAngelo Smuthers began dancing a painfully choreographed jig around the charred crater that marked the location of the detonation. The terrorized expression on Cecil Wright's face was only outdone by Roger Greeley's as he imagined what it would be like to spend his retirement in prison.

"Great job, Blue Jay, but maybe a little less explosive material next time. We don't want to kill anybody," DeAngelo said, arm in arm with his demolitions expert. "I say, ladies and gentlemen. The final piece of the puzzle is now in place. It's now time to let the games begin!" DeAngelo posed triumphantly next the three-foot wide ground zero and grinned maniacally. He was proud of his group's accomplishments and even more proud of his self-appointed leadership. The Torcadero Yacht Club would no longer be laughed at on the city streets, sneered at while seated at their table in Porty's, nor plotted against after this year's so-called Humpy Fest. DeAngelo had readied a master plan and his terror cell would reign supreme. He stood with his legs apart and thrust his fists into the air. The ladies began to applaud. Cecil finished his examination of the hole in the exterior of his home and commenced with a coughing fit. Roger whimpered. Blue Jay farted.

36

"I heard about your little raid. Way to screw the pooch on that one, Wekle," were the first words out her mouth when she picked up the phone. Captain Reesa McEwen didn't beat around the bush. "I suppose you didn't call me to get blasted about your investigation. What do you want?"

Jim sat at his desk with the phone cradled between his shoulder and ear. He was in his office alone with the door closed and readied a pen and paper in case he wanted to jot down notes.

Jim asked, "What can you tell me about my predecessor?"

"Ah, I wondered when this call might come. Later than I figured. Jim, look. It's always hard to be the new guy, and especially hard to be the new guy on a small island."

Jim interrupted, "No, not what I mean. I want to know about the circumstances around his retirement. Mum's the word around the office. Most locals think he retired. Some say he was forced that way. I want to know what happened."

Reesa McEwen's tone was frank and even, "I supervised Dan Potter for several years. He wasn't a great trooper nor was he a great station lieutenant. The locals liked him, his staff tolerated him, and he generally kept the peace over there. I heard several rumors in the last year or two about odd behavior, but never anything substantial. Hell, Jim. He never had a U.S. Senator crawling up his ass like you do."

"Former U.S. Senator. So what happened at the end?"

"He was nearing retirement anyway. He wasn't that old, but you know Alaska; we retire cops and teachers quicker than any State in the Union. Anyway, how I understand it, a kid was riding her bike along the highway. It was a rainy day with limited visibility. Dan Potter smacked into this kid with the very same cruiser that you drive around in every day. Kid survived but had to get Medivac'ed down to Seattle. Banged up pretty good."

Jim asked, "So it was an accident?"

"According to the record, yes. Tavis ran a breathalyzer on Potter and it rang in at a zero."

"So how does an accident lead to a forced retirement?"

"Well, about those rumors I kept hearing. Word was that Lieutenant Dan Potter was quite the pill popper. I believe he was doped up when he rammed that poor girl. I gave him two choices; retire or submit to urine and blood work. I guess he feared the test results, so he decided to hang it up himself. Potter was ready anyway, burned out from Alaska like many of us get. He had been flying down to the lower forty-eight almost every month for his so-called weekend getaways."

The report hit Jim Wekle in the gut like a sucker punch. Jim asked, "Did Potter happen to retire to the Seattle area?"

Reesa answered, "Yep. Some suburb on the outskirts. I think he already had a place down there before he left. So what's up, Jim? Why the twenty questions about Potter?"

Jim answered, "Still putting the pieces together here, but I think he's part of the puzzle. Can you describe him to me?"

McEwen offered, "He's an odd duck. Built like a turnip, bald as a bowling ball and talks in that high, whiny voice."

"Thanks for the info, Cap."

"One more thing, Jim. Make sure the puzzle pieces fit completely before you exercise any more futile search warrants, especially if it involves one of my former lieutenants."

"Got it." Jim hung up the phone. It made sense. *Dan P.* was not Dan Pringle, but rather Dan Potter as Alice Pringle had suggested that morning at the barge search. Potter was already a pill fiend. He made monthly trips to Seattle. Neither Tavis nor Shelly talked about him around the office. Almost as if they didn't need his memory.

Captain Reesa was right. Usually, the new guy hears constantly about how the guy he replaced used to do things. Jim had received hardly a word about the way things used to be around the office. Dan Potter was involved in this case, Jim was certain of it.

Jim was also fairly certain that Tank was involved as well. The missing box the morning of the container raid confirmed it. Kram insisted that every name he wrote down on his crayon list was correct. The bill of lading had been replaced and the box had been removed. This happened sometime between being loaded onto the barge in Ketchikan and Jim's execution of the search warrant in Craig. Had Tank been tipped off about the court order and impending search? Jim wasn't sure. Any number of people at the courthouse could have alerted Tank, or even the mysterious, container-hopping crazy man in Ketchikan could have merited a call to the boss. Or had the box and lading slip been dealt with as part of their usual MO? Maybe Tank makes a habit of meeting that monthly barge when it docks at midnight and taking his drug shipment. Jim wasn't sure of the details, yet, but he was almost positive that he had identified the ringleaders. He was certainly positive that the drug trafficking led to Shane Ketah's death, and he had a hunch that it also led to the Debbie Simms murder. Now he just needed proof.

Gavin Donaldson had been a game warden for close

to two decades. He had performed his duties diligently, serving Prince of Wales Island while being a dedicated husband and father. The State didn't make him rich, but paid him enough to live comfortably on his isolated island. His wife raised two kids, homeschooling them both while making the home a comfortable and clean place to live. Gavin ran boats, flew on float planes, drove four-wheelers up old logging roads, talked to hunters and fishermen, and occasionally needed to practice law enforcement. He rarely had anyone looking over his shoulder. Life was perfect. Until his perfect daughter got desperately sick.

The diagnosis of osteosarcoma came just two months after her fifteenth birthday. It was bone cancer, and it was aggressively progressing. Like any good father, Gavin Donaldson put his life and career on hold. A temporary Wildlife agent was stationed on the island to fill in while the Donaldson family made multiple trips south, meeting with every oncologist and pediatrician worth their salt. Gavin's insurance policy covered most of the standard treatments on his daughter, but as the cancer progressed, the Donaldson's got desperate. They flew their daughter to New Mexico to meet with a renowned naturopathic healer. They flew to a specialized children's cancer clinic in Las Vegas. Gavin even flew in a self-proclaimed spiritual healer in a dramatic moment of total despondency.

Finally, when all hope had vanished, the Donaldson family returned to their home in Hollis, Alaska. With his daughter bedridden and riddled with pain, and his savings and retirement accounts drained and credit cards maxed out, Gavin Donaldson watched his daughter die a slow, excruciating death.

In the final weeks of her life, the young cancer patient needed high doses of pain medication in order to survive without moaning in agony. Their local doctor prescribed medicine at will. Gavin found it all too easy to call any of the half-dozen doctors he had met with to order additional prescriptions. Stockpiling pain medication became an obsession for Gavin. The devastating impact of helplessly watching his daughter get eaten alive from the inside manifested itself in Gavin Donaldson in the form of Ahab searching for his white whale. Only the white whale happened to be a multitude of small white pills. Whether it was the deep seeded belief that the pain meds could ease his little girl's suffering, or possibly the well-needed distraction, Gavin exhausted every resource in obtaining his precious medicine horde. The contacts he made during his drug obtaining obsession formed relationships that would prove profitable for him in the future.

It didn't happen instantly. Gavin Donaldson didn't just wake up one morning and decide to become a drug dealer. In the weeks following his daughter's funeral, the bills began to pile up. He was in debt tens of thousands of dollars. A local church offered a spaghetti dinner fundraiser, the State Troopers Auxiliary made a modest donation, and the local guild of commercial fishermen hosted a smoked salmon benefit. But the good intentions of all concerned barely made a dent. When his neighbor sprained an ankle after stepping on a slippery rock, Gavin Donaldson made his first drug deal.

It was too easy. He started dealing away small amounts of his personal stash by carefully placing a few comments here or there. Gavin's contacts were vast throughout the island. He had the perfect cover. He could fly from one end of the island to the other in a day, meet with a dozen people or more, and be home in time for dinner. He consorted with fishermen and hunters, old salts and loggers, some of which were not the most upstanding of sorts. Within a matter of weeks, Gavin had a distribution network established throughout the island and his small illegal enterprise was ready to expand.

"I still don't know why you insisted on coming back here. We have a perfect system established and it doesn't include you being here." Gavin Donaldson sat at a table across from the fat bald man. Several large sacks of white pills sat on the tabletop between them. They were counting out hydros in batches of fifty and dropping the separated doses into individual Ziploc baggies.

The bald fat man replied in a high-pitched voice, "This is your largest shipment yet. We both know that our supplies run thin by the end of the month, thus the extra load this time. Between our increased distribution and the apparent heat that our little operation has stirred up, I think you can use some help."

"What do you plan to do that I can't take care of myself?"

Former Lieutenant Dan Potter stroked his bald head then licked the opiate-laced powder from his fingers and said, "I plan to pay a little visit to my old station. That new guy they got, he seems pretty sharp. I think it's time he had a few new leads to follow up."

"What do you mean, *new leads*?"

"You know, old case files that I forgot I had when I left town. I doctored up a few in order to completely bamboozle the clown. What's his name? Wendle?"

"Wekle."

"Yeah, whatever. I plan to head in today."

Gavin Donaldson shook his head, "I think that would be incredibly stupid. You need to stay hidden here, crashing on this couch until I convince you to fly back home. Everything is under control without your help."

"I noticed how under control everything is. You know, the Seattle papers even picked up the story on Shane Ketah's death. Pretty soon, things are going to be completely out of your control. Unless..."

"Unless, what?"

"Unless there was an arrest."

"Who? An arrest for what?"

"What Lieutenant Wendle needs..."

"Wekle."

"Whatever. What he needs is a suspect, some evidence and a highly publicized arrest in one of these murder investigations." Dan Potter laughed in a high-pitched whine.

"I hope you know what you're doing, Potter. Because if this thing blows up in our face..."

Potter interrupted, "It won't. Now trust me and hand over some more baggies." After licking his fingers again, Potter asked, "Have you ever tried licking this stuff? This powder is amazing. My tongue feels like a sea cucumber."

37

Former Senator Carl Travors went blasting through the station's security door as soon as Shelly hit the magnetic release buzzer. A tall, silver-haired man wearing a fishing vest and Xtratufs followed closely in tow. Travors barged past the reception desk and stormed by Tavis without as much as a nod. He flung open the door to Jim's office and entered without an invitation. Jim was typing on his computer when the intrusion took place.

"Do you know who this is?" Travors asked, pointing a thumb over his shoulder at the silver-haired man. "This is your boss, Wekle. Say hello to Major Franklin Stotts. You might recognize that name."

Jim nodded and said, "Major."

Stotts shrugged and said, "I retired five years ago."

Travors continued, "As of this morning, Lieutenant Wekle, you are officially on probation. One screw up and you're out of here."

Stotts said, "He forced me to make a few calls. Sorry about this, really."

Travors ranted, "This comes from the top down. Your boss's boss, Wekle. You are screwed now. You hear me?"

Stotts shook his head, "I lost a bet. Carl and I go way back. He invited me down for a little fishing, and the next thing I know, I'm on the phone with the Anchorage headquarters. Really, sorry about this."

Ignoring the retired major, Travors continued, "Go ahead and call that little red-headed Captain of yours in Ketchikan. She'll confirm it. Probation, Wekle. You pop one pimple without following procedure and you'll be on the next plane to Point Barrow where you'll spend six months a year in darkness writing citations for building code violations to people that live in igloos."

Travors turned and stormed out of the office. The silver-haired retired major shrugged again and said, "I lost a bet. Sorry."

Jim hollered out his office door, "Thanks for the visit, Carl. Next time, stay long enough for the coffee to brew."

Jim closed his eyes and rubbed his temples with his elbows planted on the top of his desk. A knock on his open door frame was followed by Shelly leaning in, "Someone else is here to see you."

"Now what?" Jim said under his breath.

Holding his hand out with great enthusiasm, a short, pudgy bald man walked straight past Shelly into Jim's office. Shaking hands vigorously, the man spoke in a bird-like timbre, "Jim Wettle. How nice to finally meet you. How's my old chair treating your backside? Used to give me pain in my lower back, but Shelly kept insisting the pain would go away if I ate a few more salads. Hah."

"Wekle." Pulling his hand away from a shake that just would not end, Jim said, "You must be Dan Potter. I have to say, I'm a little surprised to see you. What brings you back to the island?"

"Just catching up with old friends." Over his shoulder, Potter said loudly, "Like my boy, Tavis, out there. You make any big busts yet, Tavis?" Tavis averted his eyes and went back to filling out paperwork. Turning back to Jim, he continued, "Yes, just catching up with friends. And, you know, August is the only month worth visiting up here. Highest chance of seeing that old blinding light in the sky. The rest of the year, you can have the rain, wind, and darkness. Not for me anymore."

"Yes, I hear Seattle is quite the sunshine Mecca." Jim's sarcasm was lost on the man.

Dan Potter helped himself to a seat in front of Jim's desk. He placed three dark blue file folders on top of the desk and said, "Had to stop in here and drop off some old files. Must have brought them home and packed them up by mistake when I left here. Not sure if they will interest you or not. Ongoing investigations that I had in the works, nothing definitive, of course, but still thought you might be interested in some leads."

"Leads about what?" Jim asked.

"This and that. Three people in general. You'll see.

It's all in the files. Sorry about accidentally stealing those. I'm sure you bring your work home with you sometimes. Well, it's great to meet you." Standing and hollering through the office door, "And great to see you two again. Shelly, keep brewing that burnt coffee. Hah! And Tavis, hope you hit puberty soon. Well, I'd better get a move on."

Just as Potter passed through the open office door, Jim said, "Oh Dan. Just a minute." Potter paused and turned back toward the desk. Jim asked, "I'm just curious. Why did you ship a package up on the barge to Tank at the end of last month?"

Dan Potter squirmed and searched for a replied. "I haven't a clue of what you're talking about. I haven't shipped anything on the barge since I moved off this rock."

"Oh, sorry. My mistake. One more question, if you don't mind. Where are you staying while in town?"

"With a long-time friend of mine over in Hollis. Just catching up with old acquaintances, like I said." Dan Potter continued his exit from the station. He waved goodbye to Shelly and Tavis and continued through the security door.

Jim went back to rubbing his temples. His phone rang. He answered, "Wekle."

"It's Captain McEwen. I have news."

"Carl was kind enough to tell me."

313

"It's for real. Came from the top brass. Don't screw up, Jim."

"I don't plan on it." He hung up the phone.

Another knock on his door frame, "What now?"

It was Shelly, "There's someone else here to see you."

"Of course there is."

Tank Spurgeon walked into the office. Jim offered him a chair.

Tank sat down and said, "I've been an Alaskan for my entire life. I drink, I smoke, I cuss, and I chase women. I ship all kinds of stuff, sight unseen, all over this great land we call home. I am, what most would call, a hardened man, but I've run an honest business. I've raised my nephew out there since he was smaller than a lingcod. I don't steal. I don't cheat. I don't deal drugs, and I sure as hell don't kill people. I know you're in a hard place, Trooper. I know that you have some serious shit that you need to deal with on this God-forsaken rock. But I'm not your man."

Tank stood. His flannel shirt hadn't been washed in days. It spilled over a bloated belly. His face had three-day-old stubble and featured hardened wrinkles next to his bloodshot eyes.

Tank spoke again, "You get your court orders, and I'll open my containers. You come bother me during peak hours, and I'll give you short, to the point answers. I know your barking up my tree, but I'm clean, Trooper Jim." He turned and left without waiting for any kind of response. Jim looked back at his computer screen and sensed there was someone else standing in his doorway. Looking up, he saw Tavis Spurgeon standing in full uniform just outside his office. Jim sighed.

Tavis said, "I told you that Uncle Tank is innocent. He's a good man, Jim."

Jim replied, "Patrol time. Go."

Tavis grabbed his Stetson and keys to the Jeep Cherokee and walked out the back door of the station. Jim got up and shut his office door, unplugged his desk phone, gazed out the window, and recommenced the head massage.

The files contained handwritten notes on three residents of Craig. The first file outlined details of former Trooper Dan Potter's speculation into Tank Spurgeon's illicit drug trafficking. Notes about shipment dates, where he kept the drug stash, his efforts to grow, harvest and distribute marijuana buds, and his known associates suspected of distribution and sales were all neatly written in perfect chronological columns. The second file alleged Hauler Steve as the main player in getting the drugs distributed across the island. Notes detailing surveillance missions that uncovered multiple package drop-offs along the highway between Craig, Klawock and Hollis indicated that Dan Potter had secretly followed Hauler Steve on several occasions. The third file really caught Jim's attention. Potter's notes contended that the *Port of Call* was a central distribution point in the individual sales of the illegal pain pills. Maggie and Shane Ketah were listed as prime suspects.

The files were organized, efficient, and written in clean handwriting with a blue ink pen. It was all very convenient. And none of it made sense.

Jim picked up the phone and dialed a number that was written on a yellow sticky note. Jim said into the receiver, "It's Lieutenant Wekle. I think we need to talk."

38

Just inside a red metal door, a man paced nervously back and forth next to a table filled with dozens of baggies full of white pills. The man had a wad of cash stuck inside the left front pocket of his blue jeans. He pulled a hat down low on his forehead exposing straight black hair above the back of his neck. More pacing. More tugging on the bill of his hat.

There was a knock on the door. The man pulled open the deadbolt lock and cracked the door open. Two one hundred dollar bills were pushed inside through the crack in the door. The man stuffed the bills in his front pocket, grabbed two baggies from the table, and passed them through the door to his buyer. The door was shut and the deadbolt clicked back into the locked position.

Two bucks a pill was the going rate; a hundred bucks for a baggie of fifty hydrocodones. The man went back to pacing. He hated selling. Hours of nervously killing time, knowing that he was overstocked with illicit drugs and carrying a wad of cash. He was one crazed druggie away from getting shot for his stash, or one anonymous tip from being handcuffed and thrown in jail. He stopped pacing and counted the baggies again and compared it to the cash in his pocket. The numbers were correct. He checked the gun tucked into the back of his jeans. It was still there, and it was still loaded.

Another knock. This time five twenties slid through. One baggie was returned back through the door crack. The night continued in the same manner, sometimes a half hour or more between buyer knocks; sometimes less than five minutes.

It was the first Monday night after the 3rd of the month. Like clockwork, the small, one-room shack that sat on the dock hidden next to Sea Tank Marine Lines, with the red metal door lit up by a single hanging bulb, was the place to go for pills. The shack was perfect for selling. The main path leading to the red door was guarded from view as it skirted the side wall of the Sea Tank warehouse. Cars could park two streets up and customers could either circle around following a sidewalk that skirted a seldom used street or cut through the trees and walk the stairs down from the Stockade. Either way, foot traffic to and from the red door was under cover.

The man selling pills would easily rake in more than ten grand that night. Sales had been steadily increasing with each month, and now with an increased stock, the man doubted he would run out of product anytime soon. There were only three days per month that the red door was open for business, and the man knew sales totals from the three days would push close to thirty-five grand. The market was growing. Product was increasing. Customer base was expanding. Pressure was mounting.

Another knock on the door. This time four hundred

was pushed through the opening. Business was booming.

"He's lonely, Kram. See? All he does is eat now."
Jim and Kram sat atop Lookout Rock. Oscar the mink
scurried over Jim's left shoe and up his leg to snatch a
tortilla chip out of his hand. "Look at his belly, Kram.
Oscar's getting fat."

Kram was shoving spoonfuls of salsa into his mouth,
spilling chunks of onion and peppers down the front of his
Q*bert t-shirt. "No, he's not getting fat."

"What are you talking about? You killed all of his
friends. Now, all he likes to do is run up on my lap, steal
whatever I'm eating out of my hands, and run under the
boardwalk to eat it."

Kram abandoned the spoon and started slurping
salsa straight from the bowl. "No, he's not eating your
food. She's nesting."

Jim paused for a moment, the asked, "What do you
mean, *she's* nesting?"

"Well, that fat, as you call it, is actually anywhere
from four to six little mouths that Oscar will have to feed
in another week or two. And the food stashing, well
that's just instinct. The summer's coming to an end in a
few weeks. These animals know how long winter is
around here and they start stashing away food early,
especially if they have a family to feed."

Jim chewed off the pointed end of a tortilla chip, "Are you saying the Oscar is really an Oscareena?"

"That's exactly what I'm saying. Jim, you're going to be a father soon."

Jim thought about dipping a chip in the salsa but decided against it. "Well, I don't care. I'm still calling her Oscar."

Oscar the mink scuttled over to the base of Kram's shoe and looked up at the bowl of salsa he cradled in his arms. Kram growled and barked like a rabid dog protecting his food. Oscar jumped for cover underneath a skunk cabbage leaf.

"So what are you going to do about her?" Kram asked.

"Oscar? Well, I guess just let her carry her kids to full term and watch her raise the furry little guys."

"Not that *her*. I meant *her, her*."

"Oh, Maggie. That her. I don't know, maybe date number three sometime."

"Didn't Colonel Potter try to say that she was part of the whole drug thing? You know, I guess she could be mixed up in some way, you know, since her brother was obviously involved."

"That's total BS. I'm sure of it."

Kram lifted the salsa bowl to his lips and sucked

down a large chunk of green pepper. "How are you sure of it?"

"I've been around cops for years. I've read many police files on many different suspects, and never once were they so neat, organized, concise and for that matter, even written with the same ink pen. Most files are full of sticky notes, random scribbling on bar napkins, and crudely drawn diagrams with coffee and cigarette stains on them. These files were, well..."

"Too perfect?"

"Exactly."

"Well, maybe the fat man with the girl's voice is a neat and organized sort."

"Does that guy seem like a neat and organized dude to you?"

Kram scowled and said, "Squat and gaseous, more like it."

"And Kram, you should have seen Tank when he came to talk to me."

"He claimed innocence?"

"Yes, he did."

"They all claim innocence, Jimbo."

Jim started peeling the wrapper off of a fresh cigar, "But there was something... Something in his eyes. I bought it."

"So what you're saying, basically your prime suspect is no longer your prime suspect."

Jim pulled out a pair of handheld cutters and snipped the end of the cigar, "And my predecessor is now my prime suspect."

Just as Jim was lighting the end of his cigar with a butane torch, a loud, blasting horn sounded from the direction of the boat dock.

Kram leaped to his feet, "Hot damn!"

"Hot damn, what?"

Kram was trotting away toward the skiff, "That's the band. They've arrived."

"What band?" Jim hollered.

Kram yelled back through the trees, "Beer Swig and Humpy Fest is right around the corner. You don't mind if the band crashes on Mink Island for a few days, do you?"

39

As the weekend drew closer, preparations at the *Port of Call* flew into full swing. Frankie and Johnny Ross busily worked on the roof of Porty's constructing three giant slingshots. Tank Spurgeon, Hauler Steve, and a few of the other locals set up the massive outdoor barbecue grill underneath an awning overlooking the breakwater. Extra cases of booze had been ordered and Maggie had hired a couple of guys to help her stock the cooler shelves, and with a lull in the fisheries openings, Lip Rings and Neck Tattoos had accepted the extra work with open arms. Dan and Alice Pringle carried several of their fish tubs over to the mouth of the stream and readied them to be filled with dead humpies. Deck chairs were positioned next to where a diving board had been secured for prime viewing of the Porty's plunge. The only thing missing was the life ring that was usually tossed to the plunge participants. For some reason, flotation devices seemed to be scarce this summer.

Outside of Porty's, across the breakwater in marina slips twelve through fifteen, members of the Torcadero Yacht Club continued with last-minute preparations for the annual Torc Regatta. Cecil Wright polished up the revolving trophy awarded to the race's winning vessel. DeAngelo Smuthers mended his spinnaker sail. Roger

Greeley moved furniture around the interior of *The Cyclone* to offset the new weight strain that had been bolted to his starboard bow. Ferny and the other ladies made pasta salads and finger sandwiches to stock in each of the boat's ice boxes. Blue Jay Haverford was nowhere to be seen.

With Craig's most festive weekend approaching fast, the entire town seemed to be buzzing with excitement. Even the weather was playing along nicely with sunny skies and mild breeze predicted. Humpies splashed in the water as they waited out the high tide. Eagles circled high above the stage that Kram and the boys were constructing next to the *Port of Call*. Jim and Tavis walked up the street in uniform, pleasantly monitoring the hubbub.

"I put the Coast Guard on notice like you asked," said Tavis.

"Good job. I called the Captain and requested a few extra troopers. She told me no. So I called Gavin Donaldson and asked him to join the fun."

"So it will just be the three of us?"

"Not really. Gavin said that he was too busy to help out."

"So it's just the two of us again."

Jim nodded, "Two will be plenty. These guys just want to have a little fun."

Tavis asked, "Boss, you're not going to make me drive around drunk people again are you? You know how much puke I had to scrub out after the Fourth?"

"Let's play that one by ear, Tavis. But, just in case, make sure you have a full tank of gas in the Cherokee."

A circular object flew high over their heads. With a splatting sound, a water balloon smashed into the side of the cannery building. Loud cheering and "woohoos" accompanied by high-fives occurred on the roof of Porty's. Frightening Frankie loaded up another balloon in one of the giant slingshots, this time aiming for the marina. He walked backward holding the balloon in place while stretching the long elastic bands. Releasing his hold on the bands, the slingshot instantly flung the balloon arcing high into the air. About a hundred and fifty yards away, the balloon burst on the side of the docked *Cyclone*, spraying an irate Roger Greeley who was standing on the top deck. The Ross boys cheered and high-fived, hooted and hollered then went for another balloon.

"I have a feeling this is going to be quite the party," Jim said as he continued his stroll up the street.

Tavis said, "It always is, boss. You just wait."

Dan Potter used the edge of a metallic halibut jig to crush a pill into a pile of white powder. He rolled a crisp one hundred dollar bill into a tiny tube and stuck one end into his nostril. After snorting most of the pile of opiate dust into his brain, he smacked the table with his spare hand and emitted a squeal that resembled a dolphin's mating call.

"You have got to try this. Enters the bloodstream immediately. Whoooosh, I think my teeth are starting to vibrate."

Gavin Donaldson was counting out money and separating the cash into three even stacks. Gavin said, "Potter, stopping being a dipshit. Isn't it time for you to fly home yet?"

Potter started mashing a fresh pill and replied, "Not yet. I'm having too much fun. I'll head back in time to ship up the next box, don't worry. It's party time now." He finished pulverizing the tablet then wondered aloud, "I wonder what it would feel like entering through my eyeball? Hey Gavin, you want to blow this dust pile into my face?"

"Moron!" Gavin needed some air. He walked out of the red metal door and up the path next to the warehouse wall. After making a few turns, he found himself strolling down the main drag, pondering how his life had turned out so miserable.

Up ahead, something, or rather someone, caught Gavin's eye. He quickly ducked into the open cannery doors, concealing himself from being spotted by Jim Wekle who was walking up the street, straight towards him. Wekle and his counterpart, Trooper Tavis Spurgeon,

continued up the sidewalk past the cannery doors. Gavin
remained hidden from view until the troopers were long
gone.

"I think I'm going a little crazy here," Gavin said to
himself. He eased his paranoia with several deep breaths
before jogging back out the cannery doors and hightailing
it back to the shack with the red metal door.

Waking up on a pile of cushy life preservers was
usually a joy. It was an occurrence that he typically
looked forward to each and every day; something was
different about this day, however. It was close to noon
and he guessed that it must be nice out as sun penetrated
the closed blinds of his Coachman RV. Everything should
have been perfect, except for one small detail. Bill
Fetcherson had an excruciating headache.

It wasn't just the dull pain that his frontal lobe
usually endured after a full night of swilling Alaskan
Ambers. This was a disorienting, mind-numbing,
throbbing, bash your head against the wall kind of pain. It
was something that Bill Fetcherson had not experienced
since becoming a bachelor, night watchman,
kleptomaniac drunk who lived in a rampaged, immobile
recreational vehicle parked in a wood-planked industrial
lot. This was certainly a new development.

His mouth felt like shag carpet and his tongue felt
like leather. He was parched. Bill staggered to his feet
and shuffled through randomly colored flotation pillows

until he reached the Luxury refrigerator. No water. Oh well, beer will have to do. He popped the top of a brown bottle and swallowed down half of its contents. He shuffled to the small bathroom and looked at his face in the mirror.

"Holy shit!"

Bill gazed at his reflection but could barely believe it was his own. Despite not shaving or showering for several days, the real shock came when he gawked at the reflection of his eyes. The area surrounding his pupils was more red than white. The centers of his pupils were wide black dots the size of chocolate chips. Scanning down, the texture of his lips resembled the surface of the moon. There appeared to be barf stains on the front of his shirt. Bill Fetcherson was a complete disaster.

"What the hell happened to me?"

He plopped down on a blue neoprene vest, thrust his face into the palms of his hands, and searched his brain for any indication of what might have occurred the previous night. Bill worked backwards through the night. There was no memory of returning to the Coachman, nor was there any recollection of vomiting. What was the last thing he could recall? Arms around shoulders, strolling down Dock Street singing. What was the song? Something about parties. How did that go? *You got to fight...for your right...to paaaaartaaay!* What the hell kind of song is that? Better question, who the hell was I singing with?

Memories were extremely fuzzy. He decided to scan his earlier memories. The night started out normal enough; meat lover's pizza, a couple of beers, locked up the Ross Land and Sea gate and shop doors, another beer, made the first security sweep up the street, few people still at Porty's but all in all a quiet night, back to the Coachman for another beer, it was after one in the morning, second security sweep, random people... That's it. Strange, random people walking down toward the water close to the barge company.

Bill remembered stumbling onto a hidden vantage point that overlooked a side path next to the warehouse building. At first, it was just one person that walked down the path only to return a minute later. There was nothing alarming about that, but then another, and another, and the pattern continued. Bill thought about calling in the suspicious behaviors, but he rationalized that really it wasn't worth dialing 911 over. These were just people walking down a dark path, one at a time at random intervals in the middle of the night. What was the harm in that, right?

But before he could make his decision of whether or not to call in his observations, Bill Fetcherson felt a tap on his shoulder. It startled him, and he jumped to his feet and turned around. Standing before him was a rather short, plump bald man, grinning ear to ear with glazed eyes and a distant expression.

In a high pitched voice, the bald man asked, "Have you ever tried snorting hydrocodone dust through a hundred dollar bill?"

40

Three tents had been erected and interspersed among the trees surrounding the drum shack. The music rehearsal by the aging band members had finally ended at close to two in the morning. Kram swam back to shore leaving Jim alone on Mink Island with a leather-jacketed bass player, a drummer in purple spandex, a curly–haired and shirtless lead singer, and an impregnated mink.

After only a few hours of sleep, Jim was at his kitchen counter making breakfast. It was going to be a long day. The sound of a toilet flushing followed by a shirtless man in his mid-sixties standing in Jim's living room didn't surprise him one bit.

"Jimbo, good morning. I like my eggs sunny-side up."

"Of course you do. Yes, good morning." Jim yawned and poured a cup of freshly ground coffee for his guest. The shirtless man with curly hair straddled a chair positioned backwards and took a sip from the coffee mug.

"Your name is Spike, isn't it?"

"That's top secret information there, Jimbo."

"You know, I used to listen to Axe Attack while cruising in my first car as a teenager. You guys rock."

Spike winked and said, "I cannot confirm nor deny the validity of your comments."

Jim asked, "Why all the secrecy? What's the big deal if people find out that Axe Attack likes to play gigs for a couple hundred people on an island in Alaska?"

"It is a big deal, my man. First off, Grand Music Corp owns the rights to every hit we've ever recorded. Our agent and record label own partial rights to the band's name. You know how much we'd have to pay out if Axe Attack were officially booked to play this gig? Look man, as far as you, I and everyone else on this rock is concerned, we are a no–talent, hack cover band called *Kiss My Halibutt* that just happens to play a few tunes that you might recognize from your youth."

It made sense to Jim. He slid two eggs from a frying pan onto a plate and handed the dish over to Spike.

"Has Kram always been this crazy?"

Spiked laughed with an open mouthful of egg yolks. "Yeah man. Actually, that dude has mellowed considerably. Back in the day, well, let's just say his best friend probably wouldn't have been a cop."

"A little drug use back in the day?"

"We were rock stars, what do you think?"

"And how about now? I think you would understand what it might look like if you guys were toking it up in the front yard of a State Trooper."

Spike finished off the eggs and replied, "Naw, man. That's all ancient history. Gruel, the bass player, has a wife half his age and three kids. He lives in a swanky suburb of San Antonio and just got re-elected to the school board. Rupert, the drummer, owns the company that makes his spandex pants. He randomly tests his employees for drug use every month. He eats only organically-produced foods and donates to Mothers Against Drunk Drivers."

"What about you?"

"I'm a retired physical therapist. Had my own practice in a small town north of Detroit. Used my share of the *Blood Brothers* tour to fund three years' worth of college anatomy classes."

Jim was impressed. If only the photographers for Rolling Stone Magazine could see these guys now. "And then there's Kram."

"Yeah, and then there's Kram. That man's a genius, you know. He invented the hammer-on technique. We all know that's the guitar move that Eddie Van Halen gets the credit for, but who do you think taught it to Eddie?"

Jim cleaned the dishes and gathered what he needed for a long day of police duty. "Kram is something special, I'll give you that."

"He's crazy about you, Jim. Considers you his closest chum on the island, next to Deloris, of course."

"Of course." Jim was kind of happy about the

comment. He wasn't used to being called a *closest chum*.
Donning his Stetson, Jim said, "You guys help yourselves
to anything in the fridge. I'll see you on stage this
afternoon."

Spike was already digging through the cheese
drawer, "You got it Jimbo."

Blue Jay Haverford was exhausted. He had worked
through the night and now only had a couple of restless
hours to nap before needing to be in place for the day's
activities. An entire season's worth of frozen herring had
been transported and planted strategically in concealed
locations surrounding Porty's. Explosive charges had
been wired to radio controlled fuses, and a central
command post established in the belly of his sailboat.
The *Creighton Swish* would not be competing in this
year's Torc Regatta as usual. Instead, the sailboat was
relocated in the middle of the night. A small kicker engine
that hung from a mounting bracket on the transom had
been fired up and the boat puttered from its usual
moorage in the marina to a prime anchorage just outside
the breakwater.

The *Creighton Swish* swung gently on its anchor
chain as Blue Jay Haverford intermittently snoozed in a
hammock that hung sandwiched amid sail masts.
Between moments of slumber in the morning sun, Blue
Jay cracked his eyes open and squinted toward shore. His
vantage point was perfect. Porty's hung over the rising

tide supported on pilings like a beacon in the fog. Blue Jay smiled and drifted back to sleep. His large ass was barely supported by the hammock and wafted ever so gently just a half inch off the top deck of his boat.

Carl Travors was confident and prepared. He donned a safari-style tan vest and stuffed the zippered pockets with a notepad, pencils, digital camera, water bottle, granola bars, pocket knife, chewing gum, and blood pressure medicine. With the dawning sun, Travors smirked as he groomed his thinning grey hair. He was confident that today would be the day that he executed his power and removed what he considered to be a worthless and ineffective cancer of a public servant. His personal vendetta against Lieutenant Jim Wekle started with the trooper's unwillingness to prosecute the scoundrels that he handed over on a silver platter. What more could the lieutenant want than gift-wrapped felons? The mere fact that Deloris, Kram, and the rest of the island nut jobs were allowed to roam free was evidence of the trooper's complete incompetence. Couple that with a recent string of murders and rumors of rampant drug dealings on the island, and it was proof that Jim Wekle was a useless tool.

Carl Travors knew that the day would bring a plethora of out of control behaviors. Public drunkenness, lewd body gyrations, aquatic projectiles, hypothermic belly flops, and a string of other such infractions would each potentially be worthy of prosecution. And Carl Travors knew that it would all happen right under the nose of the lieutenant. Such behaviors would not only be allowed by the trooper, but encouraged.

Travors would be there to document the entire debacle. A few well-placed snapshots of the local morons at their worst, a personal journal complete with names and a timeline, and a sworn affidavit by a United States Senator should be enough to send the fool trooper packing. One click on an email loaded with incriminating photographs and Jim Wekle would be on the next boat off the island.

Dan Potter was as giddy as a school girl. The whole town was building toward the summer's climax that was Beer Swig and Humpy Fest, and for the first time in his life, Dan Potter could experience it as a civilian. No more feigning stoicism as he paraded up the street in his tight-fitting uniform, diligently putting on the show of defending law and order. No more would he be responsible if an intoxicated fool drowned after diving into the bay in order to procure free beer for the rest of the afternoon. Dan Potter could now enjoy the whole scene as a patron; copping a cool buzz and mindlessly cheering on the slime-laced assault on suspecting sailboaters. Life was good!

Preparations were in order, though, if a full day of debauchery was to take place. Three full baggies of white pills were dumped into metal bowl and pummeled into powder with the rounded side of a ball peen hammer. Two eggs, a cup of milk, a tablespoon of oil, and a carton of brown mix were whisked on top of the white power to make a chocolate batter. Thirty-five minutes later and a tray of gonzo brownies were cooling on the table next to a stack of hundreds. The pudgy fat man, washed down a handful of pills with a glass of straight vodka, divided the brownies into individually packed Ziplocs, and crammed the wad of cash in his pants pocket. Dan Potter was completely armed for a day of insanity. He crashed out the red metal door carrying a grocery sack full of laced dessert treats and made a beeline for Porty's. The party was about to begin.

41

The Torc Regatta got underway with the blast of a handheld boat horn. A small crowd on Porty's deck had already amassed and they politely raised their middle fingers as the boats hoisted their sales and steadily drifted away. Either no one noticed or no one cared that there were only three boats participating in the Regatta this year. Few party-goers even looked past the rock wall of the breakwater to spy the fourth sailboat anchored and bobbing in place.

The crowd in and around Porty's steadily grew through the lunch hour and into the early afternoon. The weather was perfect: sun, mostly blue skies with a few puffy clouds floating, and just enough breeze to fill the Torc sails. By two o'clock, the temperature was warm enough and the crowd was lubed enough that the diving board started to be utilized. Hearty Alaskans lacking any kind of aquatic technique whatsoever took turns flopping off the diving board into the frigid waters, only to climb up a ladder and claim their status as conqueror of the Beer Swig Belly Flop. The swimmers were given a shirt to wear that stated, "I got wet at Porty's!" and didn't pay a dime the rest of the day for foamy cups of Bud Light from a tapped beer keg.

As usual, all regular float plane flights for the day

had been grounded, the cannery closed, and barge lines locked up. The whole town seemed primed to celebrate their very own holiday in their very own style. Kids played touch football on Main Street, smoldering cedar limbs crackled in the metal trough of large barbeque, a band was getting tuned up on a stage surrounded by stacks of speaker cabinets, and a red-haired float plane pilot readied himself on the diving board for a cannonball. A group of teenagers had been dispatched to the stream carrying large plastic tubs with instructions of procuring several dozen dead humpy carcasses, and an older woman wearing a pink nightgown and a blue Captain Crunch hat tended to marinated fillets of halibut on a smoking grill.

"Be careful, Jimbo. That little prick, Travors, is prancing around here somewhere." Turning her head away from the grill, Deloris launched a brown wad of chew spit from the corner of her mouth.

Dressed in full uniform, Stetson and all, Jim had been passing by the barbeque grill on his way to inspect the diving board. Scents of fresh herbs mixed with the smell of cedar smoke drifted up his nostrils as he scanned the perfectly sizzled halibut chunks. "I'm not too worried about Carl. What's the worst he could do?"

Deloris flipped a fillet and said, "He could get you fired. Or worse yet, transferred to the Arctic Circle."

Jim plated a halibut piece and tore into the flaky white flesh with a plastic fork. The outer edge of the fish had been perfectly crusted and zinged with flavors of rosemary and chilies. The inside of the meat was moist and bursting with citrus tang. Hints of cedar smoke, mild garlic oil and a tinge of spicy heat filled out the palette. Jim's mouth exploded with essence, and his nose cleared and eyes watered. It was a burst of harmonious flavor unlike anything he had ever tasted.

"Deloris, this is... This is just amazing. How did..."

"Pretty good shit there, huh Jimbo?" She spat again.

Jim forked in another bite of fish and asked, "How did you learn to cook like this?"

"It was another life, long ago, and not here."

"Where, when, how? Oh man, Deloris. This is so good."

"Let's just say that I used to be a chef for some famous people. Then I retired and moved here. I don't cook much anymore. Only for special occasions." She hocked up something from the back of her throat and asked, "What do you care, anyway?"

"Just curious, that's all. I continue to be amazed at some of the people that live on this isolated island. The talent pool here, well, it's just surprising, that's all."

Once word had spread that Deloris' grilled halibut fillets were ready to be served, a line began to form next to the barbeque. Jim wandered away with his plate and fork. He decided to inspect the bandstand.

Gruel was adjusting knobs on a bass amplifier, Rupert spun a wing nut onto the tip of a cymbal stand, and Spike removed his shirt and began fluffing up his curly hair. Kram seemed lost in a maze of patch cords and foot pedals. The band seemed close to being ready to perform and Jim decided to leave them to their devices. He strolled away from the stage around the corner of Porty's toward the front entrance.

The bar was packed. The floor was wet. Several soggy patrons donning new t-shirts sat happily among a talkative crowd sipping their beverages. Maggie and Lip Rings worked behind the bar frantically filling red cups of foamy beer. Neck Tattoos slithered amongst the crowd clearing empty cups from tables and delivering fresh baskets of popcorn throughout the bar. A group cheered from the corner of the bar as Frightening Frankie shot two arms into the air after piercing the bulls-eye with his final dart. Frankie wore his "I got wet at Porty's!" t-shirt and his typically red hair was dark orange and matted against his skull from the saltwater.

Jim nodded at Maggie. She paused for only a second to smile back, then busily went back to work keeping her customers happy. Jim walked back out the door and into the sunny parking lot. Beer Swig and Humpy Fest was up and running full steam, and everything seemed to be functioning smoothly. As far as law enforcement was concerned, the town was going about their festive ways in a perfectly acceptable manner.

Jim hoped the day would continue without incident.

Jim was as pleased as the town he had just observed. The emotion hit him like a ton of bricks. He was experiencing happiness, a feeling of belonging, a sense that his part on the big blue marble had value. He had only lived on the island for a few months, but he already knew many of the residents. For as quirky as they tended to be, it was the island inhabitants' unique personalities and fascinating way of life that appealed to Jim. For the first time in his life, Jim felt as though he was in the right place and at the right time. Jim Wekle felt as though he had found a home.

Leaning on a wooden rail overlooking the diving board, Jim smiled as he finished the last bite of halibut from his plate. His contented sensation was fueled even more as he observed a pony-tailed man jumping from the bandstand and running full steam toward the waterfront. The crowd cheered loudly as the man overtook the diving board without breaking stride. Jumping high into the air then arcing back down toward the water's surface, the pony-tailed man emitted a boisterous call the whole way.

"Hot daaaaaaaaaammmmmmnnnnnn!"

Former United States Senator Carl Travors knew that time was in his favor. The more time that passed, the more likely he was to capture the incriminating evidence that he sought. The morning melded into afternoon, and, unfortunately, everybody seemed to be behaving moderately well. Carl snapped a couple of pictures of people diving into the sound and several snapshots of people slamming down cups of beer inside the bar, but none of the actions so far could be construed as "out of control." He needed evidence of pure lunacy. The crème d' le crème would be a snapshot of some lunatic tearing off her clothes in front of the bandstand with Trooper Jim Wekle in the background smiling. Carl thought, "if only I could be so lucky."

Passing through the crowded bar in Porty's with his camera poised at the ready, Carl Travors bumped into a familiar face. Former Trooper Dan Potter was bouncing through the throngs with his portly belly bumping into random people. Travors thought it was odd to see the retired lieutenant, but Dan Potter explained that he was back on the island to see old friends.

"Here, have a brownie." The bald man said in dolphin tone.

Carl was actually a little hungry as he refused to accept a halibut chunk from his insane neighbor, Deloris, out fear that she would hock a brown spit wad on it. He scarfed the delicious chocolate treat down before the crowd dispersed enough to allow Dan Potter to move away.

"Hey Potter, that was pretty good. Do you have any more of those brownies?"

Sitting on the edge of the Ross Land and Sea dock, Bill Fetcherson let his legs dangle over the wood planked rim. He was still in the throes of a bad opiate induced hangover and nursed what was only his third beer of the day. His mood was dark as he pondered the current state of his very existence. What had come of his life, now reduced to a common drug fiend? Beer was one thing, but how could he have let himself snort powder up his nose?

Bill Fetcherson only knew of one drug that could be snorted in white powder form. The strange man with the high voice had to of supplied the previous night's binge with cocaine. Bill Fetcherson feared that he was now an addict; that the horrible headache that persisted was a withdrawal symptom and that his life was spiraling down the toilet.

Gazing at the half-empty bottle of warm Alaskan Amber cradled in his hands, Fetcherson decided that his life had to have more meaning than this. The alcohol abuse led to drug use. He knew what the drug use would lead to. Bill feared death and knew that with his aging years, a drug addiction would only speed that inevitability along. He had to change his ways before it was too late. Bill took one last swig of warm beer, swished the liquid around inside his mouth, and spit a spray of foam off the dock. He looked at the bottle in his hand, stood and chucked it out into the water as far as he could throw.

MINK ISLAND

42

The band rocked on stage as the afternoon progressed. The crowd inside Porty's migrated out to the deck overlooking the bandstand and people danced and cheered through multiple guitar solos. Each song was performed in extended form with improvisations, drum and bass grooves, vocal scat solos and all out stage pandemonium. As the aging rockers crescendoed into the climax of the tune *Passionate Pirate Piñata from Panama*, a loud air horn was blasted from a tugboat out in the bay. The band played a final chord and people went scurrying in all directions like a fire ant nest that had just been kicked.

The air horn from the tugboat signaled that the end of the Torc Regatta was near. The sailboats would be coming into range shortly as the finish line markers floated just outside the breakwater. Once they crossed the finish line, the boats would drop sails and putter into the marina past the breakwater directly in front of the crowd massed at Porty's.

Men hoisted tubs of dead fish onto the roof next to the giant slingshots. Patrons rushed the bar for quick refills of their keg cups. The band went dormant and amplifiers were clicked off. The crowd surged to deck railings all along the waterfront. The epic pinnacle of the summer was about to unfold and the entire town was electric with anticipation.

"Thar she blows!" Johnny Ross yelled from his rooftop vantage. The first sailboat had just come into view as it crossed the regatta's finish line.

Completely lubed after multiple quantities of laced brownies mixed with a dose of blood pressure pills, Carl Travors' lunacy hit full tilt boogie. His quest to take pictures of scandalous acts turned into a fanatical obsession mixed with total paranoia and fear. With his brain completely fogged, Travors became convinced that he must hide from the world and take his candid snapshots from a covert vantage. Searching for his hiding spot, Carl mumbled to himself as he staggered back and forth on the outskirts of the crowd.

"Must find cover..." He bumped into a woman who scowled and pushed him away.

"Must stay hidden... Take my pictures..." He reeled into a stack of fish boxes and giggled as they tumbled over.

"More brownies..." He wobbled away from the crowd, groping the zippered pockets of his safari vest.

Off to the side of the crowd, Carl Travors found a small mound covered by a camouflaged tarp. Like an alley cat looking for a spot to curl up, he snaked his way under the tarp and climbed to the top of the mound. Extracting his pocket knife, Carl cut a small, rectangular hole in the tarp in front of his face. He felt triumphant. He had found the perfect hidden vantage, just off to the side of Porty's and inconspicuous enough to be unnoticed yet close enough to witness all the action. He readied his digital camera and chomped down on the last of his magic brownies.

In his altered state, Carl was completely oblivious to the noxious combination of odors that swirled, trapped underneath the tarp. Thousands of rotting herring simmered in the oven-like atmosphere of the tarp under the sun. The foul smell of decomposing fish mixed with several gallons of unleaded gasoline to create a stench that would expel most normal humans, but Travors' senses were dulled past the point of functionality and he remained at his post, poised for his triumph.

The game was simple. Hit a boat with a dead salmon and you score a point. The team with the most points wins. The winner gets their business name on the plaque that hung above the bar in Porty's. For three years running, Ross Land and Sea had etched their name on the coveted trophy and Frankie and Johnny weren't about to let that change. They manned the left outside slingshot and stood at the ready, waiting for the nose of the first boat to drift into range.

The middle slingshot was sponsored by Sea Tank Marine Lines, and Hauler Steve and a couple of the dock workers busily selected their humpy carcasses in order of most aerodynamic.

The right outside slingshot was backed by Porty's bar. Maggie's brother would normally have been in charge of the humpy flinging, but in his absence, Maggie nominated Lip Rings and Neck Tattoos for the duties. They eagerly accepted the job and Neck Tattoos neared the point of giddiness as he slipped a slimy fish into the netting pouch of the giant propelling device.

The crowd pushed closer to the edge, focused on the incoming boats and ready to let forth with roaring applause. The lead boat had already dropped its sail, started up its kicker motor and slowly turned in towards the marina. Salmon had been placed into launching position, rubber arms stretched back and the onslaught was poised at the ready.

The nose of the lead sailboat cut through the water closer and closer. A hush came over the crowd. Almost there...

"YEEEEEE HAAAAAAW!" Frightening Frankie let forth with a scream as he released the first shot. The fish flung high into the air, flip-flopping as it fluttered across the bay. It barely missed the hull of the boat and the crowd groaned as it splashed landed into the harbor. But the mêlée had begun and fish began flying across the small channel from the rooftop vantage. The boat proved challenging to hit at first, but eventually, the marksmen zeroed in and dead humpies started to impale the white hull with a splattering thud that evoked elation from the onlookers.

Kram and Deloris were honorary judges and scorekeepers. A wooden sign had been erected and Deloris spray painted tic marks below company names in order to keep track of points. Kram peered through binoculars and jumped every time a fish blasted the side of the boat. Hauler Steve's accuracy proved on as the Sea Tank group took the early lead. The Ross boys were in a close second. The Porty's duo had yet to land a point.

43

The plan was in full swing and Blue Jay Haverford was primed to perform his duties. The land charges had been placed in the dark of night, the crowd was in the perfect location and the boats had just started to drift in. His palms became sweaty and his heart raced. It was almost time for his role in the Torcadero Yacht Club's epic revenge on the Porty's Humpy Fest onslaught.

The first sailboat, Cecil Wright's craft, was already through the channel. It had gotten pummeled by dead fish, just as planned. Cecil agreed to be the first through the chute as it meant he would have to be declared the winner of the Torc Regatta. It was an honor that he eagerly accepted, even if it meant that the slingshot crowd would be in full lather when his boat came within range. DeAngelo Smuthers reminded him that the whole thing was staged and winning didn't matter this year. Cecil still intended on having hats made up publicly declaring his victory.

Smuthers' boat would be the second place winner and would have to endure the usual onslaught of flying fish. He didn't mind as once again scrubbing off humpy scum from his boat's outer hull was a small price to pay in order to have a prime vantage point for their ultimate revenge.

The third and last boat would be *The Cyclone*. Roger Greeley would be standing proudly on the bow of his craft as his wife, Ferny, would guide the small engine from the stern. Roger would have in place everything he needed for quick reloads. The cannon would be primed and it would be pointed directly at Porty's.

The plan was to give the impression that *The Cyclone* was firing live cannon rounds at strategic points surrounding the crowd at Porty's. They hoped to strike fear into the hearts of the Porty's crowd and watch them scramble in chaotic terror. The Torcadero Yacht Club didn't really want to maim anybody. The cannon would be firing blanks; simple blasts that would fill the ears of the onlookers, but not actually send projectiles flaming through the air from the sailboat. The charges on shore had been placed beneath Styrofoam chests full of rancid herring and the plan was to ignite the herring bombs in progressive order, thus filtering the crowd closer to each successive blast and fully dousing them with bits of the exploded bait fish.

On cue, Blue Jay Haverford placed his finger on one of the triggers of his radio-controlled igniters. In the guise of night, Blue Jay had placed his charges, coolers of herring and camouflaged tarp coverings in the assigned places surrounding Porty's. The plan seemed perfect in every way, until Blue Jay Haverford got nervous. During the night, Blue Jay's apprehension surrounding his felonious title of demolitions expert caused him to second guess his volatile TNT estimations. Feeling as though his explosive charges were not sufficient enough to plaster fish bits into the masses, Blue Jay took it upon himself to procure a five-gallon jug of gasoline. He had placed the plastic container of extremely flammable fuel next to the last of the explosive charges before covering it with the greatest mass of bait fish that he could muster. If the first three explosions proved to be insufficient, Blue Jay was certain that the added firepower to the final bomb would do the trick.

Blue Jay crouched down on the aft deck of the *Creighton Swish*. In organized fashion, he laid out all four remote detonator switches in order. The second boat was passing, getting impaled with dead salmon from the Porty's slingshots. Blue Jay knew that *The Cyclone* was just about to cross the finish line and lower its sails. The time was upon him. He hadn't felt this kind of nervous excitement since his old playing days. It was almost as if the score was tied and he was at the free throw line with one second left on the clock. The ball was in his hands once again and Blue Jay Haverford was poised at the ready, sweat in his palms and stains in his armpits. It was time.

The Cyclone passed in front of the breakwater with Roger Greeley standing stoically on the bow. The shiny silver metal barrel protruded from the side of the boat like a glistening atomic missile. Fish began flying from the rooftop. The first couple of humpy projectiles sailed high over his head. The third salmon plastered the side hull of *The Cyclone*. It was a direct hit and it was a perfect sign to

Roger that it was now time for payback.

Roger Greeley yelled, "Suck on this, you infantile bastards!" He lit the cannon's fuse and a sparkling blast rocketed from the barrel opening.

Two seconds later, in near perfect rhythm, an explosion erupted near the south end of Porty's hotel. Shards of tail fins, herring eyeballs and white Styrofoam flew into the sky. Shock quickly overcame the crowd. Most dropped to their knees and covered their heads, while others ran away from the blast. The second cannon shot, soon followed and a second explosion on shore, sent the masses into a frenzied panic. Half-blitzed patrons wearing brand new, wet t-shirts ran in circles. Some dove underneath the bandstand, while others made a mad dash for the covered barbeque area.

The third cannon blast and subsequent shore explosion caused panic from the rooftop fish hurlers. The shock wave shook the building's foundation and gave the impression that the *Port of Call* was about to collapse. The slingshot crews from Ross Land and Sea and Sea Tank Marine Lines practically jumped off the back side of the roof while fighting each other for turns down the ladder. Lip Rings sought cover underneath an overturned humpy tub, while Neck Tattoos simply stared down at the fracas with jaw slackened and pupils dilated.

The sound of explosions triggered Jim's brain into

emergency response mode. Lieutenant Wekle was half a block down the street when the blasts started reverberating. He placed his hand on his sidearm and quickly sprinted up the street toward Porty's. Without knowing the exact details of the situation, Jim began instructing people to get down and seek cover. After fighting his way through a fleeing crowd, Jim reached a waterfront vantage and observed what appeared to be a sailboat launching live cannon rounds towards shore.

Jim grabbed his radio and immediately contacted the United States Coast Guard, Prince of Wales Island dispatch. Seconds later, a fully armed Coast Guard forty-footer was diverted from its shoreline patrol and blazed a path through the water at full throttle. Jim knew that it would be on scene within minutes, but he feared that minutes might be too late.

Peering through the small opening in the tarp that he had cut, former Senator Travors was elated at the sight of explosions and mass hysteria. He snapped pictures of residents running amok through his narrow view. Carl giggled each time he clicked the button on his camera. The scene was perfect for him to capture on film. His brain fogged with drugs and an incessant drive for vindication, Carl Travors continued his surveillance without registering the fact that he was currently sprawled atop a virtual powder keg of explosives and gasoline.

"Run away in chaotic accord, you drunked up whores of a society corrupted," he cackled to himself as he snapped another picture from under the tarp.

When he heard the third boom echoing from across the harbor followed by the third explosion on land, he quickened his snapshot pace. Click, click, click. More screams. Click, click. More people ran. Cackle, click, click. More ducked for cover.

"There you are, you swine-cop." Carl caught a glimpse of Lieutenant Wekle frantically motioning to people while talking on his radio. "The perfect picture. Incriminating, damaging, career-ending." Carl maniacally laughed as he framed in the trooper's image for the shot he had been waiting for.

The stars had aligned. Everything that Carl Travors had hoped for came to fruition. He punched the zoom-in feature on the camera. Smoke rose steadily behind the Trooper's image while drunks fled in the foreground. Carl placed his finger on the camera's shutter button. Just as he snapped the image, capturing it forever into the brain of his camera, a fourth blast rang out from the sailboat's cannon.

The former Senator yelled, "I've got you, you son-of-a-bitch!"

When Blue Jay Haverford punched the button on his fourth and final radio controlled igniter, the resulting eruption was nothing close to what he expected. Buildings that lined the coast visibly shook. A sonic boom hit him in the chest. Waves rocked out from shore. A fireball mushroomed into the sky towering far above the roofline of any structure. And flaming bits of herring meat, Styrofoam, camouflaged tarp, safari vest and the charred morsels of a former United States Senator rained down from the heavens upon the crowd.

44

When jellied bits of incendiary materials fell from the sky and began sticking to the skin, hair and clothing of the crowd, panic from the explosions quickly morphed into an immediate need for extinguishing fire. The simple stop-drop-and-roll method failed to work, as the combination of flesh and enflamed gasoline proved near impossible to snuff out. With skin becoming quickly scorched, the bulk of the crowd made a beeline for the edge of the dock. Nearly fifty men and women bypassed the diving board and cannonballed their way into the sea. This immediately put out any flaming pieces of herring, but it created an entirely new problem. There were way too many people treading in frigid water and only one small ladder that rose from the sea.

Upon witnessing a herd of humans resembling lemmings jumping off a cliff, Bill Fetcherson's new-found desire to better humanity kicked in. The several dozen people bobbing in the icy Alaskan waters were in desperate need of a flotation aid. Bill sprinted from his vantage point straight for the Luxury Coachman Plus. Moments later, he burst through his RV doors, emerging with an armload of life preservers and flotation pillows. He ran full speed to the edge of the dock and hurled them at the masses below. It only took him three trips back and forth to the RV before every person in the water had something to hold on to.

The Coast Guard vessel blew past the *Creighton Swish* in a froth of water and descended upon *The Cyclone* with a row of armed men on the bow. Blue Jay Haverford sheepishly watched Roger and Fern Greeley's boat get boarded. Both were shackled and moved over to the forty-footer at gunpoint.

Blue Jay quietly pulled anchor and raised his sails. Nobody seemed to notice as the *Creighton Swish* discretely navigated its way through the small surrounding islands and out of sight.

After helping Trooper Wekle extract the last person out of the water safely, Bill Fetcherson couldn't help but feel proud. His new-found desire to clean up his act and aid his fellow man couldn't have come at a better time. It was his heroics and quick thinking that kept forty-seven people afloat while one person at a time ascending a single ladder up to the dock from the water below.

"That was some quick thinking there. Glad you knew where all those life jackets were located." Jim said as he sat down on the edge of the dock next to Bill Fetcherson.

"Uh, yeah. Good thing I knew where to find all those."

Jim asked, "You're the town's night watchman right?"

"Yeah, that's me. The glorious night watchman. Supposed public servant and protector of the night."

"You don't sound so sure about that."

Bill shook his head, "I've completely ruined my life. I was supposed to be on a retirement vacation with my wife. Instead, I've wasted away my summer on this damn rock, drinking too much, and being a complete idiot."

Jim felt a little bad for the man in pathetic throes of self-pity. Jim said, "Well, at least you helped a lot of people today. That's got to count for something, right?"

"Sure, I guess. I've still been an idiot, though." Bill sighed deeply. People passed by wearing blankets over their shoulders, giving Bill a thumbs-up and a smile.

Attempting to make him feel a little better, Jim said, "Well, those guys don't think you're an idiot. You just may have saved their lives."

Bill wasn't convinced, "Just take last night, for example. Instead of calling you to report this steady stream of dubious people down by the barge lines, I get caught up with some doofus and his magic nose powder."

Jim's head shot up.

Bill said, "Yeah, I know. Arrest me for that nose powder stuff. To tell you the truth, I'm not even sure what it was."

Jim intently said, "I don't care about the nose powder. Tell me about the steady stream of people? Where and when?"

"Well, you see, I've learned to hide pretty well over the past few nights. You know, spots that I can see pretty good from without being seen. To tell you the truth, it was more out of a desire to sit and drink booze alone in the dark, but I soon found that I was able to spy on most of the town from some of these cool little spots."

Bill went on to explain to Jim about the suspicious chain of events: person after person, walking down the secluded path next to the barge lot, knocking on the red metal door, exchanging something through a crack in the door and returning up the path to disappear into the night.

Jim ordered, "Show me this little shack with the red metal door."

"Now? What about all of my life jackets?"

"Now. Forget about the life jackets. Let's move."

45

The wind had just started to kick up as Bill Fetcherson led Jim Wekle to one of his secret lookout spots. The wind had blown in a layer of clouds and the once sunny day was quickly getting overcome by dark evening skies.

"It's not far. Just up this staircase and through those berry bushes over there." Fetcherson led Jim half the way up the stairs toward the Stockade, and then he bushwhacked through a thick outer strain of thorny branches. Just on the other side of the vegetation, a clearing gave way that was nestled atop a narrow dirt trail that descended down the hillside. The trail terminated at the far fenced edge of Sea Tank Marine Lines. From the clearing, Jim had a full view of the side of the barge company's large warehouse and a dark path that led down the warehouse perimeter to a cabin-sized building. The building had a grey shingled roof, dark brown siding and a red metal door positioned below a single hanging light bulb.

"Told ya. You can see things from here that you can't see from the street."

Jim patted Bill on the shoulder and asked, "Is that the place that was so busy last night?"

"You bet. Person after person. I was pretty sure that something wasn't quite right. I know I should have reported it earlier, but I, uh… I've been going through kind of a tough time recently."

"It's alright, Bill. You did the right thing by bringing me here." Just then, a man came into view. He was walking down the path that skirted the Sea Tank warehouse. With the cloudy skies and hidden walkway, it was hard for Jim to see any detail, but there was something oddly familiar with the way the man walked. Jim knew he had seen this person before, but it hadn't yet registered just who it was. The man stopped at the red metal door, paused while he dug out a key, and then he unlocked the door. Just before stepping inside, the man turned to look over his shoulder. Jim's heart sank. He knew the man. It was Gavin Donaldson.

"You can head back and look for your life jackets now, Bill."

"What are you going to do?"

"I am about to go see a friend of mine."

Leaving Bill behind, Jim hopped onto the dirt trail that led down from the lookout. It didn't really make any sense to him. Why would Gavin be involved in dealing drugs? And he couldn't possibly be involved in the murders, could he? But the location fit perfectly. It was close to the barge lines for easy access to the drug shipments. From this little shack, you could sit and watch the midnight barge come into port. Heck, you could probably step out of the shack and jump over the boat rail directly onto the barge surface, unload your personal shipment in the cover of night and no one would ever know.

Plus, the location fit perfectly for the Simms girl murder. Debbie Simms left the Stockade and never returned. Maybe she tried to get drugs; maybe she walked into the shack for some reason. Who knows? But the location fit.

Jim quickly skirted the edge of the warehouse wall. As he neared the red metal door, Jim unsnapped his pistol and placed his right hand on the gun. He thought that there had to be a good reason that Gavin Donaldson just walked into this building. Maybe it was his friend's place? Maybe he kept Fish and Wildlife gear here? Jim also considered the worst. What if he was the drug dealing murderer and what if Jim was about to go head to head with a stone cold killer?

Jim approached the door and stood silently for a moment. No sounds of any kind came through the door. He knocked twice with his left fist and waited. No answer and no sound from inside. Jim stepped to the side of the door and knocked again.

This time a voice from inside yelled, "We're not open. Go away." It was Gavin's voice. The fact that he "wasn't open" pretty much confirmed Jim's fearful suspicions.

"Gavin. Open up. It's Jim Wekle. I need to speak with you," Jim hollered in a strong voice. He heard some shuffling from behind the metal door. Jim kept his hand on the butt of his gun, but did not draw it. The last thing he wanted to do was to provoke a shootout with his colleague. Jim hoped for a peaceful encounter.

After almost a minute, the door cracked open and Gavin Donaldson's face appeared in the crack of the door frame, "Jim. Good to see you. What's up?"

"You going to let me in, Gavin?"

Gavin stared silently into Jim's eyes. They both knew that Gavin had been caught. They both knew it was only a matter of time before Jim would get legal permission to access the building. Gavin could legally deny him entrance, and Gavin could flee in the time it took Jim to get a court order, but where would he go? It was over and they both knew it. Gavin stepped aside and held the door open.

Jim walked in cautiously. The first thought was to scan the room for any potential dangers. They were alone. There were no signs of weapons. There were no direct signs of pills or other drugs, but there were baggies and stacks of bills on the table. White powdery dust had been wiped from the table, but residue still existed. There were several chairs, a refrigerator, microwave oven, a couch, an exposed toilet and a sink in the corner of the small shed. A tall file cabinet stood in the opposite corner of the room with a stack of papers on top of it. A pillow and blankets had been dropped from the end of the couch next to a severely damaged suitcase, obvious that someone had been spending the night. Otherwise, the room was completely void and stagnant. A window was open that overlooked the water and the growing wind blew into the small room.

"You want to tell me about it, Gavin?"

"You want to have a seat, Jim?"

"I'll stand."

A strong gust of wind caught the side the building. Siding rattled and rain began to pelt the roof. A summer storm was brewing and moving in fast.

"She died, Jim. The pain that was left, well... I just couldn't deal with it."

Jim shook his head, "I'm sorry about your daughter, Gavin. But dealing drugs? There has to be a better way of dealing with your pain."

Another gust hit the side of the shed. Wind penetrated the open window of the dilapidated building and the papers on top of the file cabinet scattered with the breeze. Jim's head turned for a second towards the flying papers, and that's when Gavin lunged. He grabbed Jim's right hand and yanked it away from its position on top of the pistol. Both men crashed into the table, spilling hundred dollar bills onto the concrete floor. Jim smacked Gavin on the chin with his left fist, but the impact was ineffective. Gavin had hold of his right arm and wasn't letting go. The table gave way and both men fell to the floor, turning several times until Gavin came out on top. Gavin landed a right hook directly into Jim's cheek. A second punch and Jim's brain began to flash darkness. Just as Gavin raised his arm to deliver another blow to the face, the door swung open and cold, damp air whistled in.

"Freeze!" Tavis Spurgeon yelled, both hands gripping his pistol and taking full aim at Gavin Donaldson. Bill Fetcherson stood awkwardly behind the young trooper, peering around with a sheepish grin. Gavin raised both arms and slowly moved from his position on top of Jim.

Jim rubbed his soon to be swollen face and said, "Tavis. Just in time. Thanks."

Bill craned his head around and asked, "Did I do good again?"

"Yes, Bill. You're on a roll."

Jim stood and tried to shake the cobwebs from his brain. The room stopped spinning, but the pain from getting smacked twice in the face was quickly mounting. The room was a mess of papers, baggies, currency, a knocked over table and chairs and a ragged, desperate Fish and Game officer sitting on his knees with his hands in the air. Jim walked over to the file cabinet and started opening drawers. The second one from the top held what he was looking for. Jim lifted up a couple of gallon sized bags full to the brim with pills. No one spoke. Everyone knew what they were.

Jim was just about to handcuff Gavin when something caught his eye. On top of the cabinet there was a familiar looking file folder. He removed the folder and examined the outer label. It had a forensics seal stamped on the outside flap and sported a fairly recent date mark. This was the file that Jim had been waiting on for weeks. Why it was sitting on top of this particular file cabinet, he hadn't a clue.

"D. Simms, Craig, AK, Ballistics Report" was displayed just below the official forensics seal. This file was supposed to be for Jim's eyes only. He assumed that Gavin somehow intercepted it, but how and when, he couldn't even guess.

Opening the file, the room fell silent. Only noise from the wind and rain outside could be heard. Jim scanned quickly down the report and his eyes settled on one single item. The sinking feeling in his heart returned. Jim looked up from the file. Gavin Donaldson lowered his arms and stood. Tavis shifted his aim from Gavin, pointing his gun directly at the chest of his boss.

"Tavis?" Jim asked, with sadness in his voice.

The forensics report indicated that the bullet that had killed Debbie Simms was a forty caliber round from a Glock-22 pistol. Fish and Game officers carry forty-five caliber guns, needing that extra firepower for protection against some of the wild animals that they might encounter. Only Alaska State Troopers carried standard issue Glock-22s.

Jim looked at the straight black hair that hung down below Tavis' Stetson. He knew the answer, but asked it anyway.

"You killed her, didn't you?"

The young trooper's hands were steady. His eyes glassy. Tavis spoke, almost as if to no one in particular, "She wasn't supposed to come down that night. If only she would have listened. We hooked up for three nights straight, but I told her not to come by that night."

Gavin yelled, "Just shut up, Tavis."

"She came anyway. Walked right into the middle of it. She walked in and saw everything. The drugs. Gavin and I. The money."

Gavin said in his gruff voice, "Tavis. You don't have to say anything. It will just make it worse."

"Doesn't matter. It's over. I'll shoot him right between the eyes and be on the next boat off the island before anybody notices. Maybe I'll shoot him in the back, just like I did Debbie."

Tavis raised his pistol and aimed it at Jim's head, then shifted it back down to his chest. He toyed with his aim, hoping to strike out some emotion from his boss.

"Ahem…" Gavin pretended to clear his throat as he nodded his head in the direction of the man that still stood in the rain outside the door. Tavis turned in time to see Bill Fetcherson slowly trying to sneak away.

"Get in here." Tavis took the older man by the arm and threw him into the room.

Jim said, "You can't just kill everyone and expect to get away with it. Sooner or later, it will catch up to you, Tavis."

Tavis spoke in a stone cold tone, "Later it is, then." He raised the pistol, aiming again at Jim's heart.

A split second before he could pull the trigger, a loud crash sounded right behind Tavis at the open door. Dan Potter came staggering into the shed after falling face first into the metal door.

"Hey... It's a party in here," Potter yelled in slurred speech.

Jim jumped to the side quickly and drew his gun. Tavis fired a shot that went through the wall of the shed. Bill jumped at Tavis, tackling him around the waist. Bill and Tavis tumbled straight back, falling on top of Dan Potter. Potter's head hit the ground hard. Tavis' gun fell from his grip and landed at Gavin's feet.

"Don't do it, Gavin," Jim yelled.

It was too late. Gavin bent over, grabbed the gun, and raised it toward Jim. Jim fired two quick blasts into the chest of Gavin Donaldson. The Alaska State Fish and Game officer flew back into the couch and landed in a heap of lifelessness. Blood oozed from below his shirt. Gavin was dead.

Jim turned his aim quickly towards the door. Bill Fetcherson was sprawled on top of an unconscious fat, bald man. Jim burst out the door and quickly took aim

down the path. It was too late. There was no sign of
Tavis. He had escaped into the darkness, wind, and rain.

46

Jim watched the medical team bag Gavin's body. Dan Potter was handcuffed and lying on the couch while being treated for a concussion and near drug overdose. Bill Fetcherson had been treated for a couple of mild scrapes and sent back to his RV for rest and to write down a full statement on the night's events.

As the adrenaline surge slowly wore down, Jim felt the reality of the situation sinking in. He came to the realization that he had been the only legitimate law enforcement officer on the entire island. His team was full of criminals. The Donaldson-Potter-Spurgeon crime triangle had functioned under his nose for the past several months, but he knew that it had existed on the island long before he arrived.

Jim suddenly felt completely alone. There was a murderous fugitive at large and he was solely responsible. There was a massive storm blowing outside, he had no idea where Tavis had run off to, and even if he did know, Jim would be completely unaided in his pursuit.

He had contacted Captain McEwen and fully updated her on the situation. He had requested immediate support, but with a full-blown Southeast Alaskan gale shredding through the night, Jim was on his own for a while. His captain reminded him that Tavis was trapped on the island due to the storm as well. Boats, planes, helicopters; it didn't matter. They were all grounded until the storm passed. She cautioned him to be careful and to be patient. Reinforcements were on the way as soon as weather allowed.

Captain McEwen knew the Donaldson's well and she agreed to contact Gavin's wife with the news. Jim was actually quite relieved. He couldn't imagine how he would be able to tell Mrs. Donaldson that he had just shot her husband after trying to arrest him for being part of a drug ring.

Jim's face was swollen, his emotions were shattered, but he still had a job to do. Potter was still in la-la land and wouldn't be worth interrogating for several hours. Jim decided to fully search the shack. While rummaging through the crime scene, Jim found a steel pipe wedge behind the file cabinet leaning against a corner of the wall. He extracted the pipe with gloved fingers and examined it from top to bottom. It was fairly clean, but he noticed a dark dried substance and several hairs on the inside of one end of the pipe. Jim let out a sigh and then bagged the pipe in an evidence pouch.

"I bet this has Shane Ketah's blood on it and Tavis Spurgeon's fingerprints," Jim said aloud, more to himself than the medics that were in the room.

"I bet you're right," answered a familiar voice at the door.

"Kram. What're you doing here?"

"Came to check on my buddy." Kram stepped into the room. Rain had matted down the hair of his long grey ponytail. His blue Space Invaders shirt was completely soaked through.

"Everything turn out okay back at Porty's?"

Kram smiled, "Yeah, pretty much a harmless prank that turned south in a hurry. Gave all of us a pretty good scare. Coasties took the sailboat brigade into custody. Impounded three of their boats. Pretty cool cannon, though, huh?" Kram smiled and turned his head to one side, similar to a Labrador. "Had to award the plaque to Sea Tanks. Hauler Steve and the boys were in the lead when the fireworks started going off."

"You get your electronics cleared off the stage before the storm hit?"

Kram nodded, "Yeah. Everyone seemed to pitch in once the Coast Guard left with the three impounded boats. You know, funny thing is, those regatta guys usually have four boats in their race." Kram stared straight into Jim's eyes and asked, "You going after him?"

Jim answered, "Who? The other sailboat guy?"

"No, Tavis. You know he's still on the island."

"Captain says I should wait."

"Captain probably doubts that you will, though."

"Yeah, me too."

373

Kram walked up and put his hand on Jim's shoulder and said, "Then I guess you'll need a deputy."

"I don't think so, Kram. Besides, I don't even know where to look."

Another voice sounded from just outside the metal door, "But I do." Tank Spurgeon stepped in from the wind and rain. "I know where he ran to." Frankie and Johnny Ross followed in behind Tank.

Tank said, "I own a cabin up on Stelikan Mountain. Always used to take Tavis there when he was growing up. I know he's up there, and we're all going to help you get him."

Frightening Frankie said, "You'll need help, too. You'd never make it up there in your cruiser. Tavis could make it up the mountain in the Cherokee, but there's no way you'll get there without four-wheel drive."

Jim looked Tank in the eyes and said, "I'm sorry about your nephew, Tank. This has to be pretty hard on you."

Tank replied, "I'm pissed off. This happened right under my nose. That boy had free access to my entire business. He knew where I kept my container lock keys, knew when every shipment came in. Hell, I even own this shack that he was dealing out of. I knew he liked to take girls here every once in a while. Figured that was innocent enough, but I guess I was dead wrong. I should've known Tavis was in on this from the first moment you walked into my office asking questions."

Kram said, "It's hardest on those who are closest. Don't beat yourself up, Tank."

Two more people walked in from the storm. Maggie Ketah and Ben Nakit stood just inside the shed with somber expressions.

Maggie said, "We're coming too."

"Maggie. I can't let you do that," Jim replied.

"Like hell, you can't. He killed my brother."

Ben said, "That bastard used me. Got me busted for watching his stupid pot grow. Said he'd kill me if I ratted him out. I believed him, too."

Jim thought for a moment, and then said, "Something about that pot bust doesn't make sense to me. If Gavin was in on all of this as well as Tavis, why'd Gavin fly us into that lake knowing that you'd be up there tending to the growing operation?"

Ben lowered his head and said, "The pot was all Tavis. Gavin only sold the painkillers. Gavin knew I was up there and wanted you to shut us down. He set me up."

"Then who bailed you out? Tavis?"

"No. I did," said Tank. "Ben's a good kid. The best fork driver I got. He made some bad choices, which he'll have to pay for, but I couldn't have him sitting in jail when I had a barge to unload."

375

Ben looked up and met Jim's eyes. "I'm a good kid. I won't screw up again, and I want to help get Tavis. He killed my friend, Shane, and he needs to pay for that."

Jim suddenly realized that he wasn't alone. He might be the only official law enforcer left on the island, but he wasn't alone in his commitment to serve the community. He had companions. He had people that he could trust. There was a job to be done, and he had a crew that was willing to help. Duty and honor in the face of a storm trumped his Captain's suggestion to wait.

Jim looked around the room. Frankie and Johnny Ross stood tall with their fiery red hair curling beneath ball caps. Tank Spurgeon looked deeply saddened, but stoic nonetheless. Ben Nakit's young face was stern and honest. Maggie Ketah had tears welling but still stood strong. Kram stared blankly into space.

Jim announced, "Let's go get this guy."

Just as the team turned to exit the shed, Tank said, "Oh, just one thing. We had better arm ourselves. That cabin of mine is well stocked. He'll have weapons, protection, a good vantage point, and he'll probably see us coming."

47

After loading up in two of the Ross Land and Sea Chevy Blazer's, Jim made a stop at the Trooper Station. He knew he was risking his career by arming his team with State issue firearms, but it didn't matter to him. Prince of Wales Island was his home now, and these people were his friends and companions. They had just as much at stake as he did. Tavis Spurgeon was their responsibility as much as he was Jim's. Tavis would be brought to justice.

Jim passed out shotguns and boxes of shells to each member of the team. He handed Maggie the gun and asked if she knew how to use it. She popped in three shells, cocked it once and stared him down.

"I guess you know how to use it," Jim said.

Kram asked, "Can I get a Taser?"

"No."

"Mace?"

"No."

"Automatic weapon?"

"No."

"Hand grenade?"

"We don't even have those."

After shotguns and ammo was distributed, Jim announced, "These guns are only for self-defense. I want to arrest Tavis, not shoot him. Understood?"

They piled back into the two Blazers and headed down the road. Johnny drove the lead vehicle with Jim, Tank and Kram. Frankie drove the second rig with Maggie and Ben. This was by Jim's order as he wanted Maggie and Ben to hold back in case gunfire actually ensued.

After a few miles on the pavement, Tank instructed that they turn onto a dirt logging road. The wind blew violent bursts of sideways rain through the trees. The night was very dark and the headlights were dimmed by streams of rain. The road was bumpy and tree limbs brushed the sides of the vehicles. They ascended the mountainside slowly. Water rushed over the road in several places.

"Look!" Tank pointed forward. The headlights illuminated fresh tire tracks in the muddy road. "He's up here, alright."

Several slow miles of switchbacks finally gave way to a short downhill run. The two Blazers followed the road down and then curved sharply to the right as the road skirted a stone cliff.

"Whoa!" Johnny said as he slammed on the brakes. The lead Chevy skidded in the mud to a stop. Directly in their path, the white Jeep Cherokee with the State

Troopers logo on the door sat parked in the middle of the road. It appeared to be empty. Carefully, with guns at the ready, Jim and Tank jumped out of their vehicle. They each ran to opposite sides of the Cherokee, watchful for any sign of Tavis. A Sitka spruce tree had fallen in the storm and blocked the road. Tavis had abandoned his vehicle.

Tank yelled through the storm, "He went the rest of the way on foot. It's only about a half mile to the cabin from here."

Both Chevy Blazers were turned off and parked directly behind the Cherokee blocking it in against the downed tree. The team stood in a circle as rain pelted their exposed cheeks.

Jim gave the marching orders, "We'll go on foot from here. We only have two flashlights. Tank, Kram and Johnny, you come with me. Frankie, take the other flashlight, wait a few minutes then you guys follow us up. Tank says it's only about a half mile to the cabin."

Kram said, "Excuse me, boss, but I have a suggestion. Let me run ahead to take up an aggressive vantage. I'll be in place long before you guys ever show up."

"Kram, I'd rather you stick with us."

Tank interjected, "It's okay, Jim. I think you can trust this guy in a battle."

Kram said, "Jim, I've been through some pretty

379

intense stuff back in the day."

Tank said, "He fought in Vietnam, you know."

Kram said, "And Jim, it wasn't just regular infantry, either. I don't really like to talk about this, but... Back then... In the war... If they wanted to take someone out, my team was the one they sent in. We were highly trained and we were highly effective. Trust me, Jim."

Jim thought that Kram had never looked more coherent. He said, "I want him alive if at all possible."

"I know that. But you need to accept the fact that he may need to be killed."

Jim paused for a moment, then said, "Go." And Kram disappeared in an instant.

Just as Jim's group turned to go up the road, Maggie said, "Jim. Be careful."

He looked back at Maggie and replied, "You too."

Lanterns glowed from inside the cabin. A fire had been lit in the wood stove. The structure was small with only one room. There was an outhouse off to one side of the log cabin and a lean-to shed covering firewood on the other side. Otherwise, it was desolate and surrounded by wilderness.

Even though Jim was cold and soaked to the bone, the one advantage of the storm was that the wind and rain helped mask any sounds of their approach. Jim, Tank and Johnny took cover behind a mossy stump that rested about fifteen yards out from the cabin's front door.

"What's the plan, boss?" Johnny asked.

"I'm going in. Tank, is the front door locked?"

Tank said, "Not a chance. We only lock it on the outside with a padlock. Just push and it should open."

"Johnny, you stay here and cover me. Tank can you take cover behind that woodshed? I want you close in case I need you to help talk him down."

"Got it." Tank quickly ran to the shed while Jim and Johnny kept an eye on the door.

Jim stayed in a crouched position while making a straight trot for the front door. He was halfway there when the shot rang out. The deer rifle's barrel had been stuck through an open window on the front side of the cabin. The bullet ripped through Jim's right thigh sending a shock wave of pain through his body. Jim fell to the ground ten feet in front of the cabin, completely without cover and totally immobilized. A metallic clicking sound signaled that the hunting rifle had been reloaded.

"Get the hell out of here now, or the next shot will make a hole in his forehead." Tavis' speech was slurred. He had either been drinking or using.

Tank yelled out, "Don't do it, Tavis. It will just make things worse."

"Worse? How the hell can it get any worse than this?" Tavis began to laugh. "You have me for murder, dealing drugs, the list goes on. Now get the hell out of here Uncle Tank, or I'll take you out next."

Tavis fired another shot. This time the bullet hit the ground a foot away from Jim's head. Writhing in pain, Jim attempted to line up a return shot. He fired his pistol once but hit the side of the log cabin a foot below the open window. He was in agony and completely vulnerable.

"Tavis, you can't get out of this one. Your best bet is to lay down your gun and come out alive," Jim yelled, grimacing through the misery.

Out of the corner of his eye, Jim caught a glimpse in the darkness of something moving around the corner of the cabin by the outhouse. The image moved steadily, silently, and had a long ponytail. Kram kept low and out of sight. He slipped below the window that Tavis had been firing from.

Tank yelled, "Tavis, I still care about you. I don't want to see you dead tonight. But you know that's what will happen if you keep firing." Tank and Johnny both lowered their shotguns. They had also seen Kram sneak up and didn't want to risk hitting him.

Tavis yelled through the window in a slurred voice, "Go to hell, Uncle Tank. You too, Lieutenant."

Tavis clicked another round into the rifle chamber

and pointed the barrel back through the window. He was going for the kill shot, this time. Before Tavis could discharge the round, Kram grabbed the barrel with both hands and yanked down hard on the gun. The rifle slipped out of Tavis' hands and into Kram's possession. Immediately, Kram burst through the front door of the cabin. Tank bolted for the door, and Johnny ran fast from the moss covered stump. Tank and Johnny entered the cabin to find Tavis, a trained Alaska State Trooper, completely submitted face down on the floor, hands behind his back, with Kram pressing the rifle hard into the back of his neck.

"Hand me that rope," Kram ordered. Within seconds, Tavis was hogtied and completely immobile. Turning to Johnny, Kram said, "Go get Jim."

Kram had just started to administer first aid to Jim's leg when Frankie, Maggie, and Ben walked into the cabin. Ben jumped down to the floor and started to help Kram with the bandages.

They had just stopped the bleeding when Jim hollered out, "Maggie, no!"

All eyes turned to find Maggie pointing her shotgun directly at Tavis' head.

She said softly, "He killed my brother. He deserves to die."

Jim quickly replied, "That may be, Maggie, but you

pull that trigger and I can't help you. You will pay the rest
of your life for that. But I assure you, Maggie. You put
down that gun and Tavis will pay the rest of his life for
what he has done."

Tears ran down both of her cheeks. Her hands
trembled. She pressed the barrel of the shotgun against
Tavis' temple.

"You killed my brother. You deserve to die."

Jim made one last appeal, "Maggie, think about the
boat ride. About eating apples on Mink Island. I was
really hoping to have a third date. Please, Maggie. Put
down that gun."

48

The storm had passed. Jim had been treated and released from the medical clinic. The bullet had missed the bone, but tore through a lot of muscle tissue. His leg would heal, but it was going to be a slow and painful process. His left cheek was red and his left eye swelled with a dark bruise. He had definitely seen better days.

"You know, you really should take some medical leave and have a doctor down south look at that leg." Captain Reesa McEwen stood in front of Jim's desk. He was seated with his bandaged leg propped up on a pillow.

"You flying them out today?" Jim asked.

"Yep. We leave in a half hour." Four State Troopers escorted a handcuffed Dan Potter and Tavis Spurgeon from the holding cell into the back of a Crown Victoria Cruiser. "I'm leaving you a couple of guys to help hold down the fort while you recover."

"You get them some rooms above Porty's?"

"Absolutely. Nothing but the best for our men in blue." Reesa stood across from Jim's desk, sipping on a cup of coffee that Shelly had delivered. "It might take a week or two, but we will get you a full-time replacement for Tavis soon. Also, Fish and Wildlife is sending in a new agent tomorrow."

Jim smiled and asked, "You guys doing any kind of background check this time?"

"No more than we did on you. How is your ex-wife, by the way?"

"Very funny." Jim looked out his window at cloudy skies. "You mad that I went in and got him last night?"

"Officially? You should have waited until I could bring in some help. That one will have to go in your file, Jim." She turned to walk out the door, but stopped and said, "Unofficially? I wouldn't want anything less from my star lieutenant. You know, headlines of this drug and murder bust will probably make the Seattle papers. You're a big hit."

"So does that mean I'm off the hook with that probation thing?"

McEwen tilted her head, "Strangest thing. Senator Travors had contacted me a few days ago and said that photographic evidence of your shortcomings would be crossing my email inbox soon. Since then, nobody has heard from the guy."

"Maybe he's learned to lighten up a little bit."

"Maybe. I wouldn't worry about it if I were you. Seems like you've got everything under control here to me." Captain McEwen waved goodbye as she left the station.

Jim picked up the phone and dialed a phone

number that had been pinned to the wall next to his desk.

"Mr. Simms. Yes, this is Lieutenant Jim Wekle from Craig calling. I just wanted you to hear it from me. We got him, sir."

Maggie was still cleaning the inside of the bar from the Beer Swig and Humpy Festival. She had sent Lip Rings and Neck Tattoos out to scrub herring chucks off the outer siding. Tank Spurgeon and Hauler Steve sat at the bar, sipping on small glasses of yellow beer. Jim hobbled in on crutches and sat on a stool next to the other patrons. Maggie poured him a cup of coffee.

Tank said, "You look like hell."

"Feel like hell, too." Jim turned toward Maggie and asked, "You holding up okay?"

"I'm doing fine. I'm just a little ashamed, embarrassed, mad and sad, all at the same time."

"Maggie, I think all of those emotions are understandable." Jim looked down the bar and asked, "How 'bout you, Tank? Doing okay?"

Tank finished off his glass then said, "I couldn't even go watch them load him into the plane. I can't help but think this is my fault in some way. I'm the one that raised him. I'm the one that basically enabled him. I'm the one that used my connections to get him stationed back home, here."

Jim slurped his coffee and cringed at the flavor, "Tank, raising a boy the best you can and helping out a young man who's just starting out his adult life doesn't make you responsible for his every action. In the end, it was Tavis himself that chose to become a drug dealer and to commit murder. Tavis should pay for this, not you."

Tank said, "I know that you're right, but it doesn't make it any easier."

Jim replied, "Yeah, it's not going to be easy."

Jim crutched his way out of the bar and around the side of the building where two college kids were utilizing brushes attached to long poles. They scrubbed soapy water in an up and down motion across the width of the building.

"Smells bad out here," Jim commented.

"Thanks, that helps," Lip Rings snapped back.

"You guys heading back to school soon?"

Lip Rings answered, "I am. The season's over in a couple of weeks. My semester fires up right after and I plan to be there."

"Good for you, Shawn. I think you will make a good engineer. How about you, Mr. McDoogle? You heading home soon?"

Neck Tattoos was really going after a herring tail

that had dried hard into the painted siding. He said, "Naw, man. I love it here. Got a good job working in the bar and I think the cannery will trade me free rent for taking care of the Stockade in the offseason. I can't pass on a deal like that. All I gotta do is keep the pipes from freezing in the winter and I've got a roof over my head."

"Sounds too good to pass up. I know that Maggie will appreciate the help." Jim turned to limp back to his car.

Lip Rings said, "Hey, Trooper man. I'm glad you figured out who killed Debbie. You know why he did it?"

"She was in the wrong place at the wrong time. She and Tavis were into each other. She thought she would go for a little midnight visit, but walked in on his drug operation."

"Too bad."

"Yeah, too bad."

Lip Rings asked, "Are you serious about that bear-can patent?"

"I think you should go for it. When you make it big, don't forget where it all started."

"You got it, Trooper man. We'll see you around."

Jim put on sweatpants and a light jacket. He stuffed a pocket full of crackers and made his way slowly on crutches up to Lookout Rock. He propped up his healing leg on a stump, unwrapped a fat Maduro cigar and snipped the end. Soon, blue smoke rose steadily from his cheeks. Oscar, the mink, scurried alongside and waited for her snack.

"You know, Oscar. I'm glad that he didn't turn you into a scarf." Oscar grabbed a cracker and ran under the deck. Jim could hear the squeaks of the baby minks as Oscar shared her cracker with the new family.

Kram said, "I am too. Those babies will soon grow into a full-blown coat."

"You're an interesting guy, Kram."

"You tell your boss that you deputized half the island?"

"Yes."

"You tell your boss that your girlfriend almost blew the head off your former employee?"

"No."

"You're an interesting guy, too, Jim." Kram got up and wandered off.

Jim puffed away on his cigar, continued to feed his new mink family, and stared out at the tree-covered islands in the distance. It was a peaceful evening. The water was calm. The temperature mild. The rain had stopped, at least for a moment.

"Hot damn!!!" A drum solo erupted through the tranquility, sending a family of minks scrambling for cover.

EPILOGUE

Since the weapon was fired from an ocean-going vessel, the Coast Guard claimed jurisdiction over the Torcadero Yacht Club incident. Seven elderly members of the TYC (as they were commonly referred to on cult internet forums) were indicted in Federal Court for discharging a cannon within five hundred yards of an industrial zone and reckless endangerment of an assembled mass. The members of the TYC held strong to their theory that the cannon was firing blanks and that the real blame should be placed on an ex-Navy demolitions expert. The Federal Judge ruled that their claim should logically be ignored given that there was neither official record nor any evidence at all that a Blue Jay Haverford actually existed. Despite the claims of a hysterical woman claiming to be Blue Jay's wife, the Judge sentenced all seven members to two years of a suspended jail sentence provided successful completion of six months community service. Any further mishaps and the two years of jail time would kick in immediately. Community service details were to be determined by members of the Craig city council. After a short meeting and unanimous vote, the seven members of the TYC were assigned the task of scrubbing dead herring and humpy guts off the decks and hulls of every boat in the Craig City Marina.

Blue Jay Haverford sailed off unnoticed from the Craig waterfront only to be completely consumed by a massive storm system. He skippered his vessel courageously for several hours, quartering waves and riding out the extreme winds. With the tail end of the storm escalating into gale force and every ounce of energy drained from his flatulent body, Blue Jay failed to notice a floating pallet of RV parts off his starboard bow. Twelve miles up the shoreline from the City of Craig, the *Creighton Swish* was impaled by the front bumper of a Luxury Coachman Plus RV. The two-foot gaping chasm that was punched into the hull of the sailboat quickly sucked in seawater like a Hoover vacuum. Blue Jay Haverford went down valiantly singing the Creighton University fight song at the top of his lungs.

After its owner seemingly dropped off the face of the Earth and failed to pay utility bills and property taxes, a home and waterfront property on Halibut Cheek Drive was sequestered by the Prince of Wales Borough Assembly. A neighboring property owner wearing a bear-skin hat testified at the sequestering meeting that the residing owner had not been seen or heard from in months. After the borough assembly took possession of the property, it was immediately sold without auction for half its market value. Although some residents felt the deal was slightly unlawful, most praised the decision.

Lacking a down payment, the new City of Craig Police Chief and former night watchman was allowed to issue the title for a used Luxury Coachman Plus RV as collateral. The man's stardom was still hailed in legendary status after his quick actions during the dreaded flaming herring debacle. The borough assembly voted unanimously to create the new law enforcement position and upgrade the night watchman's status. An induction ceremony took place in the rain down on the docks. While a badge was being pinned onto a new blue, button-up shirt, an inebriated saxophonist belted out a line from *The Heat is On*. Despite the rain, many of the town's residents came out for the induction. Although many wondered how the new police chief had come up with almost fifty lifejackets in less than a minute's time, no one would ever get caught speaking ill of the night watchman that saved the day.

ACKNOWLEDGEMENTS

I would sincerely like to thank my parents for giving me such a great start to my life, and for moving me up to Southeast Alaska as a child. Growing up in the rain certainly had its pros and cons, but how else would I know how to fillet a halibut.

I am thankful for my beautiful daughter, Ella. She did an amazing salmon sketch for this book.

Thanks to my fishing buddy and fantastic son, Sam, for inspiring me to keep writing as we tried to reel in the big ones.

I greatly appreciate my first critic and avid supporter, Marci (who just happens to be my lovely wife). Thanks for tucking in the kids for me, and thanks for telling me, "It's pretty good."

Thanks to my editor, Karyn Doran, for your great ideas, and for helping me with commas.

Tara Neilson is a true Alaskan and a great writer. Her help and support has been a blessing.

I am so appreciative for all the advice given to me by a wonderful author and good friend, Daisy Prescott. Check out her books. They sizzle!

ABOUT THE AUTHOR

Brent Purvis resides in Colville, WA with his wife and two kids. In addition to writing humorous mystery novels, Brent is a music teacher and regular performer of jazz and blues as a trombonist and keyboardist. He has also written, composed, and arranged a full-length Broadway-style musical-comedy, which was recently produced with high acclaim.

Teaching music for over two decades has allowed Brent to live in some of the most beautiful places in the Northwest, as well as meet some of the most amazing characters along the way.

Growing up in Ketchikan, Alaska gave Brent a unique experience with life in the Last Frontier. After high school, his musical pursuits sent him south as he majored in music education at the University of Idaho. Upon receiving his degree, Brent landed a teaching stint on Whidbey Island, where he met his wife and started his family. They moved to Sitka, Alaska before settling in beautiful Northeast Washington.

You can find Brent's blog, Kram's Perspective, at:
http://jimandkramrule.blogspot.com/

Made in the USA
Lexington, KY
25 May 2018